the faces she sees

elizabeth scozzari

Proofread by Deliciously Dark Editing

Book Cover by Elizabeth Scozzari

Character Art by Emily Jo Valiquette, Gilded River Tattoo Co.

First Edition 2025

ISBN 979-8-9987816-9-8

❀ Formatted with Vellum

~ AM, ME, & ES ~

And to all of my Arnolds, thanks for the lessons in life and the unintentional motivation to do better.

chapter one

Diana

IF DIANA HADN'T BEEN SO afraid, she would have kicked herself for clutching her chest and not her baseball bat. She waited in deafening silence for some midnight terror to burst through her door. Nothing happened. Usually, she could sleep through the constant sounds from her next-door neighbor and the trucks that rambled up and down Route 27 all night, but a thud had jolted her awake. Diana's arms slid under the pile of pillows on her bed, searching for her phone.

Her fingers felt the rubbery cord of the charger, which she used to drag the device to her. Unplugging it, she called her boyfriend, Arnold. With each ring, she wondered what had made the noise. Voicemail. Diana grabbed a water from the half a dozen she had accumulated on her nightstand. *Maybe it was just a dream?* She rolled out of bed and headed toward the bathroom.

She froze long enough to realize someone was in her house. Diana scurried past her open door and into the bathroom before calling Arnold again.

"I'm telling you, it sounded like someone was there," she tried explaining to him.

"There's no one in your house. You live in *West Islip*."

He didn't need to finish his sentence; his tone said it all. Long Island wasn't at all like Englewood, or any of the other neighborhoods in Chicago where he had grown up, but that didn't mean that bad people didn't live here, too. Not that Arnold was inclined to listen to her theories on LISK or any other true crime case. It was part of the reason she always kept her baseball bat in bed with her.

"Yeah, I guess. . ." she surrendered. "Oh no."

"What's wrong?"

"I don't feel well," Diana said as she pulled the phone away from her face and looked at the time. "It's almost four in the morning, go back to bed. I'll talk to you later."

"You sure, drunky?"

"Yup."

"Sweet dreams," Arnold said as he hung up the phone.

A sudden wave of nausea and the subsequent thought of throwing up while on the phone were more real and more terrifying than a home invader. Breathing in through her nose, she started counting to five. *One, two, three.* She knew he was right and that no one was there. *Four, five,* Diana exhaled shakily. She was spooked from her show and was currently scared in place on the toilet. Maybe it would have been better to stay on the phone until she felt calmer, better, or at least until she was back in bed.

Clips from the series finale of Pretty Little Liars flash through her head. Ann Hwang and a few of Diana's other friends had watched it the night before. It had been Diana's turn to host, and they had gone through almost as many bottles of wine as there had been plot twists. None more disturbing than finding out who the biggest A of them all had been. As Shakespeare once proved, what was in a name? Anyone could have been the big bad, just like it was equally as possible that Diana had just drunk too much. As was customary after everyone else had left, she and Ann settled into their respective seats in Diana's living room and bullshitted until they were out of wine.

A bitter taste filled Diana's mouth. Staring at the toilet paper roll across from her, she felt the blood rushing away from her face. She watched with shaky eyesight as her arms lost what little pigment they had. Whatever was happening to her was not going to happen in the bathroom on her toilet. Diana braced herself. Pitching herself forward, she rushed toward her bed. With every step, she felt her senses continue to fade away, like a battery being drained to the last drop.

When she opened her eyes, Diana was surprised to be looking up at her ceiling. She tried to roll over. She had no feeling below her hips and wondered where her legs had gone. She wasn't standing or kneeling. Her back felt as though it was supporting all her weight. In a moment of panic, she worried that she had died.

Slowly, she lifted her head as much as she could and managed to find that her legs were still attached, even if they were deadweight. As she continued to lift her head, the strength in her upper body returned. Her lower abdomen and legs were sprawled on the floor. Diana clawed herself fully onto her bed and somehow managed to get under her covers. She was chilled to the bone. Years of taunts about her low-set heat mocked her. Maybe the pipes had finally frozen, taking her body temp with them.

Diana began to sweat from every pore on her body. It was only when she began shaking all over that she decided to call her boyfriend again. Her arm felt like jelly as she grappled for her phone, but before she could grab it, her world faded to black.

Diana opened her eyes, surprised by the sunlight filling her room. She yawned, forcing her eyes shut. Her body felt achy as she stretched out. A small beat of panic started in her chest. While she was usually up before her alarm, there had been times when it was her saving grace. It was too bright not to be well

3

after 8 am. Her body shuddered, and her fingers found their way to her phone.

The screen was black, and the little button on the front was unresponsive. At least it explained the lack of alarm. Diana sighed. She wasn't sure she felt like going to work, but she had deadlines. Deadlines that were checkpoints in her career. Focusing on what happened between Ann leaving and this morning wasn't going to change any of it. It wasn't like this was the first time she woke up a little worse for the wear and unsure as to why. The unknowing was certainly better than Ann fussing over her via text all day.

Diana let out one more yawn, unfurling her body, before recommitting to herself that she would always plug her phone in by 9 pm, no matter what. Then, as she forced her body forward, she began to think of everything she had to do for work. If she was going to be late, still unaware of the time, as she worried she would be, she could at least be prepared.

She, dressed and ready, had barely reached her front door when she realized that she didn't have her lunch. Rounding the corner into her kitchen, Diana dropped her armful of things onto the breakfast bar across from her refrigerator. She packed her lunch, quickly grabbing a sandwich, a cheese stick, apple slices, a yogurt, and a large water bottle from inside.

The neat rows of planned meals were something that both Ann and Arnold teased her about constantly, but they had continued to prove themselves helpful as Diana threw her lunch into her favorite canvas bag, decked out in lightning bolts. Ann had given it to her years ago. The card had said something about Diana being her flash of inspiration or the light of her life. It was punny and cute, and absolutely perfect for Diana to throw her preassembled lunches into.

Repacked and almost feeling positive, Diana headed for the door. It hadn't been as late as she had feared. A freezing cold shower had done wonders to shock her system into an accelerated morning routine. She had shifted everything around to flip the deadbolt, but it was already unlocked. The muscles in her face dropped as her hand reached toward the bottom lock, also in its upright position. The crashing thud, followed by a clicking sound, came rushing back to her. She would have undergone a poly and passed for how certain she was that someone had been in her apartment.

Diana looked over her shoulder at her living room; everything seemed in order. The couch with the blanket crocheted for her by her grandmother, her fake fig tree and various succulent plants, and her other tchotchkes were all in place. She thought about Ann leaving, specifically whether or not she had locked the door before going to bed. Only fuzzy snippets of laughter, wine, and curling under her weighted blanket came to mind. That and the loud noise that had woken her up. Diana tried to remember what happened after she woke up, but it was all a blur. She had talked to Arnold, or tried to, but then nothing. It didn't matter, at least not in the moment.

She stepped out of her doorway and onto the front patio area. Her townhouse was the last on the block, which meant she didn't have to share the space with anyone. While it wasn't necessarily within the townhouse association rules, Diana had put an ornate, cast-iron Victorian stand where she could rest her bags as she locked or unlocked the door. She checked it three times and then made her way into her car and on the road.

Slamming on her brakes, Diana avoided hitting the car ahead of her. She had been so caught up in her own thoughts about her door and trying to remember all the details of last night that she hadn't realized the green sedan in front of her was stopping at the red light ahead. As if the intersection of Udall and Higbie didn't have enough accidents. She took a deep breath and concentrated on the light, exhaling as it turned green. Diana's stomach growled.

Looking at her dashboard clock, she decided to call the bagel store. She placed her order before she reached the next light. Passing Mojo's, her favorite hangout spot in West Islip, and probably her favorite bar on Long Island, on her left, her stomach growled again.

Her large coffee sat on the ledge next to a brown paper bag with grease spots seeping through. Diana had left everything in the car, except her $10 in cash. Leaving the money where her breakfast had been, she waved to the girls behind the counter.

"See you soon," the girl called out to Diana as the old-fashioned, overhead doorbell rang.

The smell of fried bacon and melted cheese filled her car.

For the first time all morning, Diana began to feel a level of normalcy. As she pulled into the office parking lot, her mind began shifting gears, focusing on what she had to get done and how much happier her stomach would be after breakfast.

Diana parked her car in her usual spot under a weathered tree, gathered her things, and made her way into the building. The consulting firm she worked for—Santo, Miller, and Volpe— was located in an old Victorian home that had been converted, like all the houses on the property. She settled into her office, a space that would have either been a small sitting room or a massive closet. It hadn't taken her long to get her lunch into her mini fridge underneath her desk, start her computer, and take a few nibbles of her bacon, egg, and cheese on a toasted everything bagel.

As she reached for her coffee, an internal message from "Ann Hwang" popped up on Diana's computer saying that the mail had been delivered. Diana stood from her desk, returned her coffee cup to its coaster, locked her computer screen, and walked through her office. "I'm going to grab the mail, Maria. I'll be back shortly." Maria grunted from her desk as she made a small mark on her calendar.

The air felt nice against Diana's face. Cold showers might have been the answer to jumpstarting a morning, but they chilled her to the bone. The walk down the winding path was peaceful.

Other than getting to see her dear friend, the walk to the

main building, the oldest and largest of all the houses on the estate, was her favorite reason for getting the mail. When she entered the building, Ann was feverishly typing on her phone, muttering under her breath.

She looked like she could have stayed home today, too. Maybe there was a bug going around. If there was a bug. . . Ann glanced up from her phone, and fury shot from her pupils. Diana quickly looked away as Ann scowled and glanced at the closed door behind her, mouthing the word "Sheryl." Diana tried not to laugh and gestured down the hall.

The reception area, which Ann referred to as her own personal purgatory, was the receiving bay of the mansion, when it had been considered a mansion, and the vestibule combined together for a grand entrance space. Down the hall were the modernized bathrooms, and Diana and Ann's favorite place to take a few minutes to let their hair down at work. Ann flashed her two thumbs-up as she stood up and walked over to an office space behind her desk.

Knowing all the problems Ann was having with Sheryl, her co-receptionist, Diana wouldn't be surprised if Ann snapped any day now. While it was true that Sheryl picked on her, Ann didn't do herself any favors by engaging the way she did. Diana walked into the bathroom and waited for Ann.

"I can't stand her," Ann said, entering the bathroom.

"Shhh," Diana whispered. "Old houses are known for traveling sound."

Ann pushed the door closed behind her.

"Besides," Diana continued, "I only have a few minutes to catch up before I need to head back. I want to get everything in place before tomorrow."

Her friend's eyes had softened, and no longer did she look like a crazed woman on a war path. Diana was sure Ann would give her far too many details about Sheryl when they talked later. Right now, there was a more pressing topic on her mind. As Ann started reapplying her lip gloss and touching up her hair, Diana asked Ann if she had walked her out the night before.

"Absolutely not," Ann said with a snortle. "I asked if you wanted to smoke a cigarette out front, but you really had to pee and your hands were full," she added.

Diana vaguely remembered strategically holding her wine glass and cell phone in her right hand, and what could have been a waffle in her left. She forced a laugh, but couldn't help but worry a little bit. At this point, it was hard for her to decipher what truly had occurred and what she believed had happened.

"Why?" Ann questioned flatly, her perfectly penciled brow arched high above her eye.

"Just was curious," Diana answered, shrugging her shoulders. "Can you grab our mail for me? I gotta get back."

Ann walked back around her desk, where a small stack was rubber-banded, sitting next to her keyboard. She worked for the company that managed the estate and had stakes in almost every company they rented to, including the one Diana worked for.

"Here you go!"

"Thank you, Ann," Diana said. Leaning forward, she added softly, "Text me later if you need anything." She nudged her head in the direction of Sheryl's still empty chair.

"Wait till I hit send on the mini-blog I was texting you before you miraculously appeared," Ann added in a whispered laugh.

Skimming through the text, Diana surmised that Sheryl (the lazy cow who Ann could just drown in the mud, even if it meant ruining her shoes and getting dirty in the process) had really stepped in it today. While Diana disagreed with Ann's tactics, her texts read like the transcript from a comedy show. Diana glanced at the time as she slid her phone back into her pocket. She had been gone from her desk for less than ten minutes. While it didn't matter to her boss, Diana was sure Maria was keeping some kind of scorecard.

Returning to her desk, Diana checked her cell phone as her

work computer came back to life. While she had been walking, she had received an email from Tim, her very best friend, linking to a case study on fainting. A small memory niggled in the corner of her mind. She wasn't sure why or when, but she had woken up, sweating and cold last night. Something Tim would probably flag if she mentioned. She had fainted a few times in the spring, and no one, including Diana, seemed more concerned than he was. She had probably drunk more wine than she realized. Even Ann had laughed at the thought of Diana walking her out last night.

Signing back onto her computer, Diana was happy to see a few replies to an email that she had been waiting for regarding a much larger fundraising project for later this summer. The day had passed quickly, most of which was spent preparing her end-of-month reports. Technically, the month didn't end until tomorrow, but having everything ready gave Diana a sense of preparedness and accomplishment. Even if she wouldn't be able to finalize Q2 and H1 reports until she was back next week. It didn't matter, Diana was on it! Vastly different from the girl who giggled while juggling her phone and a waffle the night before. That was a Diana that her boss, Judith, wouldn't be seeing any time soon.

Diana glanced down at the time. Judith would come in like water off the bay within the next 15 minutes, wanting to catch up with her before the end of the day. Her boss was funny like that; she exuded chaos, but every day was the same structure as the one before. Arnold's face lit up Diana's screen on her cell phone. Had they spoken since last night? Getting up, she closed her office door, ignoring a frown from Maria as she did. Diana answered the call quietly.

"Hello?"

"Hi, I'm here, can you hear me?"

"You don't have to whisper at your desk, Dee," Arnold said with a laugh. "Maria wasn't hired as the Business Operations Associate, and she's not on the short list for Senior Director if

Elizabeth Scozzari

Judith gets moved up to COO. You did, forever ago, so screw her."

"It wasn't that long ago," Diana said, mumbling into the phone. "Not that you're wrong. I still don't have long. How're you?"

"I'm good. Talking to SMV's future COO."

"Ass," Diana whispered, smiling as she said it.

"Your ass," Arnold answered. "I can't remember, did we talk about me coming over tonight or tomorrow for dinner? Because we were thinking of an impromptu guys' night."

"I don't remember," Diana began, "but to be fair, I don't remember a lot of yesterday evening. Though I might have fainted."

"When?"

"Last night."

"Was it the wine? Why didn't you say something sooner?"

"Because we talked soooo much this morning," Diana laughed.

"I have a job too, Dee. One that doesn't allow me to hang out with my best friend during the workday. What did Ann say about your fainting?"

"I didn't even mention it to her. I'm still not even sure I did faint, just like I'm not sure why you're getting so pissy."

"It's the way you say things, Dee."

"I was joking," Diana cut in.

"You can't even hear your attitude right now."

"Arnold, what are you talking about? I'm going to have to go soon and—"

"Not my fault you're too busy for me. Go, be an executive. I'll talk to you later."

The line dropped before she could respond. For as far as they had come since last summer, there were times when Arnold's behavior made her feel like nothing had changed. But each of them had grown as people, and their relationship had gotten stronger. Diana took a few deep breaths and rang Arnold's cell phone. The voicemail picked up after the second ring. She left a message, "Hi. I'm sorry. I'm very edgy. I didn't sleep great. You're probably right, the wine, all the wine, was probably just too much sugar.

You're probably firming up your plans for guys' night. Please call me before you head out."

Diana returned her phone to her drawer, ignoring two texts that had come in from Ann and one from Tim. She had a few more emails she could answer before Judith returned. Before she could read through the first one, her desk phone rang.

"Santo, Miller, and Volpe—"

"Hey, Dee," Arnold said as if their previous conversation hadn't happened. "You didn't answer your cell. I tried it twice. I figured Maria was watching you, so you put it away."

"Hey," was all she could muster back.

"I'm not calling you a bitch, but I can forgive you for acting like one." Arnold laughed lightly. "I'm glad you're finally listening to me. I know how much you hate not being right."

Diana ignored his jokes. No matter how often she expressed it, he never seemed to understand that sometimes his jokes landed like torpedoes.

"Regardless of what caused you not to feel well, you feel okay now?"

"Pretty much. Just tired and trying to get a lot done," Diana said.

"We can talk about what happened last night later if you want. I have to get ready for practice, and then after, Mark is driving us back to his place."

"Great. Have fun, okay?"

"Will do. I'll touch base with you later."

The line dropped again, and Diana returned the phone to its cradle. The front door slammed, causing her to jump. Judith darted past Maria and into her office. Diana glanced at the clock. *Right on time,* she thought to herself. Within minutes, Diana's computer dinged; it was an interoffice message from Judith.

> When you have a minute, please stop in.

Diana replied with the thumbs-up emoji. A second notification sounded. This one was from Ann.

> Have some goodies to drop off. I'll leave them
> on your desk since I'm sure you'll be in with J.

There was a flurry of GIFs of cats and laptops. Diana smiled to herself, grabbed her notebook and a pen, and headed out of her office over to Judith's. Maria was sitting at her desk, her hands neatly folded in her lap, her eyes fixed on the screen where a giant clock was ticking away.

Judith looked up at Diana, who was standing in the doorway, and a quick yet professional smile welcomed her in. The office space was decorated with purpose and subtly showcased why Judith would naturally be the best fit for achieving success. Diana envisioned her own office and how, by the time she moved into this space, assuming she kept on her current trajectory, what it would say about her.

"How's the end of month looking?"

"From a numbers perspective, it's not great, but it's not completely shot. And it's still June."

"Tomorrow. It's June until end of day tomorrow. Ugh," Judith grumbled. "Not you, dear. I'm sure you did a fabulous job. I'm more concerned that the numbers aren't as fabulous."

"I'll send you the official report tomorrow," Diana said.

"Fantastic," Judith replied, picking the top one up.

Diana smiled to herself. Judith was the poster child for businesswomen. She was tough and expected nothing but the best. She was also one of the sweetest people underneath the professional layers. A small beep sounded from outside Judith's office, followed by the soft sound of footsteps. "Night," Maria called out, the thud from the door cutting the salutation short.

"Must be 5 o'clock," Judith said, shifting her gaze.

She wasn't the only heavily routinized employee at SMV. If

Maria had ever left after 5 pm, it was because the clocks glitched. Diana relaxed her smile before she spoke.

"I wanted to give you an update on the community initiative project. If you have some time?"

A small smile tugged at the corners of Judith's mouth.

"It was one of the things I wanted to ask you about. Do *you* have the time?"

"I do," she nodded. "Although," Diana shifted the pages in her notebook, "it seems I left the printouts in my office. I'll be right back."

"Terrific."

Upon walking into her office, Diana was greeted with two wrapped sandwiches, two bags of chips, and two cookies. There was also an iced coffee and a napkin covered in permanent marker. It read:

Leftovers from a big to-do client, and iced coffee from the new coffee place next to the deli. Lmk your thoughts!

Diana shook her head and smiled. Ann wouldn't eat a sandwich with bread, condiments, or lunch meat, nor would she eat leftovers, but hell if she didn't take a freebie. And make sure that Diana was fed properly.

Everything fit in her mini fridge except the iced coffee. She removed a 1L water bottle she had started earlier in the week and made room. If it wasn't already incredibly thoughtful, it was also going to force Diana to stay better hydrated. She made a note to text Ann back a thank you. With her water bottle and spreadsheets in hand, Diana returned to Judith's office.

Taking a seat in her usual chair, Diana handed Judith her

copy and walked her through the progress and where they were at from a budget perspective.

"You're off on Monday," Judith interjected as she flipped through the spreadsheets, her eyes scouring the details.

It hadn't been a question. Diana had just drained the last of her water. While she had intended to drink it throughout their meeting, she had talked so much with such enthusiasm that she had barely stopped to breathe. It was only when Judith asked a quick question that she realized how parched she was. Now, from the sound of Judith's voice, she worried that perhaps something wasn't right with her work.

"Diana, this is great."

Her shoulders eased back, too far back. The room behind Judith rushed in a wave toward her and then swayed to the side. Diana could hear Judith's voice, but she wasn't able to understand what she was saying.

* * *

Diana tangled herself in her green and white blanket, which was designed with quotes from classic novels, and began to tie her seemingly endless hair in a ponytail. She could spend hours gathering up her long, curly locks, trying to get every strand included before twisting it into a knot on the top of her head. She sighed, surrendering to random strands falling out and running down her neck. Her hands were shaking. Diana silently chastised herself while wringing them together. Getting worked up over a few strands of hair that refused to cooperate was ridiculous. Almost as silly as thinking someone had been in her home.

Her body ached, and the pounding in her head was deafening.

At least Tim was outside, giving his own version of events to Arnold. She was grateful that Tim had been there to pick her up, even more so that he was dealing with Arnold instead of having to do it herself. She didn't want to relive why her emergency contact for work was Tim and not her boyfriend, nor could she handle grief about missing guys' night. It wasn't fair to assume he would make the joke, but she had known Arnold for years. With those years had come a level of anticipated behaviors.

She had known Tim almost as long and probably even better in some ways. Diana yawned, cuddling her extra-large, reusable thermos against her chest and nestling her body further into the couch. She pictured the two of them, her and Tim, silly sophomores, both studying business, both first-year Resident Assistants, and both enamored by the same stories from the same frat boy. *Fucking, Arnold,* she thought before she closed her eyes.

chapter two

Arnold

"THANKS FOR GETTING MY GIRL," Arnold said to Tim. They were standing outside Diana's townhouse.

"It's really no trouble," he said with a smile. "She's my girl, too."

Arnold's face forced a smile. Sharing had never been a skill of his, and he was no different when it came to Diana. Of course, he valued Tim's friendship with Diana; hell, he was how they had met. It sometimes seemed like they were closer than any two people could be.

"Besides, I was on my way to the gym. Instead of running indoors, I'll take a run to SMV and grab her car. Do you need anything?" Tim asked.

"I don't know," Arnold said. "You said she's okay?"

"She seems okay," Tim said flatly, "but does anyone know what's going on with her? Has she gone to a doctor?"

"A doctor?"

He looked at Tim. He was serious, more serious than whatever was going on with Diana. He opened his mouth as Tim held up his hand.

"I'm not trying to overstep. But this isn't new. She fainted at the baseball game last month."

"Yeah, but—"

"Twice the week of your birthday. Before that, she fainted in February and around Christmas and New Year's. You remember Friendsgiving?"

Arnold thought about it, staring at the table where Diana's outdoor plant lived. Lines from where she put down her keys or her coffee had cut through the pollen. They had been drinking. It was too hot in the house; too cold outside. There was always some logical explanation for her unwellness. Countless reasons they all disregarded what seemed to be a pattern. He tried to remember their take on Thanksgiving.

"She didn't faint at Friendsgiving!"

"No, bro, but she threw up for three days before and then passed out the day after we got back."

Arnold looked over at Tim. His veins pushed against his forehead. Tension radiated from him. Pieces loudly began clicking together in Arnold's head.

"Okay, so maybe—"

Tim's head snapped away from his hands, his eyes boring into Arnold's. "She keeps losing her keys or locking herself out. She's messed up plans at least a half a dozen times this summer. Whatever has been going on with her, it's not new. It's getting worse."

Air forced its way from Arnold's lungs. He felt his muscles, still strong under a slight layer of dad-bod, as he rolled his neck.

"When do you think it started then, Timbo?" "I don't know. . . October?"

"October!"

"I've seen her in all kinds of shape, but nothing like Friendsgiving."

"I don't know," Arnold said, rubbing his eyes. "Like you said, we had a lot going on. She's had a lot going on at work. Let's just see how things go."

"It's not your call to make," Tim's voice faded as he spoke until it was barely above a whisper, "but since we know she won't go, I guess we'll wait."

They stood there, appraising each other. Arnold jammed his hands into his pockets. His t-shirt had a few stains from the hot wings and beer. Tim looked like he was going into work, his shirt still wrinkle and stain-free. Didn't he say he had plans to go to the gym? Tim cleared his throat before asking Arnold if he was going to Mark's later.

Arnold shrugged his shoulders.

"Okay then. After I bring her car back, I'm going to head home and shower. Work tomorrow." Tim turned, stopped, and looked back at the door. "There's some chicken soup in the Crock Pot. It won't be ready until 11 or so, but she can have it tomorrow. She doesn't have too much in her fridge. You need anything?"

"I left my six pack at Mark's—"

"You have a growler inside," Tim groaned. "I'll see you in a bit, man."

Arnold swallowed and headed inside. Squatting as low as he could, he pulled the 64 oz glass container from the bottom shelf of the fridge and twisted off the cap. There was half a bottle left from whenever he had opened it. It wouldn't be the best beer in the world, but he took a sip, and it was okay. He closed the fridge and headed over to where Diana was resting on her favorite spot on the couch. Reaching down, he gently caressed her arm and picked up the remote.

It was good that she was resting now. She must have drifted off while Tim was lecturing him on how to take care of his girl-friend. Arnold sat on the chaise, turning on the television. Looking over at Diana, Arnold thought about how peaceful she looked. It was also a huge plus that he could now watch the game without Diana rooting for her favorite baseball team, which happened to be losing three to one.

It was one thing for her to love the Mets—at least they were from the area—but her supporting the Patriots was deplorable. For someone who bled green and white, he hated New England with a passion, almost as much as he hated her beloved sweatshirt that she wore year-round. At least she wasn't a Yankees fan.

Still, it would have been better if she had converted to a White Sox fan like himself.

Arnold's eyes traveled to coach Belichick's mug imprinted on Diana's sweatshirt. If he could burn it, he would. She had some strange protective quality associated with it. Probably why she was wearing it now. He wondered if Tim had brought it down to her, knowing it would somehow make her feel better, or if she had asked for it. Arnold took a sip straight from the growler, definitely not as fresh as it used to be, and wondered what he would have done if he had been the one to bring Diana home. Arnold's phone dinged, interrupting his thoughts. A message from Mark popped across his screen.

> How's she doing? I just hung up with Tim.

He typed back.

> Sleeping now. We'll see when she gets up.

The response came almost immediately.

> How are you?

Arnold rolled his eyes. Mark was worse than any annoying TV little brother sometimes. He texted back.

> Good. Everything is fine. How's guys' night?

> Good! A few of us are going out now that the wings and beer are gone. If you want to meet us later. . .

Assholes drank my beer. Thanks. I'll let you know.

He put his phone down. *Thirsty Thursday*, he thought to himself. He should have known they couldn't have just stayed in. There was a time when every Thursday, he and Mark were rattling Tim's cage to come out. Arnold picked his phone back up, glancing over at Diana. His thumb hovered above the text thread. He returned his cell to the couch, looking instead at the television. He grunted at the ref's bullshit call favoring the Mets.

Diana stirred slightly, catching Arnold's eyes. She was still curled up with her blanket wrapped around her legs. Her small fists wrapped around a humongous water bottle thing. Her long hair that had once been piled on top of her head now swam in a pool around her neck, flooding into her face. Arnold watched as she settled back into the pillow. Every few breaths, a soft murmur escaped her throat. Even passed out, she was breathtaking.

Her wide, almond-shaped eyes were almost puppy-like, but bright green with flakes of vibrant gold encased with a black band. Her skin was soft, whether it was eggshell porcelain or radiant tan. She was short and voluptuous with her hourglass figure and blessed chest.

Arnold checked the score; the Mets were leading the Marlins. His guys' group text was blowing up, keeping Arnold's eyes glued to the screen and his phone. Tim was also a Mets fan, like Diana, whereas Mark was a devoted Pinstriper.

"Hi," Diana said, her voice still sleepy and stuck in her throat.

Arnold didn't flinch from his spot on the chaise, phone in hand, muttering about the game. He heard Diana rustling off to the side. Even in sleep, she wasn't able to sit 100% still. She cleared her throat. Arnold sighed as he locked his phone screen and looked over at Diana.

"Hey, sleepy. How are you feeling?"

"Tired," Diana responded. "Come sit with me?"

Arnold stood up, looked at his phone, grumbled, and slid it into his pocket before walking over to the couch. "The game's over. They're praising the Mets." Arnold scowled. He saw the smile she was trying to suppress. He slid down next to her, lifted the giant thermos from her hands, and took a sip.

"Blehh," he said. "That's gross!"

"It's Big Yellow. It's only used for water with strawberry lemon. You like it normally."

"I like it when I know that's what I'm about to drink, and usually if it's topped with vodka."

He ignored Diana's eye roll and took another sip from the thermos. She wasn't wrong. Besides, his growler was closer to empty. He hadn't planned on sleeping over here. Switching to water was probably a good thing.

"What was the final score?"

"Six-three Mets," Arnold answered.

"Nice," Diana mumbled.

"Should you be drinking plain water?"

She shrugged, biting the corners of her lips to hold back a smile. Arnold was used to that face from her.

"Mind if I put on something goofy?"

"Whatever you want," Arnold said. Anything would have been better than a pro-Mets press conference.

"There's a marathon of that new cooking competition I wanted to watch!"

Almost anything, Arnold thought as he stood up and walked into the kitchen. He grabbed a water for Diana, shaking his head at the row of half-drunk bottles. Her intention of reusing plastic water bottles was adorable, but her execution of leaving them everywhere half empty, and then consolidating them, drove him nuts. If he was going to drink her strawberry lemon water, the least he could do was grab her a plain water. When he returned, he handed her the bottle.

"Take a few sips," he directed.

Diana didn't answer but chugged most of the bottle. "Thank you," she said, a guilty smile lighting up her face.

He could see the heaviness in her eyes already. Arnold pulled the coffee table closer to the couch, leaving the water bottle on it. With his growler tucked beside him on the left and Diana's face nuzzled into his armpit on his right, he focused his attention on the television. The last two contestants of the competition were lined up and ready to compete. There was an incredibly hot chick versus a balding dweeb.

chapter three

Diana

DIANA TRIED to open her eyes, but a weight pushed against them. They felt held shut. She tried to move, but her body had shut down. Non-responsive. Heaviness seized the air around her; her insides shook. Her eyes were fluttering, yet all she saw was black. Her head rolled forward. She could barely make out the light from the television. The room was dark. Her thoughts raced as sweat pooled under her arms.

Her head tipped back. A familiar blend of soft, sturdy muscle caught her. The vibrations of Arnold's heartbeat against her. She focused and felt his body next to her. A break in the flickering light caught her attention. Diana willed her eyes to open. She recalled being a child and trying to keep her eyes open when she sneezed. Her breath quickened.

She had to get her eyes open. She strained with all of her might. They had to open. She finally forced her eyes open for a few seconds. She was sure she had seen a figure take the corner from the stairs toward the front door. She screamed, but nothing more than a raspy croak escaped. Diana's eyelids clamped shut against her will. Darkness and despair took over. There was nothing she could do but accept the lull of sleep.

chapter four

ARNOLD JOLTED AWAKE. He hadn't meant to fall asleep. He couldn't actually remember dozing off, but without Diana's enthusiasm, the competition had put him right out. His original plan had been to switch back and forth between channels to see if the hot girl won while still catching up on sports, as long as Diana was still sleeping.

He blinked, his eyes adjusting to the light. He squinted toward the cable box; it was a little past 12:30 am. Another half hour or so, and the timer on the lights would go off, leaving them in only the light of the television. Diana was still out cold. He arched his back, stretching, but he couldn't shake the groggy feeling he woke up with.

Arnold looked down at Diana once more. She would be cranky if she woke up on her couch on a work night. While he didn't want to wake her up, his bladder wasn't going to let him stay put. As Arnold's hands slid under Diana's knees and around her back, a piercing sound attacked his eardrum, threatening to burst it. A sharp pain erupted through his jaw. Something heavy landed on the floor. His feet felt wet.

29

"Dee!" Arnold shouted. "It's me. It's me, Arnold. Relax. Relax, Dee!"

Diana stopped thrashing. He felt her muscles relax into his hands. Arnold pulled his arms back and began rubbing his jaw. He hadn't felt a hit like that since his football days as the star QB, around the same time he and Mark were known as the Brawl Brothers at Teddy's. Arnold looked down at Diana and was met with unrecognition. Tears were welling in her eyes. She looked around the room as if expecting something to come bounding out from the shadows. She closed her eyes as tears began to fall. Her small hand began massaging her head.

Arnold looked at the floor. He was standing in spilled beer. He bent over and set his growler straight up, closing the swing top with a snap.

"What the hell just happened?" Arnold asked her.

Diana murmured something.

"I can't understand you."

Her breath, ragged and wet, began to steady.

"I don't know. I, I, I," Diana sobbed. "I saw someone.

"You were sleeping," Arnold explained, sitting on the coffee table. "It was only a nightmare. How do you feel?"

"My head hurts," she said warily.

"It should, you cracked me in the jaw with it," Arnold said with a smile.

"I did?" Diana gasped, "I'm sorry, I—"

"It's okay. I want to make sure that you're okay before we put you to bed, though."

Arnold grabbed his cell phone and, turning on his flashlight, passed the light over Diana's eyes. He knew enough about head injuries, having had several himself, to feel confident that she was stable for the night.

"I'm gonna help you up. Watch the beer on the floor—"

"I'll clean it up. Just—"

"No, let's get you into bed. It's after midnight, and you have work in the morning." Arnold helped Diana off the couch and over the mess on the floor, adding, "I'll do something with the beer. I'm just amazed the glass didn't break. You are a force of your own kind, Diana."

With Arnold's hand resting on Diana's lower back, he guided her as they walked up the stairs. Heading toward her bedroom, Arnold watched as Diana steadied herself against the wall, breaking her strict *don't make the walls dirty* policy. He walked over to the corner of her room and switched on her nightlight as she began undressing. Arnold watched her cozy into her bed, noting her eyes surveyed the room.

"You're okay, Dee. You got your baseball bat?"

Diana reached behind herself, tugging the end of the bat out of the covers. It was silly; she lived in a safe neighborhood, but at least it wasn't a stuffed animal or something.

"You're all set, slugger," he said as he pulled the covers up over Diana's body. "No one's gonna mess with you now."

Her smile broke into a yawn.

"Here," Arnold said, handing her a water bottle from her nightstand, "drink up."

Diana took the bottle and lifted her head. She sipped, swallowed, smiled, and handed it back.

"Thank you," she said, her voice heavy with sleep.

"I'm going to head home. Get some rest. Call me in the morning?"

She nodded. "Text me when you. . ." her voice trailed off.

Downstairs, Arnold walked over to the couch and grabbed his beer. There was barely anything left in it now. He shrugged and chugged it, leaving the empty container in the sink. He returned to the living room. Replaying the scene from before, he sipped out of Big Yellow. Only Diana would name her water bottles and have specific drinks for them. Going to take another sip of the water, Arnold was surprised by how good the strawberry lemon water was.

Arnold sat on the edge of the couch and leaned forward, taking his phone from his pocket. He felt disoriented as the room

swayed around him. Shutting the television off, he made his way
to the front door. The lights from the living room shut off, and he
opened the door. Arnold stumbled out into the night. Maybe he
was the one concussed. The last time a little bit of beer made him
woozy, he was fourteen. Arnold shook his head and made his
way to his car. The night air felt good.

chapter five

<u>Arnold</u>

ARNOLD FELT LIKE SHIT. Lying there with his eyes closed, he felt an ache pulsing through his head. He needed a sports drink, anything, even water—which he despised—and some type of painkiller. He heard the toilet flush and water running. With as much force as he could muster, he pried his eyes open and began to look around.

He managed to focus his sight on the bathroom. There, standing in the doorway, a smidge or two taller than Diana, with shoulder-length fried-blonde hair straightened into an inward flip, was a girl. Arnold wondered if he was dreaming. The pain in his body told him otherwise. Arnold watched as she moved toward him, naked, picking up a tiny plate.

"Morning," she said as she sat down on the bed.

Arnold propped himself up on his left side.

He wasn't sure if it was fear or panic that kept him still. Looking toward the window, he could see that it was still dark out there. The day was overcast and grey, much like Amber's apartment.

A combination of modern, stoner sleek. Dark furniture, with

metallic and glass accents—pops of bright colors in crazy patterns in the artwork and blankets. Hand-crafted plates with anti-government sayings and lyrics from songs probably older than her parents took the cake, though. Amber came from a family of politicians, and she had her own plans of working for the people, not "The Man."

Amber slid her hand up Arnold's thigh. Arnold looked on the ground, searching for his pants. She must have noticed, because she leaned forward and grabbed them for him, tossing them onto the bed. Arnold dug his phone from his pocket. The screen said 4:38 am.

"Hello?" She stared at him blankly, waiting for him to respond. Arnold shook his head, feeling himself cringe as Amber sprang from the bed. "I have a charity brunch thing this morning," Amber continued as she reached up into her cabinets to grab something.

"Is that why we're up so early?"

"One of them, at least," she said disappointedly. Her eyes trailed down his body. "As a past president, I have to be there," she said, putting on her best cheerleader imitation. A fake smile breaking across her face made her look like a bitter second-place beauty queen. Returning to the bed, Amber took out a baggie and a straw from her nightstand. "Best cure for a hangover," she chirped, putting them on the plate.

Arnold pushed his phone and pants aside, making more of an effort to sit up. He studied Amber's face as she prepared the coke. She wasn't pretty. Not if you really looked at her, past the smile and nose that cost her parents thousands. Under all the makeup, her face just wasn't that pretty. But she wasn't ugly. Hell, she wasn't even bad-looking. Put all the layers back on, with her hair and nails done, her body and attitude meticulously planned, she was hot.

"Look, about last night," Amber said, before snorting a line off the mirror.

A wave of nausea overcame Arnold. He wasn't sure how he had gotten here and wasn't sure he could stomach finding out.

Amber adjusted her face and held the straw toward him. Hesitating for a moment, Arnold gave in and took a bump, bracing himself for whatever shit was bound to come spewing out of Amber's mouth.

"Don't look so disgusted, Arnold. You're the one who doesn't call, doesn't text, doesn't care. You're the one who said it's over," Amber said. Her hand raised, cutting him off from a rebuttal, "And then you just show up using my sister and her *situation* to show you care. At least you cared last night." Amber's face scrunched up, highlighting the straight edge of her nose. "And again this morning," she added with a chuckle.

There were two lines left. Amber did one and handed Arnold the straw. Maybe it wasn't the best idea, but he needed something to brace himself for what he was about to say.

"Amber," Arnold started, "it *is* over. I don—"

The sound of shattering ceramic was louder than what he had tried to tell her. Pieces of the empty plate flew to the ground, leaving a small dusting in their wake. Arnold wondered if it was more ceramic or cocaine residue.

"Get out," Amber shrieked. "You miserable prick! Just get out of my bed, out of my room, out of my life!"

Arnold jolted backward. The coke was making its way through his system. His hangover was receding to his numbed senses. Amber hopped off the bed, her feet thudding with every step toward the kitchenette. Arnold heard cabinets slamming as he jumped into his jeans. A glass whizzed by his head as he yanked his shirt down over his stomach and bolted for the door.

Arnold was tired and wired. He texted Mark.

> Tell me you're still out. . .

Almost immediately, his phone beeped.

County Line—breakfast. You coming?

Arnold threw his car in reverse, answering:

Be there in ten.

He kissed his Celtic cross for Mark and Thirsty Thursdays. Soon, he would be at the diner getting breakfast with his friends, like everything was right in the world. Cranking the volume up, Arnold peeled out of Amber's parking lot, putting another mess behind him.

chapter six

Diana

DIANA AWOKE to a pinging sound coming from her phone. Groping around her nightstand, she picked up her cell. A notification that read, "Ann Hwang" in bold letters, took up most of the bubble.

Underneath it read, "Call me on your. . ." in smaller print. Diana blinked a few times. She felt exhausted. Clearing away the unread message notification, Diana unlocked her phone and looked at the time—7:45 am.

"Shit," Diana muttered to herself.

After doing a rinse and repeat of the previous morning, Diana stopped in her living room. Sitting on the end table was a water bottle less than half-full. Diana walked over to it, feeling her foot stick to the floor. Looking at her phone, there wasn't enough time to clean it up. She vaguely remembered excitement over something the night before. She would call Arnold once she got in her car.

She began to pack her lunch, the sight and smell of food turning her stomach. Remembering the leftovers in her fridge at work, Diana left her lunch and the water bottle. Instead, she made sure she had her purse and her work bag and headed out to her car, double-checking the lock behind her. She walked to her car. As she unlocked it, her phone pinged. Reaching into her back pocket, Diana eased out her phone, once more seeing Ann's name across the screen. As she pulled down her street, Diana called Ann.

"Did you even read my texts?"

"Good morning to you, too, Ann," Diana said with a sigh.

"I'm just saying you haven't answered since yesterday—not even when I texted you about grabbing you breakfast, I might add."

"Ann—"

"Do you know how many women go missing in this country in a year? How many are the victims of some terrible 'they-never-saw-it-coming-boyfriend-definitely-did-it' crime? What if you fell from the countertop? You love climbing to get something from the top shelf, or what if you hit your head in the shower again?"

"Ann—"

"How long before he would notice? I would notice—"

"Ann," Diana cut in, her voice too loud and echoing in the car.

"Oh, don't be so dramatic," her voice sang through the speaker. "I already picked you up a sandwich. I'll give it to you at the office."

"Thank you," Diana moaned.

"Of course. Are you okay? You seem a little touchy," Ann said, pausing for a moment. "Fill me in when you grab your food," she said, before hanging up.

The sound of Diana's blinker filled the car. She remembered being afraid on the couch. Arnold had been there. She could have sworn she had seen someone else. Diana's eyebrows knitted toward each other. Tension ran through her jaw. She remembered talking to him, almost as if it were in a dream. A horn blared from behind her. Diana jumped, and, making sure there were no cars coming, she turned right on Montauk and left into the parking lot.

Diana parked her car, picking up her phone as she cut the engine. Arnold wasn't off today, but there weren't any gym classes during the first few periods of the morning. At least none that he taught. Sending him a quick text, Diana picked up her stuff and headed into the office.

The clock on Diana's wall read 9:15 by the time she had put her stuff down. Her stomach rumbled. Diana grabbed a water bottle from her fridge, making a note to take the rest of her bacon, egg, and cheese from yesterday home with her. The room spun as she stood up. Diana grabbed hold of her chair and waited for the vertigo to stop. Composing herself as best as she could, Diana slid her phone into her blazer pocket and left her office, shutting the door behind her.

"Maria, there's something I have to grab from the other office. I'll be back in about ten minutes. You can hold the fort down," Diana said with a smile.

"Of course," Maria said, taken aback.

It was clear from the look on her face that she couldn't tell whether Diana was being serious or facetious. Diana didn't offer any explanation as she exited the building. She was tired, hungry, and wanted to get as much done today as possible before her body completely shut down. Walking into the foyer of the main building, Diana heard muffled yelling. Quickening her pace, she was relieved to see Ann alone, but concerned when she saw the look on her face and the door behind her closed.

For everything Diana was, Ann was almost the complete opposite, both physically and in personality. Ann was tall compared to Diana—well, most women, but especially Diana. She had Asian and Polish roots, both of which she was very proud of, though most people could never quite pick out her nationality correctly, something Ann believed added to her mystery. Her black hair was usually tied back into a long, high ponytail with sweeping bangs across her forehead. She lived in makeup and outfits executed for magazines.

"Did you and Sheryl have another incident?" Diana whispered, nodding at the closed door behind her where raised voices were threatening to break through.

"Yes and no, this time it wasn't me," Ann said, a smile breaking through her scowl. "Sheryl might have royally messed up this time."

"We'll talk later!"

"Text me things, woman—you look like shit," Ann whispered back.

"Thanks, love you too," Diana said quietly.

Ann blew her a kiss as she took the brown bag off the counter.

Diana was back at her desk at 9:26 am. Maria's face flashed with disgust as Diana walked back into her office holding a coffee and a brown paper bag with oily spots. Keeping her head up high and her eyes on her door, Diana returned to her office.

Leaving her breakfast on her desk, Diana closed her door and took out her phone. There had been more than just texts from Ann.

Judith had texted her:

> Hope you're feeling better, Diana. If you need to take today, please do. If you do come in, I'd better not see you in the office at 2. Get a head start on the weekend and feel better. Don't worry about Maria. I'll take care of it.

There had been three more from Tim:

> I got Marked. Ended up meeting up at the bar after the gym. You better be feeling better, Dame. I'll call you later.

> Why is Arnold meeting us at the diner? It's early af. Are you coming too?

> I hate Mark. I feel like death. Had just enough
> time to get home, shit, shower, and change
> before I had to leave for work. Who am I?

Diana's stomach flipped, and the room spun. She felt as hungover as Tim sounded—what else he was expecting from a night out with Mark was beyond her. She would have to call him later. As she sat down at her desk, she texted Ann.

> Fainted in Judith's office yesterday. Arnold
> came over to take care of me. Stepped in a
> sticky pile of what I can only hope was beer on
> my way out. Memory is holier than Swiss this
> am. Thank you for the breakfast!!! Made my
> morning <3 <3 <3 Judith gave me a half day, so
> call me on your way home!

Wanting to get some work done, Diana didn't wait for a response from Ann. Instead, she pulled out half a muffin. A warm, butter-soaked corn muffin. With each nibble, her stomach felt more at ease. Maybe her leftover breakfast wouldn't make it home after all. Diana opened her notebook, and, after dating the page, she began to map out her goals for the day.

At a quarter to two, Diana's phone rang. "Santo, Miller, Volpe."

"Hi, Diana, it's Judith."

"How are you?"

"Great, just great. Listen, the meeting went well. So well, it's becoming a late lunch. I hate to trouble you, but that package for EC. It needs to be delivered today by 2:30. It should be on my desk. Can you drop it off?"

"You brought it to the courier yesterday, you didn't want them—"

"That's terrific. It's almost the end of the day anyway. Lock your office and mine and leave Maria in charge until I get there."

"But the package, I—"

"It's not a problem. You're very welcome." Grant's grandfatherly voice boomed in the background. "Grant said next time I should bring you with me. Thanks again, Diana!"

"Have a great weekend, Judith. I'll see you on Wednesday."

"Of course. You too!"

Diana laughed as her phone pinged. Judith wrote:

> The package in my office is for you. We got the account because of your idea! G was impressed. I knew you had the stuff.

Because she had powered through even though she was feeling a little woozy, they had gotten the account. Grant Santo and Judith were happy with her. An amazing way to end the month.

Diana packed up her things, including her treasure trove of food, and smiled as she went into Judith's office. A thick rectangle wrapped in brown paper with a string bow sat on her desk.

"Maria," Diana said as she flipped the lock to Judith's office door and closed it behind her, "I'm heading out now. If Judith isn't back when you're ready to close, please make sure you lock up on your way out. If there's an emergency, you can reach me on my cell."

A grimace held Maria's face as she glared at the doorknob behind Diana's elbow.

"Have a wonderful weekend," Diana added with a smile as she turned on her heels and exited the office.

Unlocking her car and her phone at the same time, Diana laughed a little to herself. Maria was definitely something out of a sitcom. She was sure Maria had already toyed with the idea of calling Judith to let her know Diana had left. Not that it mattered to Diana. She had earned her place at Santo, Miller, and Volpe; if Maria wanted to cast herself in that kind of lighting because of her own judgments on what Diana did, so be it. It wasn't going to have any bearing on Diana anymore.

Feeling empowered, Diana opened her texts. Several burst

messages from Ann and two from Tim waited for her. Ann didn't have a half day like Diana, so calling her would make little sense. Diana replied:

> You're too much lol I'm on my way out now.
> Call me whenever you're free.

Within seconds, Diana's phone went off three or four times—it was hard to tell with all of the dinging.

Diana put her purse and lunch bag down on the passenger's seat and took off her work sweater. The first message from Ann was a picture. Her designer shoes melded perfectly to her delicate feet, the designer pants she had on earlier no longer covering her ankles or calves. Diana looked at the picture for a few moments. She was as sure as the humidity in Florida that there was another version of that picture that had gone to someone else first.

Ann took a lot of pictures of a lot of things, especially herself, and in the years Diana had known her, she hadn't seen one bathroom picture that hadn't been taken for a targeted audience.

The rest of Ann's messages read:

> You're so lucky. I'm still here. Will hide in the
> bathroom for a little bit. Let me know if you're
> free later. I'll call you on my way home. Maybe
> we can meet up.

Diana sat in the driver's seat, quickly replying to Ann before starting her car. She pressed the talk-to-text button.

> "Will do. Remember, metal surfaces show
> reflections—keep your face out of those
> pictures."

With a rumble, Diana's car started. Her phone connected to her car, and a text from Ann popped up on her screen.

> Bitch 😊

47

She laughed as she called Arnold.

"Hello."

Arnold sounded like shit as he answered the phone. Diana hesitated; her breath caught in her throat.

"Hello," he said again, his patience sounding so thin already. "What's up?"

Nervousness bubbled up from her stomach, bringing a wave of nausea with it.

"Hi, babe," Diana said as evenly as possible as she pulled out of her work parking lot. "I'm on my way home. Judith gave me a half-day today. What're you up to?"

"Free period," Arnold said into the phone. "Nice that you got a half day. When did that happen?"

"Last night, before everything," Diana said, and she put her blinker on.

"Why is that so loud?" Arnold said, his voice fading as if he was holding it away.

"My blinker?" Diana asked. "Wait, are you hungover?"

"No, Dee," Arnold said. "I'm just exhausted. I was worried about you. I left late last night and got up super early this morning. Felt like shit. Mark and I went to the diner for breakfast instead of the gym."

"Oh no," Diana said with concern. She hadn't talked to Tim yet. Maybe Arnold had left early and met them at the diner before heading to work. "I'm sorry. You want me to come over later and take care of you?"

"No, but I would love it if you could shut that blinker off," Arnold said. Diana completed her turn, the clicking sound ending immediately. "Thank you," Arnold continued, "I'm just really tired and am going to rest after I get home from practice."

"Okay, well, let me know if you change your mind," Diana said.

"Will do," Arnold mumbled. "What're you doing with the rest of your day?"

"Well, I'm going to go home, eat, rest, and relax. I might hang out with Ann depending on how I'm feeling when she's out of work. And since there's some mysterious sticky liquid spilled on my floor, I'm probably going to clean that up too."

"First of all, it was you who knocked my beer over on your way to bed. Second of all, if you want me to clean it up, just say something. Don't make a cute little joke about it and try to guilt me into doing it for you. It's your floor, even if it's my beer."

"Arnold, that's not what I meant," Diana said. Silence flooded the car. "Look, let's both get some rest and maybe try to have a nice day together tomorrow, okay?"

"Yeah, Dee, whatever you say. Just leave the beer there for me. I'll take care of it. I'll take care of everything," Arnold said.

Diana couldn't gauge his temperament, but his tone sucked.

"Feel better, Arnold," Diana said. "I'll talk to you later." She ended the call.

They both needed sleep and maybe some general attitude adjustments. She would call Tim once she was home, possibly after a nap. Maybe then everything would seem normal, instead of this weird, skewed reality.

chapter seven

Arnold

ARNOLD PUT his head down on top of his crossed arms. The cool of his metal desk reached out and caressed his head. "Are you hungover?" Diana's accusing voice pounded throughout his head.

Guilt trickled down his throat around the knots of worry.

The stale taste of cigarettes wrapped around the trail of greasy bacon fat from breakfast this morning.

When he had walked into the brightly lit diner, he heard Mark before he saw him. He was in their usual seats in Darlene's section. Mark and Tim were sitting opposite each other in a large circular booth. It felt like old times, good times, when he and Mark were still doing their student teaching in the same school they were both still working in now.

Tim had just pledged their fraternity, and Arnold had put him through the ringer with clues to figure out who his Big was. He had most certainly pushed the boundaries of hazing even back then. If they had been in school now, Arnold probably would have been kicked out. In his mind though, it was a scavenger hunt, not a kidnapping. Tim had been a twenty-year-old sophomore. You couldn't really kidnap a twenty-year-old sopho-more, at least Arnold didn't think. It had worked out.

Tim had introduced him to Diana, and by the spring of 2013, Arnold was graduating from his five-year master's program in teaching, and his grand-little had introduced him to Amber.

Thankfully, as close as frats and sororities were, there was no actual relationship between bigs and littles and grands.

"Look what the cat dragged in," Mark said when his eyes locked in on Arnold. "Dude, you haven't looked this bad since—"

"I know," Arnold said, standing on Tim's side.

"You know, huh," Mark said, raising an eyebrow. "What did you do last night, Arnie?"

He could have laughed or left. Instead, he hesitated. Arnold pressed his head further into his arms as the rest of the morning replayed in his mind. Like a shark to blood, Mark took the bait.

"Or is *who* did you do last night a better question?" Mark was goading him. Mostly in jest, he assumed, but he hadn't been wrong. Arnold looked at Tim, sealing the nail in his coffin.

"I have to go," Tim snarled.

"I. . ." Arnold lifted his fist and slowly slammed it onto the table twice.

"I thought you were done with that. Thought you had chosen Diana," Tim said, his voice cutting as he stood.

"I was, I am," Arnold said, combing his fingers through his sandy brown hair. Most of the pomegranate wax he used to style it after yesterday morning's shower was long gone.

"So then, you fell and your penis landed inside her? Did it go in her—" Mark's snide remark was cut short by Tim.

"Don't," he said. He sighed, throwing cash on the table. "I can't. Enjoy my Hungry Man. I'll catch up with you later, Mark."

Arnold slid out of the booth and took Tim's seat across from Mark. Grunting, his fist thudded against the table again. This time, the silverware jumped. Darlene followed Tim with her eyes before walking to their table.

"What did you do to my favorite guy?" Her gum cracked in her mouth as she waited for an answer.

"We told him that I was going to take you to the prom this year, and he couldn't have you," Mark said, winking at Darlene.

"You two," she said, wagging her thick, calloused finger. The bright red nail glinted in the light. Darlene looked at Arnold. "What do you want me to do with his order?"

"I'll eat it—sunny side up with extra bacon if possible," Arnold said.

"Sure thing. You want extra syrup for the pancakes?"

"You know me so well, Darlene."

"Don't I know it. I'll bring your usual drinks with the food."

Arnold winked as she turned and walked away.

"So," Mark said as he settled back into the worn red and black booth, "what happened, Arnold?"

"Fuck if I know," Arnold said to the table. "Diana flipped out when I went to bring her upstairs and kicked me. She hates sleeping on the couch. I had a few beers, the growler we got from whatever that farm upstate was. I was heading to my car, and I just—I wanted—I *needed* it."

"So you were horny?"

"Sex, freedom. I don't know, dude. Either way, Diana wasn't going to give it. I'm not entirely sure exactly what happened until I texted you earlier." Arnold felt Mark's eyes on him as he stared off beyond the white and black checked walls. "I do remember being in my car. There was text after text from an unsaved number. Something about an emergency. I couldn't read while I was driving. Not that I thought I could have read at that point anyway." Arnold reached for a coffee that wasn't there. Instead, he picked up Tim's knife and twirled it on its tip against the table. "It was worse than when that crazy redhead power-texted for an hour. An address popped up, and the next thing I know, I'm waking up to Amber offering me lines and yelling at me for breaking it off with her."

Thoughts ran through Arnold's head, but nothing made

sense. Mark played with the wrapper from his straw as Darlene approached the table, their buffet in her arms.

"Thanks, sweetheart," Mark said, throwing her another wink.

The two men sat in silence as they prepared to eat their breakfast. "Emergency?" Mark asked.

Arnold noticed how his eyes never left his toast as he smeared it with butter.

"A baby emergency. . ." Arnold's voice faded. "But you haven't, I mean. . ." Mark's sentence trailed off.

The daunting feeling crept into Arnold's chest as he opened the ketchup bottle. In his memory, he could see Amber sitting on the floor, her chin resting on his bare knee. He could still feel the chill of her hands sliding up his thighs.

"Her sister is pregnant."

"I thought you weren't talking to her?"

"We're not talking. We weren't *talking*. Just," he sighed. "She's been taking it hard—" Mark opened his mouth, but Arnold ignored him. "She's been having a hard time with her sister being pregnant. We talked a couple of times when she was home for spring break. But not since she graduated, man."

Arnold studied his chocolate milk. He watched the froth slowly break down to light brown milk. Mark looked up at Arnold, waiting for an answer. Arnold put down the knife and picked up his phone. Opening his texts, he scrolled, trying to find the texts from Amber. They were gone.

"Seriously, you okay?"

"They're gone. The texts from last night. . . they're wiped."

"You sure they said something about her *sister's* baby, and not. . ." Mark jutted his chin out toward Arnold's crotch. "I'm not saying it would be, because you know Amber the way a lot of people know Amber. They say no one can fully change, bro."

"Thanks," Arnold snipped.

His heart pounded in his chest. He was supposed to be better than this, not better at it.

"I meant—" Mark's voice trailed as he shoveled his fork into his mouth. "Fuck, man, what are you going to do now?" he asked, a mouthful of potatoes trying to escape between words.

"Nothing," Arnold blurted out. "There's nothing to do. It's over. It's *been* over. It's exactly what Tim said, I chose Diana.

That's it."

"Well, here's to Diana not finding out," he said, lifting his soda. "About any of it," he added.

"Fuck yeah," Arnold heard himself say, lifting his chocolate milk. Dread and a headache crept in, overpowering the numbness the drugs had provided. After they had eaten, he had headed right to school, getting himself cleaned up in the locker rooms before students filed in for the day.

A loud bell rang out, scaring Arnold almost off his chair. Free period was over. The sound of students barreling down the hall stomped over Arnold's thoughts. At least the kids would be forced to run the mile today, and that was enough to get Arnold out of his chair and into the gymnasium.

chapter eight

Diana

DIANA ROLLED OVER, facing away from the television and the coffee table. Her nose grazed the back of the couch. Tangled in her pillows and blankets, she was snuggled tighter than a bug in a rug. She felt too aware, and still somehow completely removed. It was as if Diana was wide awake but wasn't. Her mind felt just as heavy as her body, stuck in limbo between being awake and asleep. She could hear the light rush of cars outside, her stomach still digesting her lunch, and the sound of waves. Diana concentrated on the last sound, beachy waves crashing around her, and began envisioning herself at Cedar Beach.

Her black and pink bikini popped in stark contrast to her skin tone. The sky was clear, and the sand was bright and clean, mirroring her blue and yellow towel. Diana felt the warmth of the sun on her neck as she listened to the waves. A chill ran down her back.

Empty walls molded green and stained with dirt replaced the open air. Beneath her was a dingy gray blanket. She flailed her legs, kicking them free from the rag. Once more, she was lying on her couch. She flipped over from her stomach, onto her side, her body sinking against the back of the couch. Diana wrapped her free arm around herself as she tried to listen for the sound of the waves again. For a moment, she heard nothing. Knowing that she was on the precipice of sleep if only she could just fall there, Diana waited in darkness.

The soft click of metal was followed by the whoosh of wind and the suction of a seal. Diana focused on her breathing as she waited for footsteps to come from her front door.

"Arnold."

She tried to speak. Her words got caught and warbled in her mouth, seeping like drool onto her pillow. Diana opened her eyes, throwing off the blanket as she attempted to sit up. Reaching for her phone, her hand knocked over the empty water bottle sitting on the coffee table. Taking a sip from the full one next to it, she looked at her plate of food. She had picked apart her sandwich, making it through the bacon and some of the bagel, before her eyes began closing.

Diana looked around the living room as best as she could.

There was nothing there. But the air was still pregnant with someone else's presence. Goosebumps ran down her arms. She sighed, shaking her head. Diana rolled off the couch, doing her best not to wake herself up. She kept her eyes on her feet as they padded around the couch and up the stairs. She needed the rest. Her mind was playing tricks, her body run down from stress, or maybe a summer cold.

Noises from outside startled her as she was trying to orient herself. Someone dropping something, maybe. She looked over her shoulder toward the bathroom as panic began to wash over her like a shower. A shadow moved across the light streaming in from the front door. She looked up, frozen by the sound of metal scraping. It sounded like when she left things on the table out front. She stumbled forward, ripping open the curtains that lined the door. Diana saw nothing.

But she had heard something. She knew it.

Diana went into the kitchen to make herself a cup of bedtime tea. The perfect solution to get her to sleep peacefully, especially in the middle of the afternoon. The heavy sound of her deadbolt clanked. She leaned back, her eyes focused on the door. There was something moving behind the linen fabric. The room swayed. She tried to keep her eyes locked on the front door, hoping to stop the walls as they danced around her. The rev of an engine and the sound of tires peeling away down the street broke her focus. It was too loud, too jarring.

Someone had just been in and out of her house, and they locked the door behind them. Fear took hold of her. She needed to find her phone, call someone—Tim, the cops—she braced herself against the wall. She felt weak and cold. Diana stumbled back into the kitchen. On the counter was a bottle of water. The lukewarm liquid hit her tongue. As she fell into the darkness, a strange taste filled her mouth.

chapter nine

<u>Arnold</u>

ARNOLD'S FIST clenched when he saw Ann strutting his way outside Diana's apartment.

"You-hoo, asshole," Ann shouted toward him.

Did she just call me an asshole? Arnold thought to himself. He watched as her ponytail swung the opposite way from her hips.

"Hi, Arnold."

The chipper tone in her voice sounded strained and forced.

"Hi, Ann," Arnold replied in kind. "How wonderful to see you."

Instincts from the field and his fighting days took over, and Arnold squared his shoulders, staring at Ann like a predator about to pounce.

"What brings you here?" Arnold prompted.

"As I'm sure you know, and just in case you don't, Diana is feeling a little out of sorts. I'm here to take care of her," Ann said. "I heard you didn't feel too hot yourself, Arnold. Late night?"

Ann's eyes seemed to scan over every part of Arnold's body. He wasn't sure if she was trying to gauge his temperature or laser his skin off.

"Didn't realize I needed to ask your permission first, or I would have called and told you to fuck off," Arnold answered, hatred dripping from his sarcasm.

He knew she was goading him, and yet he couldn't stop.

He hadn't always been fair to Diana, but it was Ann who championed him as the devil incarnate.

"Oh, and I would have thought you were out fucking a whore, but I'm glad you stopped by. Silly me, always rushing around, I forgot something from my car. Since I'm headed that way, I'll walk you back to yours," Ann said through a cheer-leader's competition smile. "Unless you want to come inside and join us for a girls' movie marathon. They're playing the best of the cheating husband, the stalker ex-boyfriend, and the college frath-lete who rapes someone and thinks they can get away with it."

Arnold swallowed his anger down. Diana had chosen to forgive him, and yet Ann held on to his past like a yappy dog with a bone. He thought of Amber then, and earlier this morn-ing. It was still the past, he figured. He heard his teeth squeaking as he ground them together, pushing tension throughout his jaw. Ann turned, her heels scraping against the sidewalk, and flipped her ponytail at him. If she were a man, he would have used it like a rope around her neck.

"Much as I would love to listen to you shit on me for the next few hours, I have plans with my own friends. . . ones who happen to like Diana and value our relationship," Arnold said. He had been matching her phoniness, but what he really needed was to channel his inner sorority slut. He shifted his hips, mirroring Ann's usual stance, and tried his best to mimic Amber's cheery ruthlessness, speaking to Ann in a language she could understand. "But thanks so much for the offer. You can be a good little bitch, though, and give these to Diana for me."

He tipped the cup before he finished his sentence. Ann let out a shrill yelp as lukewarm liquid slid down her ponytail and into her blouse. The entire right side of her shirt was now wet and almost sheer. Coffee trickled down her forehead, getting trapped in her fake lashes.

"You mother—" Ann growled under her breath.

"O-M-G," shrieked Arnold. "That was totes an accident. Such a klutz."

Ann rolled her shoulders back as she wrung out her long hair, watching the coffee drip from the ends.

"Thanks for your help," Arnold said, shoving the brownie into the crook of Ann's arm. "Hopefully next time I see you, you'll be in a casket."

Arnold stormed off, his stride nearly doubling what Ann's could do, especially on an uneven road. He had already messed up when he tried to be civil and failed. What was the difference at this point? Diana would yell at him when she felt better. And with Ann nagging her, it wasn't like he could blame Diana. That girl was one strap-on short of being metaphorically and literally up his girlfriend's ass.

He got in his truck and turned the volume up louder than it already was. Not even Ministry blaring through the speakers loud enough for Arnold to feel it through his seat softened his anger. He was still fuming as he sped down the causeway to meet Tim at the reservation. It had taken him less than two songs from Diana's to get here. A new record.

Arnold parked his car and whipped out his phone, his fingers pounding on the screen like a hammer on nails.

> Dee. Tried to stop by before my run w/ Tim.
> Your lil chihuahua nipped at me. The coffee
> didn't make it; hope she at least gave you my
> brownie. Call u later.

He had just hit send when he saw Tim's car pull into the parking lot. By the look on Tim's face, it seemed as though he had already spoken to Diana.

"Heard you're having an off day with your coordination,"

Tim shouted over to him through his laughter. "Maybe a nice five-mile combo will help straighten out your legs."

"I tell Diana all the time that they need to pave the sidewalk in front of her house, bro." Arnold threw his hands up in the air.

"You also tell her that Ann is the biggest piece of trash on the island and Mark is a great guy," Tim rebutted. "Look, I know Mark is your go-to for extra-curricular—"

"Was my go-to. There is no more extra anything."

Tim raised an eyebrow as he threw his arms up in surrender and continued, "But something is up. More than Ann's coffee shower and Diana's 'summer flu.'"

It was hard to take Tim seriously as a grown man making air quotes. Arnold knew how strongly Tim felt about his concerns about Diana's health. He wondered if he had yet to broach the subject with her. Arnold stretched his neck up toward the sky, closing his eyes. "You want a breakdown by player or in order of events?"

Tim patted Arnold on the shoulder.

"We got five miles, brother, you might as well start at the beginning."

"Funny," Arnold began, "I almost wish Diana were telling you her version instead of updating that shrew she calls a best friend."

"I'm not a shrew," Tim said. Arnold picked up his pace to match as they made their way toward the parking lot. "And Ann's not actually her best friend. But I am waiting to impartially judge you."

Arnold laughed, feeling the difference in his breathing when they stopped jogging and started to run down the sandy path.

"Yeah," he said, "might as well get the full version since you can—I guess it all started the other night when she woke me up at three or four. . ."

chapter ten

ANN DOWNPLAYED her run-in with Arnold as best she could; no need to make an under-the-weather Diana even more upset. After a quick wash up and a shirt change, Ann settled them on the couch and put on a movie while Diana updated her.

"So, wait," Ann said, hitting pause as their movie returned from commercial break. "Let me just make sure I understand this correctly. You woke up after I left because you heard a noise—"

"Correct," Diana said.

"You called Assclown, who did nothing useful." Ann held up her hand as Diana opened her mouth and continued, "You then found your door unlocked, went to work, and that's when you fainted in Judith's office?"

"Right so far," Diana said, laughing as she broke off the corner piece of her brownie.

"Assclown—"

"You can just call him Arnold, you know? I'll still know you hate him."

Ann rolled her eyes and shook her head.

"Asshole tucks you into bed, disappears, and then has the

audacity to be cranky when he clearly left you sick at home to party with that ape-like creature he calls a friend?"

Diana frowned.

"You hadn't thought of that," Ann stated.

Diana shrugged. Ann's heart melted a little. Her friend was snuggled up on the couch, picking at a brownie on the verge of tears. Even after everything, Ann always seemed to catch on to his antics before Diana did—the downside of being a good person, she supposed.

If Arnold had been Ann's boyfriend, well, she wouldn't have taken him back after the first time he cheated. Or the second. Or the third. Especially not when his "cheating" was another relationship. What Arnold had with Amber seemed like the real deal, not just someone he fucked when his girlfriend was doing her own thing. *And still, he thinks he deserves someone like Diana.*

She would always see Arnold as someone who wanted to do better, because she knew they could.

Not someone with a massive chip on their shoulder and a bad case of entitlement. Just because he grew up in Englewood, one of the most dangerous neighborhoods in Chicago, and had worked his way up to an apartment on Long Island, didn't mean he was entitled to shit. He didn't even work that hard, if her impression of his college days was right.

Not that she *had* to work, but she did. Diana had started at Santo, Miller, and Volpe after graduation. The first few weeks without her bestie had been brutal, until there was an open position for a receptionist. So lucky that both her parents had treated at least two of the three founding partners.

"You know what, it's probably all these movies we're watching," Ann said, shrugging it off. "I mean, really, how many movies deep can you go before you start seeing everyone as the bad guy?" Ann added, waving her hands about.

"Here," Ann said, picking up Diana's hot cocoa from the table. "Bottoms up, bitchy," she added with a wink.

Diana's eyes closed, and color rose to her cheeks. Ann smiled.

She couldn't fix all of Diana's problems overnight, but at least she could cheer her up. Give her a little comfort after a harrowing few days.

Her eyes fell to the coffee table as Diana returned her mug.

"What's this?" Ann asked, picking up a book in some kind of plastic sleeve.

"It's from Judith. It's a signed copy. Her husband is a lit agent and had some connection to hers. She knows how obsessed I am with her and all of her books. I was planning on starting it yesterday, but I barely remember even taking it out of my bag."

Ann turned the book over in her hands, dropping it back where she found it. She slid her fingers against the blanket on Diana's couch before picking up her own hot cocoa.

"You know, bosses don't typically give their employees presents. Are you sure she's happily married?"

"Put your eyebrow down." Diana laughed before breaking off another piece of brownie. "You're right, you know? If we don't stop soon, I'll start thinking you've run off with Mark next time I don't see you at work."

Ann pretended to puke and sat back down on the couch next to Diana. After making sure she was tucked in tightly with a water bottle in reach and her cell phone nowhere near her, Ann started their movie. It was a shame that Arnold couldn't be a better boyfriend to Diana. Not that he tried to hide any of his indiscretions.

Later, she thought.

Her best friend was under the weather, and it was going to be her favorite gal pal to get her through these dark times, even if Diana refused to see that any time she spent with Arnold was a massive raincloud against her bright future. The surprise coffee shower was a gift.

Walking into someone's home with sopping wet hair and a stained blouse required an explanation. By dousing her with coffee, Arnold had unwittingly given Ann a chance to save her ace card for later. The coffee beans just had to be spilled. Ann watched as Diana's eyes started to close. Then she picked up her phone and searched for *The Breakdown*.

chapter eleven

Diana

DIANA SQUEEZED her eyes shut until bursts of color popped behind her eyelids. She remembered saying goodbye to Ann. At some point during the night, the hot cocoa had turned into whiskey and cream liqueur, which had turned into just whiskey. All the while, movies featuring cheaters turned into a montage of dick pics sent from Ann's newest fling and documentaries on unsolved crimes. When they had finished all the whiskey, Ann had left.

They had made some plans for today. What those plans were, Diana had no idea. They had something to do with her upcoming party, and they were made staring up at the stars. It had been either very late or very early, depending on a person's inclination. Diana had long since dropped pretenses and her drawers. She had gotten up to walk Ann to the door, and as her friend pulled out a cigarette, Diana decided to join her, looping their arms and leading her around the building to her small porch off the back door. The perks of having a corner unit.

She stood on her deck in her teal and blue thong and her favorite cream-colored t-shirt with a coffee pun across the front.

Diana and Ann laughed as the summer air warmed around them. She remembered Ann snuggling up against her, making a "scratch and sniff" pair—coffee hair, coffee shirt. Throwing her cigarette askew and into a tree, Diana apologized to the tree. She remembered a slap across her butt as she stumbled in the doorway. Diana had maneuvered up the stairs and dove into her bed. She assumed Ann locked the back and front doors on her way out.

Somewhere, her phone was ringing. Rolling over, Diana reached around to no avail. Not even her baseball bat was in arm's reach. The other side of the bed was warm. A memory flashed in her mind's eye as tingles ran up the side of her arm. Her body reacted as if someone had been in her bed with her. Maybe she had finally outdone herself in drinking. Diana started to drift off. Warm, rich notes of coffee warmed the chilling thoughts right from her mind.

"Ann?" Diana's voice croaked as she tried to speak.

Arnold appeared in the doorway holding a brown paper bag and a large to-go cup.

"Better," he said.

He waved the bag in the air. Diana rolled around, pushing herself up. Underneath the smells of bacon and espresso, there was a hint of something familiar in her sheets, but she couldn't place it. She was being crazy. Strangers didn't sneak in for a cuddle, and Ann would have locked the doors. The time she tried to pay for a home security system flashed through Diana's thoughts. A thought scarier than any intruder.

She was sitting up and comfortable before Arnold kicked off his shoes and hopped into bed.

"Can you grab the tray? I think it's in the spare room."

"From the girl who slept with the back door open and the front door unlocked, you're still worried about crumbs."

Diana felt her stomach flip. The creaminess of the hot cocoa curdled in the leftover whiskey.

"Mm-mm," was all she could manage, pushing off the bed.

Diana stumbled into the bathroom, landing hard on the thick, wool-like bath mat. She heard Arnold close her bedroom door before her stomach wretched its contents into the porcelain bowl. Arnold hated throwing up, whether it was himself or anyone else. She knew it grossed him out, and most of the time, she preferred to be alone. And she had been, until Arnold showed up, right?

The skin on her neck pinched as goosebumps spread down her body. She wanted to look behind her, check in the shower, behind the door, but her stomach kept her pinned where she was.

Besides, maybe it was better not to know. Then what would she do if someone had been there? Arnold was nowhere to be found, and neither was her baseball bat.

Diana gargled a laugh, choking on the rising bile. She could always throw up on them. That would work. She groaned as she rested her head in her arms. Just a few more minutes, then she would soldier on, brush her teeth, ignore the monsters in her mind, and figure out if things were okay with her and Arnold. He brought her breakfast. It only made sense that he had something to be sorry for; Diana wobbled as she stood. Once she felt centered, she flushed the toilet and gave her teeth a quick brushing, careful not to overdo it on her tongue.

There was a pair of cutoffs on top of the laundry pile, along with her t-shirt from last night. Diana threw both on and shuffled to the stairs.

"I'm done, Arnold," she called down.

"I tried calling you to tell you I was here, but you didn't answer," Arnold said. He appeared at the bottom of the stairs. "You need help?"

"I got it," she said.

Diana held onto the railing and took each stair with care.

"You must have been out cold. You and Ann have fun?"

She nodded as she continued making her way. Arnold

reached out and rubbed her back as she stepped onto the small landing.

Breakfast was sprawled out on the coffee table. Arnold's already missing several bites. Diana eased herself onto the couch and snuggled under the balled-up blanket. Arnold plopped into his seat and resumed munching away.

The crunch of bacon and other chewing sounds filled the silence between them. Diana wasn't really sure if they were fighting, and if they were, she couldn't even remember what about. This wasn't new for them; this blurred area where emotions ran high and common sense ran low. The last time Arnold got out of bed this early and got them both breakfast was not since Amber. . . Diana coughed, a bite of her sandwich caught in her throat.

"You okay?"

Diana nodded, clearing her throat again. "Yeah, wrong pipe."

Arnold's face relaxed as he handed her a bottle of pineapple juice from the bag on the floor.

Diana looked back down at her sandwich. A bacon, egg, and cheese on a lightly toasted everything bagel with an over-medium egg. Her go-to favorite, and yet, Diana felt her chest tighten. She lifted her chin and turned in Arnold's direction, looking over his shoulder, and asked, "Are we fighting?" Diana put her sandwich on top of the paper bag on the coffee table and cleared her throat. "That's not what I meant. Kind of, but I want to start with thank you for the breakfast. It's perfect. You surprising me this morning was perfect. But I get the feeling that something is off, and I don't understand. It's just—"

Arnold took her hand and squeezed.

"No, we're good. I'm not mad at you. Pretty sure you're not mad at me. Unless you're still pissed about yesterday—"

"You poured coffee on her and called her a bitch."

"Yeah, she is a bitch. Shouldn't have *said* anything about it, though. Definitely shouldn't have poured coffee on her. I think the stress has taken us both for a ride."

Diana looked into Arnold's eyes and exhaled. His greasy fingertips slid across her skin, engulfing her hand. She squeezed Arnold's hand before letting go and returning to her sandwich.

Diana felt herself breathe easier than before. Her stomach growled, now craving the food she had struggled to want moments ago. He had promised her that the frat house chapter of his life was over. She didn't think he would let her down again, especially knowing that it would be the last time. There was only so much a person was willing to take. Arnold had far exceeded his limit.

"It's also scary that you've been passing out or fainting.

Whatever. But I'm here. For you, for us." He reached up, his fingers stroking the side of her face. "Just some yolk," he said with a wink. "You're my yoke."

"You're so lame."

"Hey! If I had kids, they would be considered Dad jokes. And I'd be awesome at them."

"If you had a sense of humor, your jokes would be funny."

Diana swayed as Arnold lightly punched her in the shoulder. She thought she was pretty funny, but as long as she had known him, Arnold hadn't. *Oh well*, she thought. *Tim would have laughed at that.*

"Have you seen my phone?"

"You don't know where it is?"

Diana shook her head. Her door had been open all night. Her baseball bat was missing; granted, she hadn't really looked for it yet, and her phone was nowhere to be found. She was fighting hard to keep the panic at bay, but already her stomach had turned to lead in her belly.

Arnold called it three times before they found it under the couch.

"I don't even want to know what you two were up to," Arnold said.

She could see from his rolling eyes that he wasn't kidding.

"I'm not sure I want to either," Diana answered. "I do know that we made plans for later today. Going to help with some last-minute party stuff."

Diana tucked herself back into Arnold's armpit. The same artificial smells of surf permeated her nose. Familiar, but it wasn't what she had smelled when she woke up. If Arnold had been in her bed, there would have been no question. He'd been wearing the same deodorant since she had met him in college. It didn't ease the feeling that she had smelled something—or someone—earlier.

She shook her head, nuzzling closer to Arnold, avoiding the spray on stuff as best she could, and looked at her phone. She had two dozen or so texts. Most of them were group texts from her friends still theorizing about how long the latest Pretty Little Liars plot twist had been planned, and whether, after all that, anyone still liked the show. Two were from Tim. Together they read:

> Hey, Dame. Heard you were under the weather (sorry to hear) and had a late night date night with Ann. . . Try to rest up though. . . you'll need it for Sunday. Plans for Monday yet? lmk.

She texted him back.

> Rest? Mister, don't you know the Mets and the Phillies are playing again tonight! Already missed last night's game... will let you know about Monday.

"What about you?" she asked Arnold. "Big plans?"

"Mark's still having his poker tournament today," Arnold answered. "So I'm going to stop over there for a bit."

"Nice," Diana answered. "We're still going tomorrow night, right?"

"Mhmm," Arnold said. He looked down at her; from this

angle, his eyes looked dark. Not just the color, but brooding. "Best behavior for Ann's Annual Fourth of July bash," he said.

"And no coffee spills," Diana added, patting his thigh. "I'm going upstairs to take a shower. You going to head out?"

"Yeah," Arnold said. "My sneakers are upstairs, though."

Diana rolled her eyes. She stopped in the kitchen to plug her phone in before making her way upstairs. She finished the water bottle that had been left out on the counter from last night, or maybe the night before. The tepid water made her even thirstier. Perhaps she should start labeling them with dates or, at the very least, putting them back in the fridge.

She headed upstairs. "Are you coming?"

"Can you toss them down?"

"Mhmm."

She steadied herself against the banister and finished her water before heading into her bathroom. At least the water could heat up while she grabbed his shoes. She blasted the hot water and then stood, feeling behind the door: *no towel and no robe*. She sighed, *easy enough to grab*. Diana took two steps into her bedroom when her arms weakened. They felt like two overcooked noodles.

She lifted them in front of her face, but she couldn't see anything through patches of darkness.

"Dee—what the fuck?" Arnold's voice hovered above her. "Dee—you okay?"

Diana's eyes fluttered open. "The shower," she repeated over and over until it came out clearly. Arnold ran to the bathroom and shut the water off.

"Stay lying down," he said.

Arnold pressed something cold and wet against her forehead, sending shivers down her spine.

"I'm okay," she said.

Her voice was small even to her own ears. "Maybe we—"

"Really, I'm okay," she said again. She forced herself to sit up, doing her best to sound like she believed herself. "Drinking.

Hot steam. Not enough hydration."

"Well then, looks like you're going to need some shower supervision."

"Arnold—"

"Nothing crazy," he interjected. "Just someone to watch you and support you, you know?"

The dancing of his eyebrows while his eyes remained pinned to her chest suggested something different. She thought about it, recalling the last time they had actually been with each other. It had started the same way. She nuzzled against him. They were in his apartment, and there were too many blankets stacked on top of them.

She rubbed against him until finally he sighed, reaching into his nightstand before he pulled her on top. She managed to get herself off moments before he finished, but it had been more underwhelming than usual.

Maybe the shower wasn't a terrible idea. Diana stepped in and turned to see Arnold close the lid and sit on the toilet. She leaned forward to grab her soap, angling her backside toward him, but when she looked over her shoulder, his eyes were glued to his phone. She sighed and went through her routine, letting the hot water run off the stress of the morning.

She had just started relaxing when Arnold's phone started to ring.

"It's Mark," he said. "I'm gonna take this. You're good?"

"Yup," Diana answered.

She reached for her towel, realizing she had never actually grabbed a new one. Arnold's voice had traveled downstairs. Diana ran her hand down the length of her arm, brushing off as much water as she could. She did this all over her body, laughing at how silly it was, but loving the freedom. After a solid minute of dancing around, shaking her limbs like a salt shaker, she brushed her hair and grabbed her coconut oil. She would still have to pat herself dry before she got dressed, but her nana had always stressed the importance of hydrated skin.

Diana closed her eyes, remembering the two of them rolling their skin and applying face cream together. Nana Rosa would roll over if she knew Diana had switched away from the chemical stuff to plain old coconut oil, but still. She'd be proud to know that Diana always applied the oil gently and lifted up. "Gravity will do enough damage on its own, no need to help it," she would tell her.

Throwing on a pair of shorts and her favorite shirt—a white waffle shirt with little roses her nana had made her—she headed downstairs to the living room. Her eyes drifted to the spot next to the couch. She blinked a few times and then realized what she wasn't looking at... the sticky spot from yesterday was gone. She hadn't been feeling well enough to clean it yesterday when she got home, and it slipped her mind once Ann stormed in on high.

She got closer and looked again, but didn't see it. "Arnold!" Diana exclaimed. "Arnold?"

"What? What's wrong?" Arnold shouted. He stepped out from the kitchen, his phone still in hand.

"Nothing—sorry!"

"You're okay?"

"Yeah," she said. She gave him a half-hug and whispered, "Thank you! The floor looks great!" Arnold pulled back and stared blankly at Diana. "You know, the beer. I had forgotten about it until just now, but it's—"

"Diana, I didn't do it."

"It was an accident. I know that. I just meant, who even knew you could mop?"

"No, Diana. . ." Arnold's voice trailed off. "What?" Her head cocked to the side.

"Nothing," he said with a shrug. "Mark? Yeah, no, it's good. I'll see you later."

Diana watched him end the call. His eyes were locked on the spot that had previously been stuck with dried beer.

"Don't worry, I won't tell the guys."

She laughed, breaking from him before walking into the

Elizabeth Scozzari

kitchen. He followed behind her. He was smiling, but it seemed *off*, hollow even. She didn't understand why he always felt so attacked. Diana knew—and had pointed out—that it was an accident. One day, she hoped he would believe her. Her thoughts were interrupted by another ringing phone. This time, hers.

"Probably Ann," she said.

chapter twelve

Arnold

Diana answered the phone, moving through the kitchen like she hadn't passed out earlier. At least he had been right about the shower. He tried not to stare at the floor, but Diana loved cleaning. It wasn't like she would just work on one area like most people.

She cleaned in her own weird tornado way. Starting over here, bringing this into that room, and getting distracted by something else. It was an all-day affair.

He wasn't going to disappoint her and let her know that he didn't know how to mop. He didn't even know she owned one. He sure as shit hadn't cleaned up the beer. Until she pointed it out, he had forgotten about it, the same way she must have forgotten cleaning it up. Just like she didn't remember to lock her door last night or where her phone was. It was easy to write them off as drunken silliness. Maybe Tim had a point; maybe there was more going on with her.

Concern rooted itself in his chest as he grabbed his own cell phone. He texted the guy's group text to let them know his ETA, and quickly side-barred Tim.

Are you going to talk to Dee?

The reply was instant.

Yes.

Arnold felt better knowing Tim was handling it. Diana hated the doctors as much as he hated fighting with her. If only she could forget how to do that. He laughed at himself. Unlikely. She was the most stubborn, organized, detail-oriented, and driven person, as long as she wrote it down. Left on her own without a notebook of sorts, she was apt to forget her own name. That was her, though. Arnold came up behind Diana, gently wrapping his arms around her. She gasped and then relaxed when she turned and saw his face.

"Sorry," he whispered.

"S'okay."

"Listen, I know you're going to help Ann set up for tomorrow, but you need to rest, too. The game is on tonight, maybe invite Tim over?"

Diana pulled herself away from Arnold and turned to face him fully. She was studying him, scratching her finger on the underside of her chin. There was something in her eyes, something he couldn't read. She had been a wreck when her grandmother died. Forgetting to eat for days, oversleeping, or not sleeping at all, but she pulled through. He had been *distracted*, which left her to face her grief alone. It wasn't right, but she was strong.

Something gnawed at his chest, making him uncomfortable. He had one slip-up. One Diana didn't even know about. That couldn't be setting her back. Could it? He watched as her eyes lit up.

"You that worried about me, or don't want Tim winning all of your money?"

She was teasing him. The pressure lessened, and he felt his shoulders relax.

"Both," Arnold said. "We both know Tim loves the Mets as much as you. Plus, he'll force you to rest."

"He *is* my best friend for a reason you know." Diana smiled. "And he's already been texted."

"Glad that's settled."

The two grabbed their keys and whatever else they needed before walking out the front door and locking up.

"Have fun with Satan," Arnold said.

"Could have sworn *you* were hanging out with Mark. Tell him I say hi. Seriously, though, have fun. Love you!"

"You too, Dee. If something happens, call me, okay?"

"You got it," she said as she got into her car.

Arnold watched her as she drove down the street. He turned on his car and pulled out his phone. Taking care to make sure he didn't fat-finger the screen, Arnold deleted his last incoming call.

* * *

Arnold looked down at his phone. He had just parked his car outside of Mark's and had four texts—one from Tim, and three from Amber. Arnold sat puzzled for a moment. Amber's messages sat in his inbox like a nuclear bomb. His thumb hovered over the detonator. Instead, it dropped down and opened his text from Tim.

See you by Mark's.

Arnold fired back a thumbs-up.

His thumb began to shake as it hovered above the messages from Amber. Arnold took a deep breath, the distant smell of cigars penetrating his lungs. He held it until the air burned in his lungs as he opened the texts. A small, rosy alien with massive blue eyes stared back at him. There was something about it that looked familiar and yet completely foreign.

Holding it was an older, more mature version of Amber with long, ashen blonde hair and a softness around her features, unlike Amber's, whose were as sharp as her anger. Arnold's hand released the steering wheel and dropped to his side. His heart ached with fullness. Not that he would admit it, but he saw himself holding a baby one day, like a prized game-winning football.

Scrolling down, he read the caption to the photo:

> A bumpy start, but mom and baby are okay.
> Roselynn, born June 30, 2017. 19.5", 7.5 lbs.

Underneath:

> I know we just cleared the air, and I'm sorry again. I'm not trying anything; I just. . . the other night helped. Having you here. . . We made some bad choices, old habits and all that. . . but thank you. I'm sorry that we didn't work out. I'm really sorry for HER. You know she would have been 8 months already? We've never soberly talked about it, and well, we're skipping the Vineyard this year. I'll be around if you ever need to talk. Thanks <3

A loud thunk sounded next to Arnold's ear. He jumped, his phone falling into his lap. Mark's meat hook held the neck of a beer against Arnold's window. Laughter roared in the background as Arnold fumbled between the seats for his phone.

"PARTY'S HERE," Mark shouted over his shoulder.

Dropping down so his eyes were level with Arnold's, he said, "Get your ass outta the car and grab a beer."

chapter thirteen

Diana

Diana parked the car in front of the movie theater and called Ann. While the phone was ringing, she took a sip of the half-drank water bottle on her passenger's seat. She *really* needed to stop leaving plastic in the car in the summer. She clicked her tongue, hoping it would get rid of the stale taste, but it just made her thirstier.

"Just leaving your fav place!" Ann sing-songed into the phone in place of a greeting. "Hi, dear!"

"That's not overly specific here," Diana said. She got out of her car, taking the empty plastic water bottle with her. "Where should I meet you?"

"That depends. Where are you now, and are you hungry?"

"I parked—"

"YOU DROVE?!"

"How else do you think I would get here?" Not giving her a chance to answer, Diana continued, "And I parked in front of the movie theater. More importantly, I'm hungry."

She hadn't eaten since breakfast, and her stomach was already grumbling.

"I figured you would be. Then again, I also figured that Assclown would have driven you here, but I'm sure there was a meeting of the neanderthals or something. Meet me by the large fountain. I know there's something over there, but I don't remember what."

"Sounds good. See you in a few."

She laughed to herself and hung up the phone. She didn't need Ann to forgive Arnold, but it would certainly be easier for her if she could cool down the rhetoric.

Diana didn't have to look for Ann. She saw her almost immediately walking past the fountain toward the cinema, wearing some type of romper dress with high heels. The mirrored tint on her round sunglasses made her look unreal, like a photo in a fashion magazine come to life.

Her long black hair swung from side to side as she sauntered. No matter where she went, Ann stood out, not just because of her height. It was something in the way she walked, the way she carried herself. Almost as if she were one of those rich housewives who exploited her wealth and cattiness to become the most hated on her show. It was reasonable for anyone to expect there to be a slightly older man behind her carrying parcel after parcel as she recklessly shopped on whims and wants alone.

Based on the number of bags she was carrying, it was better that Ann didn't have a backup set of arms to encourage her.

"What is all this?" Diana asked, waving her hand over all of Ann's bags.

"Just a few things for the party tomorrow," Ann said, leaning over to air kiss Diana's cheek, "and a get-well present for my very bestie! Couldn't have Judith being the only one to shower you in gifts. Though one is more of a sprinkle, no?"

Diana rolled her eyes. Ann understood the concept of money the same way Mark understood concepts like "monogamy" and "celibacy." They both were aware that these things existed in other people's lives and could be very important, but they didn't understand how or why.

"Di," Ann said as she pinched the back of Diana's arm. "You okay?"

Diana jolted. "Yeah," she said breathlessly. "Sorry, I zoned out for a minute there."

"I know," Ann exclaimed. "I gave my name to the hostess, and then came back over here, and you were totally spaced out! I was afraid you were going to faint. You're not going to faint, are you?"

"No," Diana answered, forcing herself to smile. "I was just thinking."

"Just as dangerous if you ask me. Anything good at least?"

"Not sure." Diana tried to laugh.

"Oh, honey," Ann said, somehow managing to loop her arm chock full of bags around Diana's. "Probably just worried about him being with his clown posse all day. You gonna be okay?" She spat the word "him" out of her mouth like sour milk.

"Mmm," Diana said, a wall settling behind her face.

"Oh, relax, I didn't mean anything," Ann clucked, exasperated.

"It would just be easier if—"

Ann cut her off. "Oh, you look just like Nana Rosa."

Diana raised her eyebrows slightly. It wasn't easy, but Diana had adjusted to life after she passed. Then there were days like today, where no matter what was going on, Nana Rosa was in the middle of it.

She tried to swallow and keep the tears at bay that threatened to start pouring. They had been thick as thieves. Diana's mother had burned with seething rage when the townhouse had been left to Diana. As Nana Rosa put it, "You've lived with me longer, and we made this townhouse our home. It's ours now—yours later. She'll deal." Nana Rosa shrugged her slight shoulders as she spoke. Her face was a little puffier then, tired and aged. It was the oldest Diana had ever seen her look, still stony with a rosy warmth. She passed away not too long after that.

Her smile, one that could be genuine or lethal, accented by a little dimple, was cemented in Diana's mind, along with everything else about her nana. Her mother hated that face. Before Nana had been buried, her mother had taken off for Europe and never looked back.

"Seriously, are you okay? You're freaking me out a little. . . Diana?" Ann's voice cut sharply into Diana's thoughts.

"I'm—," she cleared her throat, "I'm good. She's easy to miss. So feisty, with the biggest heart."

"Very feisty. Both traits she gave directly to you," Ann added with a smile. "Have you heard from Roberta?"

"Not since she cursed the townhouse before heading for the airport."

Maybe that's what's been running around in the shadows, Diana thought.

"Right this way, ladies," the hostess said, approaching them.

Diana watched as she partially lifted her head, as if Ann were some kind of presence to be revered. She tried not to laugh out loud.

Technically, Ann was a socialite in certain circles. Both her parents were highly successful and involved with one of the biggest hospitals on the island. She had ended up on TMZ for her fashion choices and the parties she threw. Despite the Hwang's efforts to raise an independently successful daughter, Ann had turned into a receptionist by day and an heiress by night.

They were seated at one of the square tables in the middle of the restaurant. Ann muttered to herself as she tried in vain to get all of her bags and boxes to sit still or hang neatly on the two extra chairs. Glaring at the waiter as he put down a basket of bread, she snapped, "I only have two hands and enough packages that she could have put us in a booth or something." The waiter recoiled as though he had been slapped.

"Let me help," Diana said, starting to reach forward.

"No," Ann barked. "I can't find the one that's for you. But if you see that tart cake that sat us here, get her attention."

"Yes, ma'am," Diana answered as she reached into the basket of warm bread and pulled out a piece. Dipping it into the infused oil, she smiled as she watched her friend shuffle bags on and off her lap.

After a few more minutes, Ann pulled out something over-sized and gift-wrapped. Somehow, she had managed to keep everything else on the chairs.

"We don't need the hostess anymore," Ann said, putting the package on her lap.

Diana's eyes followed Ann's quick sideways glance to the table next to them. A pack of four guys, the oldest of whom couldn't have been more than twenty-three, were seated. All of them were dressed as if they had walked off a life-size poster for various designer stores in the outlets.

Ann had barely moved, yet somehow seemed even more put together than before they had been seated. It was as if she had never been flustered by the strategically placed bags or by the hostess, Tart Cake, as she had affectionately named her. A smile and a side eye translated to Diana that she had caught someone's attention from that table, but before the lucky young man could be certain, Ann refocused all of her attention back to Diana.

"So, listen," Ann began, "I got you a little something."

"Why?" Diana pinched off another piece of bread.

"Because Judith did," Ann spat. She cleared her throat and tilted her head. "And of all the drama that's been plaguing you lately," she added, her tone coming out much softer.

Ann lifted the package, which was almost as wide as the table itself, then stopped mid-air.

"You can't argue with me over cost or whatever. I got a fantastic deal. At least," she said, looking up and doing the numbers in her head, "half off." She wiggled her fingers. Diana felt her eyes roll. "I'm just saying, don't waste time arguing with me. Now open it."

Ann ended the discussion by handing the package to Diana.

Diana peeled back the wrapped layers, surprised by a beautiful tote, one she would have never bought for herself, even if she could have afforded it.

"Ann!"

"You love it, right? You're welcome!" Ann clapped silently from her side of the table. "Now open it."

"Open it?" The bag opened to reveal a matching wristlet-wallet thing, similar to the one Ann had. Plus something black with a large ruffle. "What is this?"

"Remember that shirt I wore to the office a few weeks ago?" Diana stared at her. "The one that had a dramatic shoulder?"

"Yes! You looked amazing!"

"Well, now you can too. They had a similar shirt in your size, so I *snatched* it for you. You'll look amazing." Diana's jaw parted, but nothing came out. "Besides, when you realize I'm right, and when you've come to your senses about your dating choices, you and I will pick out some more outfits for you!"

Diana wanted to say thank you, but it was too much. Too much stuff, too much to process.

"Diana," Ann sighed. "The words are 'thank you.' And since you'll be helping me prep for the party, it's really a thank-*you* present."

"And a get well and a good job at work present too?"

"Now you're getting it! You'll be taking Judith's job any day now," Ann said.

Diana rolled her eyes and shook her head. "Not quite yet. She didn't get her promotion, and I'd like to get some actual traveling in before I have to forgo my PTO to all her responsibilities."

"Anywhere in particular?"

She had a list of places, but the gleam in Ann's eye seemed like a warning.

"You're insane, Ann. But thank you! This is, you're just—!"

"The best! I know," Ann said, throwing her shoulder into the air as a victory cheer. "Glad you came around. I couldn't return half of that, even if you wanted me to. The clothes were somehow left off the receipt." Ann threw her head back and let out a devilish laugh.

"You know, when I told you to work on saving money, that wasn't what I meant, right?" Diana shook her head and began reassembling everything into the tote.

"I know, which is why after this we're going over to that wholesale place across the way," Ann said a little louder than necessary. "What's the name of it again?"

Ann put her elbow on the table and leaned forward.

Looking upward and batting her eyelashes, she parted her lips, putting the tip of her index finger in between her teeth. Tapping her bottom teeth with her finger, she added, "It's right here on the tip of my tongue."

Diana took a casual glance at the table next to them. There was little to no doubt that the table next to them was paying attention to Ann. She saw her friend wink once before sliding to the edge of her chair. Diana picked up her menu. Ann reached out toward the young man sitting closest to her.

"'Scuse me," she whispered. "Do you know the name of the wholesale place back that way?" She pointed in the direction over her shoulder, saying, "With the red and white logo."

Diana lifted the menu up higher, hoping to conceal the laughter trying to escape. She was sure no one would notice. Two of the young men looked at Ann, taking in her beauty regardless of what she was saying. The other seemed to defer to the bigger one, the alpha—Diana felt her eyes roll—whose face Diana couldn't see. It reminded her a little of the first time she had seen Tim go out with Arnold and Mark.

Tim would have been sitting there staring, while Arnold would have deflected to Mark, or picked up the friend of the girl Mark was flirting with; she had seen it enough in real life. Diana felt her stomach turn at the memories. She lowered her menu and watched as the alpha of the group turned around in his seat to fully face Ann. "You said the red and white logo?"

"Mhmm." Ann nodded.

"RJs, DJs, TJs," he said, looking straight into Ann's eyes. "Something like that. Were you looking for something in particular?"

"Just a few things that I'd rather get in bulk," Ann said, eyeing his muscles.

"How about you give me your number, and if anything pops up, I'll let you know."

"That could work," Ann began slowly, her eyes traveling up and down his toned body. "Now that you got me going, I remember. It's BJs. How silly of me. I just love BJs."

"Who doesn't? About your number?"

"Here," she said, passing him her phone. "I'll let you put it in."

Taking her phone, the young man keyed in his number. "Name?"

"Bryan," he replied.

His fingers moved as fast as his eyes trailed down Ann's legs. She took her phone back, leaving it on the table, and extended her hand.

"Pleasure," Ann said. "It's all mine."

"Should I need an extra hand, I'll give you a call."

Ann took her hand back and turned in her seat. Her manicured nail tapped on the top of Diana's menu. Closing it, she placed it on the table, shaking her head at her friend.

"Incorrigible," she whispered.

Ann shrugged her shoulder in toward Diana, delicately placing her hand across her chest.

"Me?"

"Yes." Diana hissed. "Definitely you."

"So, what can I get you ladies this afternoon?"

"We'll get two house salads. No dressing. Thanks." The rest of lunch was as boring as the protein-less, dressing-less, bacon-less salad. Diana watched as Ann froze out the young man she had just been fawning over. His curiosity and irritation were apparent from where Diana sat. Ann insisted on speaking in low tones and wrapping up the salads to go the second they arrived at the table. Diana's stomach growled as she got into her car. Once her phone was connected, she called Tim.

"Dame," Tim answered the phone.

"Hi! Just finished *not* eating with Ann."

"My poor friend, starved again by the societal expectation of girls, and let me guess, lettuce." Tim laughed into the phone. "Did you want to switch to an early dinner date instead?"

"Perhaps," Diana said. "Mojo's?"

She heard Tim scoff at the name. It hadn't been called Mojo's in years, and while Diana knew that, it didn't matter to her what it was called; the bar had always felt like a second home.

"You know what time yet?"

"No, just heading over to Ann's now, and there is nothing quick that doesn't smell of fried oil between here and her house. Pray for me. Maybe if Mr. Hwang is home, he'll sneak me some snacks."

"You have really questionable friends, Dame."

"Present company resembling that remark," Diana quipped.

"Wowza, feel the burn."

"You know the saying about friendships that last over seven years never ending? Well, I've known Ann since the week before high school. Which was. . ."

"Thirteen years ago, Champ."

"So you see, we're stuck with her at this point, no matter how questionable she's become. She used to be almost kind of normal. She never really had any friends before we met. . ."

"And what's changed?"

"She's much better at interacting with people than she used to be."

"That's really not helping your point about why we've been friends with her for so long." Tim laughed. "On a happier note, congrats are in order. Based on your theory of seven years, we're officially locked in for life."

"Thanks for the warning. You didn't want to tell me last year?"

"Then you might have found a way out."

"So crafty. Game starts around four. I'll try to be out for then?"

"You got it. Stay textual."

"Heard."

Diana opened her prosciutto-wrapped cheese stick before exiting the parking lot of the mini mart. While not the healthiest snack, at least it had protein and tasted good. She had also bought a pack of gum to conceal the emergency purchase. Not that Ann didn't want her to eat. She just wanted Diana to eat *healthy*. Which would mean a tirade about the dangers of sodium or the downfalls of dairy if she were found out.

Nothing had been worse than the time Ann had found out her personal trainer also did meal prep. It was through some glorious miracle that he was fired for sleeping with a client. It was kind and helpful, but Diana felt terrible repurposing the plain grilled chicken and giving it soul with some Creole seasonings or dousing it in hot sauce. Ann would have died if she had known Diana had added olive oil and salt to the steamed veggies.

With her snack settling into her stomach, the drive to Syosset was calming. Diana let her thoughts drift as she drove. How different things had been last year. The Fourth of July party itself had been a nightmare. Her relationship with Arnold had hit an all-time low, made worse since Diana had barely been keeping it together since Nana Rosa had passed.

Bursts of memories flashed through her mind: Ann screaming at Arnold. Mark dragging Arnold away in a chokehold. Tim intercepting Ann. It had been too much.

At some point, Diana had wandered away from the chaos. What she did remember more vividly than anything else was the cool night air against her skin as she stripped down. The tingle of water caressing her body as she walked into the small body of water, a little pond, on the Hwangs' property. The pull of the water as she submerged herself under. The pressure building in her chest, and when she couldn't take it anymore, she stood, the night air assaulting her dripping body.

For the first time in a long time, she let everything go. Her anger, her sadness. She cried and laughed. And when she was exhausted, she floated on her back as she watched the last rays of light fade behind the trees. She didn't remember leaving the water or rejoining the party. She remembered Tim handing her a towel and offering her a ride home.

This year, things would be better.

She and Arnold were in a better place. Diana had found a way to live with her grief instead of having it define her. She was pretty sure Mark had not been invited, despite Ann telling her that he had declined. While he had seemed to help keep Arnold under wraps last year, it was more common for Mark to egg him on, something Ann said she would never forgive him for. Diana wondered if there were other reasons Ann would refuse to invite Mark, but she didn't have time to mull it over.

The large wrought iron gate that closed off the Hwangs' driveway came into view. It didn't matter how many times she had seen it; her breath caught every time as she approached it. It was supposed to prevent intruders, neighbors, and even delivery people from approaching the house. Packages, parcels, and visitors were supposed to drive around the block to the other side of the house, where a lovely man named Bruno played security.

Despite having attempted to slide through the bars with Ann one drunken night, Diana was still amazed at its presence. They had never managed to get through or over the gate. For years, she had sat outside of Ann's window on the roof, wondering if they were keeping things out or in. Pulling into the driveway, Diana parked her car behind Ann's. She had barely shut her engine off when Ann opened the car door.

"There you are! Was starting to think that you had an episode or something, and was already blaming myself for letting you drive. Come on!" She grabbed Diana by her hand. "We have plenty to do. The workers are setting up the tents and tables in the backyard, and in between supervising, we have favors to make!"

Diana took the bags from Ann's trunk and followed her around the back of the house to the pool area. The yard was surrounded by thick, overgrown trees, further secluding their property from the rest of their neighbors. Off to the left was a stone area with several fancy rocking chairs, a love seat, a fire pit, a coffee table, and, because of the party, two ping pong tables. Further down, another path of stones led to the pool and guest house. On the other side of the backyard, over to the right, was a full stone path leading to an open porch with a grill, patio set, and a minibar. Further down along the property line was Diana's little pond.

As Ann shared every scandalous text and picture from Bryan, Diana organized and stuffed pairs of American flag socks, red, white, and blue bandanas, white and blue candles, and one MK watch into each bag. Between replying to texts, Ann cut tags from pairs of red and white Converses. All adult sizes would be available for people to pick and add to their bags.

"Shit," Ann muttered, shooting out of her chair. "I have to make a phone call. You'll be okay here. . ." she said, waving her hand over the table.

Ann was already halfway across the patio when Diana nodded. All of the bags had socks and bandanas. Her plan was to do the candles next. It seemed Ann had made less progress with her sneakers. Diana reached into the Yankee Candle bag, nabbing a candle and a receipt. She was pretty sure Ann would be tossing it, but on the off chance she was going to start budgeting like Diana taught her, she straightened out the receipt and left it to the side.

Something about it caught her eye. The receipt wasn't for candles, it was for two salads. Which reminded her that somewhere there was a salad with her name on it. Diana continued wrapping candles in the tissue paper, adding one to each bag. She had been five candles deep when she pulled out a long black book. Not a book, a check holder. She groaned and saw Ann storming toward her.

"Did you steal the salads?"

"Diana," she barked. "There are much more important things right now. Everything is ruined."

"I'm sure it's okay."

"No, it's not okay," Ann said. "Mariana is out sick today."

"Who?"

"My waxer. Her kid was sick or something." Diana picked up another candle and wrapped it as she listened. "The manager is on her way over to personally take care of my wax."

"Well, that's—"

"Only because I threatened to find a new place. She's not Mariana. We can only assume that because she's a manager, she'll do a better job."

"I didn't realize you had a wax today," Diana said.

"I didn't. I just tried to make an emergency appointment." Her tone softened as she held her phone up to Diana.

"Wow," Diana said, nodding at the picture of a very erect penis. "Bryan, I assume?"

"Oh, no," Ann said, waving her hand in front of her nose. "He's too young. More like an appetizer. This is someone else. Someone my parents encouraged, actually."

Diana raised her eyebrows.

"I'm only doing what Mommy and Daddy said to do." Ann laughed, batting her eyelashes. "Besides, they're so busy with the new building, they'll have no idea."

"Ann," Diana said, standing up. "I've known you and your parents for years. They would die if they knew a fraction of what you did."

"If only I thought the shock would kill them that quickly." She shrugged as she joined in step with Diana.

"You're awful."

Elizabeth Scozzari

"I'm wonderful. And in a hurry. Don't worry about the rest of the favors. I can't remember his name, but the tent guy is going to get some of his team to work on these after they're done with the setup."

"If I stop worrying about the favors, can I worry about your dining and dashing habits? Maybe your sticky fingers?"

"No," Ann said.

Instead, she looped her arm through Diana's as she led the way back to her car.

"Ugh." Diana groaned. "Then can I at least have my salad?"

"Salad? I tossed those." Diana stopped and raised a brow at her friend. "What? You know I don't eat leftovers," Ann said.

Ann tugged on Diana's arm, causing her to trip over her toes. "It's a euphemism for—"

"Is this yours?"

Releasing Diana, Ann toed a water bottle in her direction. Diana bent down and picked it up. It looked like hers, half-drunk and right next to her car.

"Must be," Diana said, taking the water bottle and tucking it under her arm. "Since you only drink Beverly Hills 9OH2O."

"It's what my parents get! Either way, I'll see you tomorrow. Don't be late! This year is going to be a blast. You did tell Assclown to—"

"Yes," Diana said, being the one to interrupt this time. "And I'm telling you the same thing. Best behavior. His name is Arnold, not Assclown, and I fully expect you to both play nice in the sandbox, kiddies."

"Only because it's your sandbox." Ann winked.

Diana got into her car. Ann was already disappearing around the side of the house as she started it. Grabbing her phone, she noticed a text from an unknown number. Opening it, she saw a picture of her naked body facing away from the camera. She pulled the screen closer to her face. That was the Hwang's pond. The text underneath it read: Hopefully you won't have to be alone this year.

Her throat tightened as she tried to swallow. She took a sip of water, hoping to calm her nerves. Visions of shadowy figures moved through her mind. Her townhouse, filled with the sounds of doors opening and closing, of the thud that woke her up days ago. Her fingers shook as she tried to select Tim's cell from her call log. Finally, the phone began to ring as she turned her car around to leave.

"Hey—"

"Tim, where are you? Are you still at Mark's?"

"Yeah, wh—"

"Is Arnold near you?"

"Yeah, but—"

"Can you just go somewhere to the side, or the bathroom, somewhere?"

"Of course, I have a few minutes to discuss the account."

"Thank you," Diana sighed.

The sounds of beer bottles clanking and poker terms thinned in the background as Tim walked away from the party.

"What is happening?"

"I'm sorry. I was about to leave Ann's. *Am* leaving Ann's. And I got a text from a number I didn't know. One of the guys, Mark, maybe, playing a joke?"

"Diana, I don't know what you're talking about."

"It's just. The text. . ."

"Said what?"

"It wasn't what it said as much as the picture."

"Picture?"

"Of me, in the pond. From last year."

"At Ann's?" Tim asked. A noise escaped Diana's throat. Her skin prickled as sweat beaded under her arms.

"Okay. Are you driving yet?"

"No, I'm at the end of Ann's driveway." Her mouth felt dry, and she tried to cough.

"Are your windows open?"

"No, why?"

"Because I know you don't use the AC, and you're starting to breathe like a bulldog."

Diana waited for the gate to open. She turned the temperature down to low and the fan speed to high. Everything felt like it was moving too fast and not at all. If someone had been stalking her since last year—a chill ran down her spine.

"Ohh," she said. "That's better."

"Good. Before you pull out of the driveway or off her street, hang up with me and dial star-six-seven and call the number."

"What?!"

"I'm sorry, Nancy Drew, I thought this would be right up your alley," Tim said.

"You're right, but this is clearly a job for Frank or Joe," Diana retorted. "Damsels can't really rescue themselves."

"From the girl who idolizes Meg from Hercules?"

"Tim!"

He had a point. Meg was an actual badass. But she knew the monsters she was facing. This seemed different.

The car's engine pushed forward as her foot eased on the pedal. She wanted to gun it, get as far away from the text as she could. Not that it mattered; it was on her phone. The same phone she was talking to Tim on right now.

"Okay then, send me the number and I'll call it."

"Thank you. I'm oddly disappointed in myself, but it's weird, Tim. It's really weird."

"I know," he said. "You'd be shocked to know how many naked pictures I get of myself."

"Too soon, Ron Jeremy. Maybe after a beer."

"That works! You heading straight to Mojo's?"

"I guess so, I hadn't really thought about that."

"Head over there, and I'll be there as soon as I can. You feeling a little better? At least enough to drive? We all know you are kind of a terrible driver. . ."

Diana half-laughed. "You're the worst best friend. Thank

you, Mister. I can drive, both generally speaking and in the moment. Catchup later?"

"That's a mustard, Dame."

The line dropped. Diana put her blinker on and eased over to the shoulder. With her emergency flashers on, she sent a screenshot of the text to Tim's phone. Her shoulders dropped a little as she pulled back onto the road. She had almost calmed herself down when her phone rang through the car speakers.

"Go for Dame," she said, picking up Tim's call.

"Are you still driving?"

"Yes," Diana said.

"Well, keep your eyes on the road. The number for your mystery stalker has been disconnected."

"Disconnected?"

"Out of service. Not working. Probably a burner if I had to take a guess."

Diana felt her stomach twist into a knot. A burner sounded serious. "Basically, what you're saying is it's a dead end?"

"Yes," Tim said.

"Ugh." Diana groaned into the phone.

"Sorry, darlin'.

"Not your fault. Do you think your idiot friends are just playing a joke? They were both there last year."

It sounded like the shit Mark and Arnold used to do to sorority girls back in their fraternity heydays.

"By idiot friends, do you mean your boyfriend and his best friend, both of whom are my good friends?"

"Yes. Those would be the idiots in question." For the first time, she hoped Arnold and Mark had used their joint brain. The one that got both of them into tons of trouble. "I want to laugh and vomit at the same time."

Had there been someone in her bed last night? Did they have more pictures of her naked? Or was it just a stupid joke from someone *else*? There were a ton of people at the party last year.

It's not like Ann's Fourth of July bashes were known for sober and well-mannered patrons.

"Right." Tim blew out a breath. "Laugh now. If you wait to puke 'til we're at the bar, I'll hold your hair back."

"You're a real gentleman, Tim."

"So are you, Dame."

Diana laughed. "I'll see you in a bit?"

"Sounds good."

chapter fourteen

Diana

Diana didn't see Tim walking into the bar or that he acknowledged their usual bartender, Paul, who nodded toward the back-right corner. She had been focused on the two frosted beer mugs. The chill tickled her fingers as she doodled on the glass.

"Pardon me, miss, but has no one told you that babes don't go in the corner?" Tim teased her as he pulled out the stool next to her.

"I thought I was supposed to wait here for my bad-boy with the heart of a teddy bear to save me," Diana said. "How else would he know I need rescuing?" she added, rolling her eyes.

"Big words from someone who turned down a case to solve earlier," Tim said. She tried to sit still, but he wasn't wrong. She had wimped out earlier. It was a phone call, not a stakeout. "Where's the girl who knows I'm kidding?"

Diana made a cluck with her tongue and threw up her hands. "I've been trying to figure that out myself."

"Stop trying so hard," he said. "How're you doing? You still freaked out?"

"I keep trying to rationalize it as a joke, you know? But there's just been so many *things*. This is just creepy. And I don't know. I'm probably just being silly." Her voice sounded as defeated as she felt.

"We're way past sarcasm here. It's reasonable to feel creeped out when someone has a naked picture of you. Especially if it's not one you sent them."

"Well, I didn't send this one," she snapped.

"I know," Tim said. His voice remained even-keeled. Her stomach plummeted. She had sent naked pictures before—not like the kind Ann took—but a few risky ones over the years. This was something else. Knowing someone was watching her from the shadows felt wrong. Like a violation.

Like if someone had been in her home. What if they had, and this psycho-stalker picture *was* connected somehow? It's not like she had mentioned it to anyone, because it wasn't like Arnold had believed her. She hadn't been 100% lately; there were reasons other than an intruder—she could chalk it up to being an older townhouse. She shifted around in her seat, pulling up her legs onto the stool and crossing them. Her fingers played with the hem of her shorts.

"You know that, right?" He pulled her hand into his. "It's okay to be creeped out, pissed, upset that someone took a picture of you naked and is now taunting you with it. You know that, right?"

Tim's face was soft and open. He would listen to her, her crazy theories, and probably tell her they *weren't* all that nutty. Unlike Arnold, who would tell her it was her overactive imagination, her need for drama, or a puzzle to solve. The same things he told her when he was cheating on her. She hadn't been wrong then.

"Yes," Diana said. She wanted to tell him everything, but her stomach growled against the beating of her heart. Maybe she was just hungry and tired. The combination had kicked her on her ass before. "I don't know, Tim. Everything just feels a little off."

"Well, we'll get you a water and some dinner," Tim offered.

"Yes, please! Lunch was an obscenity." She gave a small laugh. "I've known her a dozen years—"

"13," Tim corrected.

"—and I'm still not sure I believe it."

Paul greeted Tim as he put down a tray of apps: Thai wings, chicken tenders, chicken and cheese quesadillas, tacos, and fries. Diana looked between Paul and Tim. Together they shrugged until Paul pointed over her best friend's head.

"I called ahead," Tim said.

"He said you were really hungry," Paul cut in. "Like Diana-hungry."

"So we got you a little mix and match," Tim added.

"Just lemme know when you're ready for dinner." Paul smiled. "Buffalo chicken Caesar salad, no croutons."

"Should I be concerned that you've nailed all of my favorites?"

"Yes," Tim said. "But only because of how often you come here."

"Well, thank you," Diana said.

Paul nodded and headed back to the bar, stopping at tables along the way. Between dunking the chicken tenders in buffalo sauce and picking off the fries one by one, Diana recounted her lunch with Ann.

"So, after the bowls of lettuce were boxed up, she got the check and sauntered off," Tim said, finishing his second beer.

"No, no," Diana said. "She got up, made sure she rubbed her ass against the kid's arm as she picked up her eighty million bags, and then sauntered away with the checkbook in one of her bags. I hadn't realized it until we were back at her house."

"So, she literally picked up the check and left with it?"

"It gets worse."

"Worse?"

"She told me she tossed my salad—"

"Woah, lady, this is a family establishment."

"—and didn't get the joke."

"Well, not everyone is a delinquent like you are, darlin'," Tim said, looking at Diana. "But I said it earlier, I'll say it again, *questionable* friends you got."

"Look who's talking."

The conversation paused for a moment. Diana returned her empty beer bottle to the table, the frosted glass sat there empty and clear, and she picked up her fork. As she began composing the exact bite she wanted, Tim waved the butt of his bottle at Paul, who quickly walked over with two more.

"Feeling better, I take it," Paul said. His brown eyes focused on Diana.

"I was definitely just hungry *and* thirsty," Diana said, smiling.

"Glad we could fix that. Just make sure this animal tips me better than his other friends do." Paul cast a side eye at Tim.

"Since it's those animals' money we'll be paying with, it'll be the biggest tip they've ever given," Tim said.

"Hope you saved some action for me. I'm headed by Mark's after. You think there'll still be money to be had after my shift."

"You've been to Mark's tournaments," Tim said.

"Yeah, and without you there, they're probably still going strong."

"It's not my fault I clean up," Tim said.

"No," said Paul. "But it is your fault that you stop playing like an adult."

The chatter continued, but Diana felt eyes on her. Somewhere, a door closed. Her fork froze midair as her breath caught in her throat. She forced an exhale and looked up. Tim was staring at her, almost like he could see her thoughts racing through her mind.

"What?" Diana said.

Looking back at Tim. Paul was already back behind the bar.

She left her fork on her plate—the perfect bite just waiting for her.

"You sure you're okay?" Diana picked up her beer mug and took a gulp. She wasn't okay, but maybe if everyone stopped asking her every two minutes, she might be. She took another gulp and returned the mug to the table. "Diana?"

"Yes! I was for a minute, a whole minute of just being and not worrying or thinking or—" She took a deep breath. "Now, I just. I have no idea," Diana said.

"I didn't mean it like that," said Tim. "Paul said goodbye, and you didn't even move. You look exhausted. You're jumpy as hell. Something is wrong—"

"I don't know," Diana said.

"—I just want you to tell me. I can't fix it if I don't know what it is."

"Who said you have to fix it?"

"No one," said Tim. "But you need to let someone in, and if I can do anything, you know I will. Same as you would for me, kid."

"Bet your ass, chief."

Even as she tried to force a laugh, a tear rolled down her cheek. Silence settled over the table. Each took a sip of their beer, avoiding the conversation still hanging in the air.

"I'm always here for you," Tim said, his gravelly voice thick with emotion.

Diana reached over and placed her free hand on top of his. "I know you are. And I love it. I love my life, my job, my town-house, but Tim, I'm tired. Physically, mentally. It's like I'm losing pieces of myself. Leaving them behind, not sure where I've left them." She swallowed, trying to push down the lump in her throat. She squeezed his hands, taking a grounding breath before she continued. "I've been throwing myself into work because I thought it would give me purpose.

"I'm happy, I am. But I don't want to be fought over or claimed. It was one thing when Arnold and I started dating. I

115

almost understood the unspoken rivalry between him and Ann. New boyfriend vs best—

"Hey!"

"—friend. From her perspective. But since everything with. . . It's gotten so much worse. Somewhere along the way, everyone, including me, seemed to forget that I don't want a white picket fence with two-point-five children and a golden retriever. I don't want to be a housewife. I sure as shit don't want to keep passing out or falling apart. I want an old house to restore to new glories, preferably with my partner. Not as someone's doll or someone else's caretaker. Dogs, multiple dogs—slobbery and stubborn, not picture perfect. And trees, so many beautiful trees.

"All of the property! A reading room for me and a fireplace in the bedroom, with an out-of-place, fancy as fuck latte and a mini-fridge. A place to grow into and invest in. I'm not there yet, trying to save now, buy later, and then build my dream. A long-term investment, something so real I can almost touch it. . ."

Diana felt Tim's hand under her own, drawing her back to the moment. His touch grounded her. She watched as his face came into focus. The small smattering of freckles just on the sides of his nose, the end of it scrunched a little. His eyes stared out into the distance. She felt her cheeks flush. She couldn't remember the last time she talked about her dreams, what she wanted. Her heartbeat echoed in her ears.

"That's incredible," he said, interrupting her thoughts. "Not surprising for everything I know about you. But have you seen the website that lists cheap old houses?"

"Yes!"

"I've always thought that would be so cool," he said. "You're not just teasing me?"

"No, why would I?"

"Have you met Ann or Arnold? You have definitely heard about Maria."

"Point taken. Maria would have you committed. Ann, too. Don't know what she'd do with half a closet," Tim said.

"She wouldn't know what to do in a modest mansion, let alone a tiny house."

"Point made and taken. But Arnold?" Diana shook her head. "Agreeing to be with him, to make it work, every day it feels like I've cashed in my dreams in for his. Which aren't even dreams—they're sports teams and Mark. Don't get me wrong, I love Arnold," Diana took a big breath, "and Ann and you and even Long Island, but I don't want to settle into that life. At least Roberta left. Granted, she rode the coattails of a rich man to get to the fancier coattails of another, but you get the point. That sounds terrible, doesn't it? I'm rambling. We should shut me up."

"To quote you, 'I know nothing.' But for what it's worth, it suits you. Your dreams. Your big ideas."

Tim stood and pulled Diana into a hug. She breathed in, the familiar smell bringing with it a sense of calm.

"Thank you!" she said into his chest. "Better keep it to yourself, or I'll have to bury you in the back with the trees."

"Whatever you say, Dame," Tim said. He let her go, hovering for a moment. "Whatever you say."

Diana reached for her water glass and realized it was empty. She turned and dug into her purse. There were a few sips left in the one she had almost left in Ann's driveway.

"You know we could just ask Paul for some more water, right? It's free, but if you ask him really nicely, he might be obliged."

"Shut up." Diana waved him off as she finished the last of the bottle. Tim turned toward the bar, nodding at Paul while pointing to Diana's water bottle. Diana could see Paul's dramatic eye roll. She had to pee, and since there was more coming, it seemed like a good time. Diana stood up quickly. As the room dropped, Tim's arms wrapped around her.

"You okay?" He shifted her weight so he could face her.

"Yeah," Diana said, still holding on to his arm. "Just stood up too fast."

"Your hands are like icicles," Tim said, putting his other hand over hers. "More than normal."

"Ha ha," Diana said, shaking the feeling. "I'm fine. I'm going to pee. When I come back, we'll do another round?"

"Sure," Tim said.

"Seriously, I'm okay. Already feeling better," Diana lied. "I'll drink more water before I even look at another beer."

As Diana walked toward the bathroom, she felt Tim's eyes upon her. The look of concern in his eyes caused a pang in her chest. More than anything, she wanted things to be normal between them; she could pass it off. She could ignore the tingling in her arms, space moving around her like a dance partner. She could just be drunk! Sure, she wasn't a lightweight, and together they had eaten a pound of food. People stood up too fast, which was exactly what she did. Everything was okay.

Diana tapped the tips of her fingers together as she walked. Thumb to index, thumb to middle, thumb to ring, thumb to pinky, and back again. No monsters hiding around the corner, no fainting or losing control. Just her and her best friend eating dinner at their favorite bar, watching the Mets beating the Phillies.

Opening the bathroom door, Diana took an uneasy step inside. It was still a surprise to her that the walls weren't mod-podged with pictures, newspaper clippings, and the works, like they used to be when this place was Mojo's. Now they were sleek and gray. The sounds from the nearby kitchen rattled her.

Diana braced her hands on the sink and kicked the door closed. Splashing some water on her face, she tried to regain her composure. Feeling stable enough, she turned around, locked the door, and sat down to pee. Focusing on her breathing, she managed to make it onto her feet and back to the sink. As the hot water ran over her hands, the soap foaming between her fingers, Diana watched as the steam from her hands crawled up the mirror. Shapes began forming. The soap washed away from

Diana's hands, but she couldn't stop looking at the shapes. They were letters, a word.

HI D

Diana gasped and jumped back. Staring at the wet letters, she killed the water. The words began to drip and fade. The breath caught in her chest released in short, heaving puffs. Swallowing hard, she turned back toward the door. Everything was okay. Her thumb compulsively began touching her fingertips in rapid succession. *The floor is white tile. The cabinets are stained dark brown. The wall is gray and white. This bathroom is hideous.* She made her observations, hoping to reset her brain. Diana willed herself to get a grip.

She reached for the door. The knob jumped back and forth as the door violently shook. The muscles in Diana's chest pulled closer, forcing themselves inward. The pain intensified, sending her forward. Doubled over, she tried to count the tiles. "One, two, three, four—" The door stopped. It had probably been someone waiting for the bathroom. She looked over her shoulder; there were no letters now. Just a scared, pale version of herself.

Diana grabbed for the lock, fumbling, and then finally unlatching it, she tumbled out of the bathroom. With her eyes locked on Tim, she practically ran to their table. Diana fell into Tim's shoulder and gasped, "I think I need help."

chapter fifteen

Tim

Tim had listened inside the bar as she rambled on about the door and her sudden dizziness. She had relinquished her grip on his arm and reattached it to her beer. He wasn't sure it was progress though. He could see her hands were still shaking, her beer foaming from the sloshing, as she spoke. She had barely formed a solid sentence when he waved Paul over for the check.

"Dame's not feeling well, too much excitement about the Mets game," he explained. "Going to get her set up at home."

Paul looked at Diana, and Tim could see the concern shadowing his forced smile.

"Well, at least she's in good hands," he quipped. "Even if her team sucks."

Tim laughed as he paid the bill.

Now they were sitting in his car, driving back to Anthony Drive. Only the sounds of radio commercials filled the car.

"Tim," Diana said quietly. "I could have—"

"No," he interrupted. "Technically, yes. I'm sure you could have driven your own car. But it's silly. We're pulling down your block now. It would have taken longer for us to argue about it than to get here."

The blueish-gray color of the complex appeared as they turned onto her block. Tim slowed down as he approached her unit.

"I'm going to get you settled inside and then figure out how to get your car back here. Okay?"

More alarming than her state was that she nodded. How many times had she *let* him take care of her *without* a conversation? Tim couldn't think of many.

"Come on," he said, shutting his car off. "You okay?"

Again, Diana nodded. "Mhmm."

Tim looked over as Diana unbuckled her seatbelt and grabbed her bag from the floor. Her eyebrows were knitted tighter than he had ever seen them. Her usual smile was gone, replaced with a clenched jaw. Taking his keys from the car and his phone from the cup holder, he exited the car and walked over to her.

The tips of her fingers brushed against his as they walked toward her door. Tim heard the keys jingling in her hand as she struggled to get the key in the lock.

"Here," Tim said, as his hand covered her own. The coldness of her fingers surprised him as they softly vibrated underneath his. Diana wasn't known for having warm hands, a fact that Tim's mother always found appropriate, given her warm heart.

Apparently, it was a thing: cold hands meant a warm heart. These were as cold as death. Together, they unlocked her door.

"You go change. I'll make you some hot cocoa, okay?" Diana looked back at him, her eyes somewhat glazed.

"Diana?"

He studied her, watching as she came back to the moment. "Yeah," she said. "Sounds good."

Tim waited until he heard footsteps on the stairs before taking out his phone. He texted Arnold.

Hey. We're at her place. I think you need to be here. Something's not right. Can u drive?

Pulling down Diana's oversized blue mug, Tim waited for a reply. He filled the mug to the top with whole milk and put it in the microwave for three minutes. He saw her as she was earlier that evening, sitting in the corner of the bar in jean cutoffs and her embroidered long-sleeve thermal shirt, her hair curled and wild.

She looked like an extra from an '80s bar movie. He had watched as she ran her fingers through her hair and flipped it over her back where it belonged. She was so beautiful. He sometimes forgot she was his best friend.

When they were eating, he looked closer at her. The skin under her eyes was more purple than usual, and her lips were a pale pink with deep grooves running down the center. Whenever a door opened or closed, he watched her shoulders pull further up to her ears. He had noticed the bruise on her leg from what he presumed was her fainting earlier.

The microwave beeped, and Tim started making her hot cocoa. As he reached for the packet, his phone dinged.

Yeah, I can be there in 20. She okay?

Tim texted back.

She's upstairs changing. Going to tuck her in on the couch. We can talk on the way to Mojo's. Left her car there.

The reply was instant.

Just drunk?

Tim sighed and wrote back.

123

Nope—she freaked out. Almost passed out.

Three dots appeared as Arnold typed. His message appeared.

Damn. . . See you soon.

chapter sixteen

Diana

Diana stood in her bedroom, vaguely aware of the microwave beeping downstairs. The air around her felt cold and hollow, like someone else had been there and left with Diana's essence. Her closet door was closed. Water bottles cluttered her nightstand. The pictures of her family—Arnold, Tim, Ann, and Nana Rosa— all lined her dresser. Happy faces watched as they waited for her to do something.

A light layer of dust surrounded her broken necklace—the rose gold one Arnold had given her on Christmas last year—and the jewelry dish where Nana Rosa's engagement ring sat on her late husband's gold chain. Everything from her ceiling fan, with its lights on, to the one messy corner of her bed she never quite made in the morning—all of it looked as it should. The daunting feeling of exposing herself while changing kept Diana's feet frozen in place. It looked the same, but it felt wrong.

"Dame," Tim called up the stairs. "You okay?"

Footsteps followed his voice. Diana waited, staring at her nightlight in the shape of a baseball. Tim had given it to her years ago in college. No team, just a plain, simple baseball with a switch for ON/OFF on the front. The Christmas after Nana Rosa passed, he had given her the baseball bat.

Diana screamed as something grabbed her shoulders. "It's me!"

Tim had jumped back with his hands in the air.

Diana shook her head, her beachy curls dancing side to side. She rubbed her hands over her face, leaving her hands pressing into her smooshed cheeks. Helplessly, she looked at Tim and said, "What is happening to me?" She felt hot and embarrassed. She pulled at the sleeves of her shirt. Her arm caught. She was stuck.

Tim wrapped his arms around her, and she leaned into him. His touch calmed her. She breathed deeply against his chest, feeling his body tighten around her. He smelled like soap with a woodsy undertone. When she had steadied herself, she took a small step back. Without words, Tim's fingers slid under the cuff of her shirt and eased it down, freeing her hand. Her eyes stayed glued to his small Adam's apple as he swallowed.

"I'm going to change, can you just. . ." Keeping her eyes anywhere but his, she turned and took a few steps to her dresser.

Diana opened the bottom drawer and grabbed a pair of blue PJ bottoms with yellow flowers and her sleeveless Mets t-shirt.

"I'll be right here."

He nodded, then turned to face the hallway. He filled the doorway. She smiled, aware of the threat of tears, and kicked off her shorts, replacing them with the cotton boxers. She peeled off her shirt and bra, tossing them aside, and pulled over the jersey. She'd clean up the small pile later. She walked up to Tim's back and knocked like he was the door. He turned to face her.

"Thank you," Diana said.

"Of course."

Downstairs, on the coffee table in front of the couch, was a mostly full water bottle and a large mug of hot cocoa. Diana walked around front, plopping backward onto the couch, and watched as he bent down and slid her baseball bat under the coffee table. Yellow and gray pillows surrounded her as Tim draped her literary blanket over her legs. Handing her the clicker and her cocoa, he forced a smile.

"Diana, whatever this is, we'll get through it," he said, squeezing her shoulder. "I'm going to grab your car. I'll have my phone if you need me. Drink some water, enjoy your cocoa, and watch the game. Okay?"

"Yes, Dad," Diana said.

"Dian—"

"Really," Diana interrupted, "I mean it. You're always here for me, protecting me, whether it's with baseball bats, hot cocoa, creepy stalker photos, house restoration, whatever. I'm trying to say thank you without making it weird. So much is weird. And. . ." Diana's voice trailed off as she looked up at him. Tim's soft brown eyes were filled with worry. She studied his broad shoulders, flexed and tight.

"You're okay. For right now, you're okay. Get some rest, and Monday, before the game, we'll have a very long talk about it."

"You're assuming that things don't get weirder before then."

"And if they do, we'll talk about those on Tuesday. Small bites, alright?"

"Okay," Diana said.

A smile lifted her features for the first time since dinner. "I'll be back soon. Catchup later, Dame?"

"That's a mustard, Mister."

Diana leaned back into the pillows and pulled her feet onto the couch. Alternating between her hot cocoa and her water, she watched her team bat.

chapter seventeen

Arnold

Arnold pulled up in front of Diana's townhouse. He saw Tim's imposing figure pacing back and forth in the dark. His fists, like softballs, were grinding against each other. Arnold's passenger side door opened, and Tim jumped into the front seat.

"So, what happened?"

Tim reached back for his seatbelt as Arnold pulled away from the curb. The engine of his Ford F150 revved in the background.

"She was freaked out before we got to the bar. A text she had gotten—"

"From who?"

Arnold thought about his random texts from Amber.

"Not sure. It was an unknown number." Arnold's grip lessened on the wheel. Tim continued, "She got there first, sitting in her corner. She seemed okay. We were bullshitting. She gets up to go to the bathroom and looks like she's going to topple over. Then she nearly fell over herself running back to the table because there were smudges on the mirror and someone tried to open the door."

"Did she say what happened, like to her?"

"She said she got up too fast."

"About the bathroom?"

"She panicked."

Arnold heard Tim's breath coming heavy and fast.

"I know what's wrong with her," Arnold said.

"You do!"

"Why do you sound so surprised?" Arnold surprised himself as his words came out in a low, harsh tone. "I just didn't know having an overactive imagination was contagious." Arnold looked across the truck to Tim. Anger radiated off his body.

"I agree that she hasn't been the *healthiest* person, but she stood up too fast and panicked. And you both react like she's won the affection of Michael Myers or something."

He stopped at the light and put his blinker on. Diana's car was visible from where they were. Pulling down the side street, he pulled into the dirt-covered parking lot and parked his truck. Tim's breathing filled the car. Arnold watched his fists, clenched and ready to throw a punch, flex in his lap.

"If you have something else to say, just say it, man," Arnold said.

"Yeah, *man*," Tim spat. "I told you a few days ago that something wasn't right with her. In the past handful of days, she's either fainted or freaked out every day, at least once if not twice. You're going to sit here and tell me there's nothing seriously wrong with that?"

Arnold thought back to Wednesday or had it been Thursday? Diana had fainted at work, and he had ended up with Amber. She had gotten weak before getting into the shower earlier, but it had happened to him at the sauna before. What was Tim noticing that he wasn't? As if he could read Arnold's thoughts, Tim continued, "Maybe if you hadn't been with your head between someone else's legs, you would have noticed on your own."

"You're wrong," Arnold growled.

132

"Oh, sorry," Tim snapped. "I forgot you don't actually provide pleasure for the women you're with."

Arnold punched his steering wheel. The horn blared, and pain zipped between his fingers. Had Diana told him that? *Traitor.*

Anger burned white hot throughout Arnold's body. Tim was *his* friend, and—he took a deep breath—probably had said something to the same effect in the years they had known each other.

"Whatever," Tim said. "Look, you guys have had a lot of other stuff going on, and she makes it so easy not to worry about her. If she doesn't want someone to notice something, they don't."

"You noticed," said Arnold.

Tim's mouth closed like a bear trap. "My mom," Tim said, the tension from his voice gone and replaced with sadness. Arnold looked at him, unsure of what to say. Tim was trying to move past their moment, and it wasn't like Arnold was going to duke it out with him. If Tim could be civilized; at the very least, he could try. He was saved when Tim sighed before he continued, "I think the calls might be coming from inside the house, so to speak."

"Whatever Hollywood bad guy you want to—"

"No, dude." Tim sighed. "It could be blackouts, hallucinations, all the same stuff my mom experienced with her dementia."

"I'm sure she's going to be okay," Arnold said, patting Tim's shoulder. "It sucks about your mom, but Diana doesn't—she's young, she'll be okay."

"She will," Tim agreed, now unbuckling his seatbelt. "I'll get a list of doctors together. She'll go to someone."

Arnold's biting laugh filled the cab. Disbelief hung in the background.

"You've known her longer," Arnold said, turning his car back on. "I guess if anyone can get her to do something, it would be you."

He hated the defensiveness in his voice—so much for letting things go. It seemed like maybe Tim hadn't noticed.

"Yeah, well, you said it before, my parents. She loved them, and they loved her. I'll talk to her on Monday."

"Monday. Are you coming to Ann's party tomorrow?"

"No. Believe it or not, after last year, I was specifically not invited," Tim said.

He stood outside Arnold's truck with one hand on the open door. "Specifically, how?"

"By invite. Mark and I both got one. It looked normal except it said, 'You are **no longer invited** to the annual Fourth of July party held by Ms. Ann Hwang. If you are caught on-premises, you will be removed by the Syosset police.'"

"What did Diana say when you told her?"

"I didn't," Tim said.

"What?"

"Ann told her that Mark and I RSVPed no. Instead of making it a thing, especially with the other stuff on Diana's plate, we let it go. Sometimes it's okay to let things roll off." Tim raised an eyebrow at his friend.

"I've been telling you that for years. You should listen to me. I'm old, much more mature. Lots of wisdom for you to take in," Arnold said, wagging his finger at Tim.

"You're full of something," Tim said, closing the door. "Have fun tomorrow. Uncle Sam wants you to be the best you can be."

"Sounds good," said Arnold.

He revved the engine and popped it into drive. "Remember, she's my best friend," Tim called after him and began walking toward Diana's car.

"Now I'm offended," Arnold shouted out his window as he passed Tim and exited the parking lot.

His laughter faded, leaving him with the ache of jealousy.

He *was* offended, if he was being honest with himself. The relationship Tim and Diana had was so different from their own. No matter how close he got to either, they were always closer.

That didn't mean that he wouldn't notice if things were really that bad with Diana. If she were really *that* unstable, he would have noticed. She had the same flair for dramatics as her grandmother.

Maybe she wanted the attention. See who would stick with her; maybe she was testing them.

He had given her enough reason to doubt his loyalty; Ann was constantly reminding her of that—and a million other ways everyone else was failing Diana. He slowed down as the light changed from yellow to red. Things with Amber hadn't been a test for Diana, but he had learned a lot. She was willing to give up everything for him.

Amber hadn't been.

Jealousy turned to molten rage in his chest.

He wasn't going to up and leave the only person he could count on to stay with him. He would go to her townhouse—not Tim—and check on Diana, spend the time with her, and see if he could make heads or tails of the situation. Hopefully, the Mets vs. Phillies game was over. Even he had limits to his patience. He shot Tim a text telling him the change of plans; he could drop off the car tomorrow when he went for his run. It wouldn't be the first time.

chapter eighteen

Diana

A crash pierced Diana's ears. Her arms flailed as she panted. Her living room was dark, save for the glow of her television.

Something caught her eye on the floor. The back had fallen off the clicker, exposing the battery. She had dropped the remote. *Silly.*

She was just being silly. Tim had tucked her in tightly, and there was nothing to worry about. She took a long drink from the water bottle nestled into her arm.

Diana's lids sagged down over her eyes. Her breathing returned to its sleepy-time cadence. She scrunched up into a tighter ball, her knees practically against her mouth, and fell back asleep.

She startled awake again. This time, a sound from the other room caught her attention. She felt dizzy and disoriented. Diana's breath was as wild as her heartbeat. She tried to wake up from her dreamlike state. There was another noise. Reaching around for her baseball bat, Diana panicked. It wasn't there. She squinted her eyes, hoping it would help her in the dark, but she didn't see her bat anywhere.

The room spun and pitched around her. Maybe she couldn't see the bat, because she couldn't focus. She tried closing her eyes, but the world still felt off kilter. She had woken up before when the clicker fell. She peeked, but the clicker wasn't there either.

Another noise, this one closer. Diana blinked, trying to orient herself. A figure sloshed its way out of the kitchen and toward her. Scrambling backward on the couch, Diana struggled to come up with a better idea.

"Hey, baby," Arnold said, his voice filling the room.

His figure stepped into the soft light of the television. A small cry escaped her throat. She sat straighter up and pulled her knees into her chest. Her forehead rested on top as she tried to collect herself.

"It's just me. It's okay."

"When did you get here?" Diana asked.

"Not too long. Was going to let you sleep for a bit." She looked at the television. The Mets were in the outfield.

"The game's still on," Diana said.

"Yeah, I couldn't find the remote." Diana looked down at the floor again.

"It was on the floor. I dropped it when I was sleeping earlier. What time is it?"

"It's late, you want me to tuck you into bed?"

She was exhausted. Physically, mentally. It felt like she was running on empty. She nodded slowly.

"Do you see my baseball bat?"

Arnold's gaze swept the room, coming back to her. She was mid-yawn, bed did sound really nice.

"It's not here, Dee."

"What?" Diana gasped. "It has to be. Tim put it under the table earlier."

"Okay," he said. He took a deep breath before continuing. "Are you sure, though? Because it's not here."

"Maybe it's under the couch," she said. "Like my phone was?"

Diana went to lean forward, the room pitching with her. She grabbed the arm of the sofa.

"Let me look," Arnold said.

His eyebrows were pinched. Diana wondered if he was concerned or annoyed at her insistence.

Arnold shook his head as he stood. "Nope, not there."

Diana took slow, even breaths in through her nose and out through her mouth, doing her best to remain calm.

"Babe, it's probably upstairs where it always is."

"No," Diana snapped. "Tim put it under the coffee table for me. And besides, it wasn't in the bed this morning. I don't know where it is."

She tucked her head back onto her knees. It wasn't fair; he wasn't listening to her.

"Diana," Arnold said. His voice thin and weary, "If you didn't know where it was earlier, how would Tim know? It probably fell off and rolled under the bed."

"Maybe someone was here—" She lifted her head.

In Arnold's hands was the clicker.

"And moved your remote and baseball bat?" He raised his eyebrows and coughed. "If they were, you should say 'thank you.' It was right here next to the TV on the stand. Your bat is probably safe and sound upstairs. In your room. Where you should be."

"Why don't you believe me?" Her fists were balls. She pressed them into her thighs. "I have always believed you," she continued.

"No, you haven't," he interrupted.

"Only *after* you had given me a reason not to," said Diana. "And even then."

She sighed. It was like the past was taking over the present. Next thing, someone would be calling to tell her that her mother was dead instead of Nana Rose. Diana choked back a sob.

"Look, Diana—" This time she cut him off.

"The bat wasn't up there earlier."

"Then how would Tim have had it to put it under the table?" Diana watched as Arnold shifted his weight. She had seen him coach, easing into the same position of authority or whatever. "Baby, it's not that I don't believe you, but you're not making sense. It's been a rough couple of days. You're not feeling well, and I think it's better if we just go upstairs and get you in bed. I'll look for the bat, okay?"

Diana's heart sank deep into her chest. If it sank any lower, it could settle in alongside her dinner. Maybe she would puke both up. Before she could respond, she was lifted into the air, Arnold's butt flexing in front of her face.

"I used to do this to my little cousin when she didn't want to go to bed."

"You used to flex your ass for your cousin?"

"No, weirdo, that was to keep you distracted. I don't want to fight you, Diana. I just want to get you settled in for the night."

She studied the stitching in the pockets as they bounced their way up the stairs. He hadn't been given much in the packing department, but he could thank an All-American sports career for a nice ass. He plopped her onto her bed.

"Thanks," said Diana.

Arnold helped pull the covers over her body, and, leaning forward, he got onto one knee and looked around under the bed with his phone's flashlight. He stood, walked over to her night-light, and flicked it on.

"Ahha," he said, "your bat! Right next to the baseball where it belongs."

That isn't where it belongs, she thought to herself. She reached over to her nightstand and picked up a water bottle. Arnold slid the bat under the covers and walked around the bed, taking the empty water bottle from her.

"And these?" he said, his hand gesturing to the nightstand, "have to go. There are almost a dozen."

In one swoop, he gathered all of the bottles except one and walked to the door.

"Good night, Dee," Arnold said as he pulled the door closed.

"Good night."

Diana felt the pull of darkness before she heard his footsteps hit the stairs. No longer able to stay awake, she drifted off, facing her bedroom door. There was a soft click from the other side of the room, and then the sounds of carpet swooshing. As she rolled over toward it, a shadow moved through the pitch black to the door. Their feet cut through the light seeping in from the hallway under the door. Diana tried to open her eyes, but she was stuck in the dark.

chapter nineteen

Diana

Arnold whizzed past the gate as he strategically parked his oversized truck between a white car and an SUV. Diana saw her car parked in its usual spot this morning. She assumed Tim brought it back from Mojo's. They had stopped at the liquor store and picked up a bottle of wine for Ann as a thank-you gift for having them over. The car ride was filled with off-key singing and laughter; whatever weirdness had been plaguing them the past few days seemed to be behind them.

Diana hopped down from her seat as Arnold killed the engine. Standing on the step, she reached in for her beach bag, a white and blue canvas bag with brown leather straps and "Let It Snow" printed across the front.

"I still find it comical that you have extra gift bags for bottles lying around in your car," Diana said.

She closed the passenger side door and walked around the bed of the truck to Arnold's side.

"She says as she flaunts her 'Let It Snow' beach bag," Arnold said, digging under his seat.

"You keep gift bags in your truck. You don't even wrap

presents!" She laughed as she poked him in the side. "You don't see the humor here?"

"Coming from someone who keeps a receptionist travel kit in her car, I find this conversation stupid," said Arnold. There was a tone to his voice that Diana hadn't missed. She did have a tightly packed pencil kit with pens, a pack of sticky notes, a bottle of ibuprofen, markers, and assorted general notes in her center console. Most of it had been accumulated by mistake, but it proved handy. Diana kept it there, adding to it every few trips in and out of her car. Especially when she forgot something, which was starting to become a common occurrence. She blew out a rush of air and forced a smile. Arnold slid the wine into the gift bag and continued, "Besides, the ladies at work always give me tons of bottles as an end-of-the-school-year gift. On the off chance either Mark or I have forgotten or have gotten something appalling like tequila—"

"I love tequila!"

"—we swap out the bags. No one can tell a re-gifted bottle when it's in a different bag!"

Diana's eyes rolled into the back of her head. Arnold grabbed her duffel and his overnight bag. Unlike Diana, he wore his swim trunks to the party and could figure out the rest later. The two finagled the stuff they were carrying and headed down the driveway that looped left for additional parking and swung back to the right, facing the left side of the house and the backyard. While Diana was used to coming through the large gate, anytime the Hwangs had an event, guests were directed toward the large archway where an intricate wooden gate broke up the fence that separated the front and back yards.

chapter twenty

Ann

Dr. and Attorney Hwang were on the deck picking at appetizers with their friends. Like in previous years, as the day eased into the night, they would move inside, some of them taking their overly whipped offspring with them. *Gross.*

Ann left the deck, having properly greeted all of her parents' friends. Inhaling in a quick, sharp breath, she forced the air from her lungs and relaxed her face. Her cheeks throbbed from the fake smile she had been wearing all morning. The worst kind of accessory, in her opinion. Compared to their protégés, Ann was a loser, the disappointment, the underachiever, the "townie" of her private high school, which was especially asinine when they all came from different parts of Long Island. That didn't change how her high school friends and their shitty, pretentious parents saw her. They didn't even try to hide it.

"Oh, you're still living at home? What post-graduate program are you enrolled in?"

She wasn't. They knew that, but it didn't stop them from asking. Every year, she fantasized about spiking the champagne.

Not that she would waste the cases of Louis Roederer Cristal 2012.

She hated all of them, the parents and their offspring, as much as they judged her for her high-fashion, underachieving life. Not that it mattered much. They were nothing more than entitled eggs—plain, not like Fabergé. Not a single one of them had grown up with an original thought or their own personality. Just like the money, it was all pre-planned and handed down generation to generation. Ann's parents had made all of their money, and while they grew her future assets, Ann developed her own personality.

Just like she had made her own friend.

Diana had been perfect from the moment Ann had seen her. The week before freshman year. They were sitting through orientation, a small group of girls, none of whom Ann could be bothered to talk to, and then her. Short, wild hair and eyes that looked at everything through rose-colored glasses. Ann was surprised they were green and not some freak shade of pink. They exchanged email addresses. Ann had been so angry when Diana had said she wouldn't be attending, opting instead for public school—*ugh*—but they stayed in touch. They became friends.

Ann started school with chemically stripped hair, making it an ashy blonde and a perm. She had been so young, so insecure in herself. She had even tried saying "Ann" was short for "Diana." Until school authorities blew up that rumor. That was then.

Now she was, Ann—signature black hair, straight and frizz-free, with more high-fashion looks than Teen Vogue. Let the rest of them fake their way through their master's and doctoral programs, all the while knowing Mommy and Daddy were writing a check for their success. Let them work themselves into their shallow graves. Ann would stay young and beautiful in her kingdom. She opened her eyes, and even through her sunglasses, it was a bright, beautiful day.

Ann adjusted her black romper and skimmed the party. There were two small groups surrounding the beer pong tables in what was clearly a game of the white-collar class versus the liberals from her college days. She noted they were only using one of the two tables. In her peripheral vision, she saw Diana walking toward her, holding her ridiculous *winter-themed* beach bag in one hand and Arnold's hand with the other. Her choices in accoutrements were disgusting. Ann scoffed and focused on the positive: she was here.

"Ahh!" Ann screamed. Raising her arms into the air, she headed toward Diana. "You're here!"

"We are! We are." Diana laughed.

"Hello, Arnold," Ann said. "How are you?"

She was pleased with her tone. She had practiced earlier this morning. Cordial, with most of the disappointment being kept at bay.

"I'm good. Yourself?"

"Great, now that Diana's here. Most of these people I haven't liked in years."

"You say that every year," said Diana.

"If you want, Arnold can drop the stuff off in the guest house. I set it up especially for your stay."

"Do you want help?" Diana asked Arnold.

"Don't be silly. He's fine. *We* need to make sure you eat, especially since there will be drinking. Plus, you should see how cute the appetizers came out," Ann said, grabbing Diana's hand.

"Arnold," Diana said, resisting her pull.

"No, I'm good. I'll catch up in a few," said Arnold.

Ann's eyes followed Diana as she watched Arnold make his way to the guest house, his butt flexing as he navigated the uneven stone path. "Barf," she said, wrapping a free hand around her arm, whisking her toward the food table. Diana was still smiling at her boyfriend's backside. *Such an asshole*, Ann thought.

149

chapter twenty-one

Arnold

Arnold gave a look over his shoulder. Ann's long, tentacle-like arms were wrapped around Diana. He continued down the large stone path, around the pool, to the guest house. He entered through a door on the left side. Straight ahead, there was a bedroom. The bathroom was off to the left. If he remembered from last year, which, if he was being honest with himself, was a big stretch, one of the doors on the far wall led to the living room space, which opened up directly to the pool area.

Every year, he hoped to get Diana naked in the pool at night, after everyone else—including Ann—had dipped out. It always seemed like she had an excuse. After he had taken up with Amber, he wondered if she had been cheating on him. Sex with Amber had been different, blew what he had with Diana away.

Maybe this year would be different. So many other things had changed. But not Diana's love of the water. When they were in college, it was a rarity that Diana had been able to keep all of her clothes on, least of all when there was a pool, hot tub, ocean, or anything of the sort.

Arnold dropped their bags against the wall in the guest

room. Remembering to take his keys out of his pocket, he tossed them on top of Diana's bag. He was going to test this other door after he went to the bathroom. Going back through the door, he stood facing the window as he relieved himself. *The Hwang's property must be a small fortune to manage*, he thought. Giving himself a quick shake before putting his swim trunks back to rights, Arnold headed through the bedroom and tried the door.

Locked. *Probably better*, he figured. This way, people wouldn't be coming and going through their space. Arnold left the pool house and made his way out to the party. He could see Ann's body moving as she jabbered at Diana. He caught her eye and made a face. Better her than him.

Movement from the trees caught Arnold's eye. He remembered her rambling on about an intruder and Tim saying something about a random text Diana had received. He hadn't been specific about the details, only that it had bothered her. Arnold was happy Tim wasn't there today. It was great that he was her best friend, especially when it saved Arnold from doing something he hated.

How many black and white movies was a man expected to sit through? Or worse, a book that had been turned into a movie. The ropes course through the woods, the goat yoga class, kayaking. . . the list went on.

But when had Diana started relying on him instead of Arnold? Had she ever? Tension passed between his shoulder blades, and he drew back his arm as a guy wearing socks and sandals emerged from the trees holding a white ball in the air. Arnold felt the pressure in his knuckles from his fist. *Dweeb*.

"Arnold!" Diana shouted. "Hey!"

Arnold turned around and saw Diana and Ann heading in his direction. Both had drinks in their hands.

chapter twenty-two

Diana

"None for me?" Arnold asked.

"Didn't want it to get warm," Ann said coolly, raising an eyebrow. "No one likes a warm beverage."

Arnold waited until Ann's eyebrow had returned to its normal position before looking at Diana.

"Well, actually, I wasn't sure what you wanted," Diana said. "*Annnd* we were thinking of playing pong next!"

"We figured you could watch," Ann added.

"I'd much rather watch Diana play by herself than with you, but she is a great partner. You probably could use the hand," Arnold said with a wink.

That's not helping anyone, Arnold, she thought. Diana took a large sip of her drink as she waited to see how Ann reacted. Her green eyes passed back and forth between them. Ann stood there with her hip jutted, shoulders at a slant. Her dark hair swayed behind her like the tail of a jaguar.

"While I'm sure Diana is great with her hands, I already have a partner, and I'm certain he's better than you," Ann said, her nose crinkling. She let go of Diana's arm and took a few steps backward before she continued. "We already have the next game."

Diana took another sip of her drink, trying to keep her nervous laughter at bay. Her eyes bounced back toward Arnold, who was standing straight, with his hair perfectly set on top of his head and his chest puffed out, arms by his sides, reminding Diana of a bear standing on its hind legs.

"If you have a partner already, you won't be needing mine," said Arnold, matching his tone to the same condescending one as Ann.

With a Cheshire smile plastered across her face, Ann flipped Arnold off and turned around, making her way back toward the bar. Vodka tickled up Diana's nose. While it was still undetermined who would win in the real world, the jaguar seemed to have taken this round.

"Are you okay?"

Diana coughed, clearing her throat. "Yeah," she answered. "It could have gone worse, I suppose. Can I just ask why you do that?"

"Do what?" Arnold asked.

"Taunt her, using me as some weird sexual bait."

"Oh, you mean pointing out the obvious? Dee, it's not *my* fault that your bestest girl friend over there wants to be me. She probably hates me, Mark, and Tim, all because she has penis envy."

"Mark hooks up with one psychology major, one time," said Diana. She took a gulp of her drink, adding, "couldn't have opted for an English major or future science teacher, huh?"

"Hey, she's the one who needed a historian. Not Mark's fault."

She made a face like a monkey, her Solo cup hovering near her ear as she pulled them out.

"Both of you are just—"

"Amazing," Arnold said.

"—impossible."

"Like a mastermind," said Arnold. "Come on."

He wrapped his hand around her free one and led her toward the bar.

"More like incorrigible?"

"Genius," he said.

She stood next to him as he fixed himself some kind of whiskey drink.

"Ingenious?"

Across the way, Diana watched as Ann shook out her long black hair from its ponytail. Next to her, a tall man in a salmon-and-white polo shirt and khakis with long dreadlocks tied back was filling a glass from the keg.

"Something like that," Diana laughed. "You must have really pissed her off. She only does that when she's flirting."

"You mean this?" Arnold said, as he mimicked the way Ann giggled, playing with her hair. "Her signature move."

Diana exploded with laughter.

"Careful, they say imitation is the highest form of flattery," Diana said, breaking off into more laughter.

"You're welcome," he said.

He reached back and grabbed Diana's butt. "Thank you," Diana said.

"Let's top yours off, while we're here," she said.

She looked down at her cup. It was halfway gone from the verbal sparring match between Ann and Arnold.

"What's with the shoulder thing anyway?" He was looking over at Ann and her potential boy toy.

"Oh, that," Diana said, "She thinks it shows off her bone structure. She once made me practice with her for close to an hour to find the 'perfect' angle to accentuate her clavicle and cheekbones."

"She should show off her arm muscles from softball. Guys would be too afraid not to fall in line."

"Don't be a dick," Diana said. "There's nothing wrong with being athletic."

"I'm a Phys. Ed teacher," Arnold persisted, throwing his hands up in the air. "I get it. I'm just saying a lot of the younger, less developed boys in my classes would kill for that kind of bulk and definition."

Diana groaned and walked off a few paces in front of him.

He pinched Diana's butt as he walked past her toward the pong table.

"Think maybe you should have started with beer?" she asked.

"You were blessed with an amazing body," he replied with a wink.

"Well, hopefully that's enough to convince you to play with me, especially since you chased away my root partner. You in?"

Diana noticed the lines in Arnold's face, gone as quickly as they had appeared. Usually, she would wonder what he was thinking and who he was thinking of, but today she wanted to have fun. She wanted easy.

She took a gulp of her vodka drink, grimacing as she swallowed. She needed to not let Arnold make any more of her drinks.

"Of course," Arnold said. "You are one of the best pong players I've ever seen."

As he put his arm around Diana's shoulders, kissing the top of her head, he threw a quick glance toward the bar area. Dreadlocks had handed Ann her drink, and the two were leaning close, talking.

"Save our place, I'm going to top off my drink."

"The one you just got?"

Arnold chugged half the cup, making Diana's stomach turn.

"You really are a child," Diana laughed. "You could just say you're going to eavesdrop, you know?"

She watched him walk toward the bar. It was nice to see Arnold in such good spirits, especially with Ann in his field of vision. She wasn't exactly sure when Ann started hating Arnold, but she did remember the day she first expressed her feelings.

They had all been hanging out: Ann, Arnold, Tim, Mark, and herself. She got a knot in her stomach just thinking about it. She tried washing the horrible memory down with a sip of her drink.

She kept her eyes on Ann and her boy toy, who were on the other side of the table, as Arnold, leaning in close, whispered and laughed like two old besties. Hopefully, Arnold could hear what they were saying; it seemed like they were both enjoying the conversation. Diana silently crossed her fingers and turned her attention back toward the beer pong table. The other had become a makeshift table for drinks, refills, and side betting. Arnold saddled up next to her right as the game ended.

Ann gave them her spot; apparently, whatever they were talking about took priority over party games. Before Diana could ask Arnold if he had heard anything, they started playing. A little while later, she and Arnold hadn't lost a game since. The teams they had beaten had slowly been sucked into a growing crowd. Ann, with her new friend in tow, joined the group.

"What's everyone gaping at?"

"Them! They are undefeated," a tall, goofy guy wearing a t-shirt with cutoff sleeves and cargo shorts answered Ann.

"For how long?"

"Since you gave them your spot. It's crazy, man."

"Ugh." Ann rolled her eyes. "Tommy and I have the next game," she shouted, yanking the arm of the dreadlocked guy next to her straight into the air. The tall guy smiled and nodded his head as he started to rock on his feet.

"Contenders," he said in a rhythmic tone.

* * *

"That was so much fun," Diana said, plopping onto the outdoor couch, laughing. "I can't believe how intense everyone was. You guys had a nice winning streak for a little bit there."

"It was," Ann said with a smirk. "It's too bad you threw that last rematch game."

"We did not!"

"I didn't say you and Assclown, I said you," Ann said, as her smile began to fade as she sat down next to Diana.

Diana looked down. "Everyone should have gotten to play. And if we were going to lose eventually—"

"I get it, you're trying to do something helpful and selfless," Ann said with a wave of her hand. "You owe me nothing. Next time, just miss all the cups and run the naked mile," Ann said as she burst out laughing.

"You wish," Diana said, teasing.

"You wish what?" Arnold walked over in front of them, passing Ann her drink with a smile. "Truce?"

Ann looked at the cup and then at Diana.

"She wishes you had gotten me a drink as well," Diana said, as she raised her brow.

"M'lady," Tommy said as he approached the trio. "Since we drink the same drink, I sent Arnold back with his and Ann's."

"Well, thank you, kind sir," Diana said, scooting over for Arnold to sit down.

Tommy handed Diana her drink, nodded, and headed to sit next to Ann. Diana looked around the party. There were a handful of stragglers, mostly friends of Ann's parents.

"What are you looking at, Dee?"

"Just who's still here and how many people have left," she replied.

"You look like you're planning something," said Ann.

From the corner of Diana's eye, she watched Ann casting a daring look toward Arnold.

"She does have that look in her eyes," Arnold weighed in.

"I do not," Diana objected.

Everyone was laughing as Mrs. Hwang approached the group. Even after a day of festivities, Mrs. Hwang looked just as poised as she did when Diana and Arnold had arrived—an impressive feat, since everyone in their little group had drunk enough for Arnold and Ann to be amicable with each other.

"Ann, can I talk to you for a minute?"

"I'll be right there," Ann answered her mother.

As Mrs. Hwang and Ann chatted, Diana and Arnold tried to get to know a little more about Tommy. Only a few minutes later, Ann rejoined her friends with a large smile spread across her face.

"So, excellent news," Ann began, "the Stewarts invited my parents and the rest of the other protégés' parents still here to watch the fireworks from their boat."

Ann beamed. Diana saw the gleam in Ann's eyes and tried not to laugh as she turned toward Tommy, pulling the end of her ponytail forward and over her shoulder.

"Maybe you can fall asleep, snuggled inside," she said. She rested her hand on Tommy's thigh. His face froze like a child watching Santa come down the chimney. "You know, with me?"

Ann giggled as Tommy nodded; the color came back to his face.

"Sounds like it's going to be a good night for all," Arnold said, and he lifted his glass in a mock toast.

chapter twenty-three

Arnold

As much as it surprised him, he had to give Ann credit. She knew what she wanted and how to get it. He remembered a night early on, back when Mojo's was still Mojo's. Diana and Tim were still at the show they had gone to at the Patchogue Theatre. Something dreadful she had asked Arnold if he wanted to see. Instead, Tim took the ticket, and he and Mark got an early start at the bar. He did a double-take when Ann walked through the door, not realizing it was her at first glance. He waved her over, shouting her name. She had given him a hug, and he made room for her to stand between himself and Mark.

She had waved her hand at the gesture. "Thanks," she said, "but no girl gets picked up when stacked between two good-looking men."

She had winked at them as she said it.

"Honey, no one wants to get picked up here," Mark had said, waving Paul over. "Especially not when this guy's working. He brings in such trash."

They had all laughed. *Was it really so long ago?* Arnold would have bet a round for the whole bar that Ann and Mark had left together that night. Not that it mattered. These days, Ann went as far as to formally not invite him to her party. Mark had finally been banned from somewhere, and it wasn't actually his fault. It had been Arnold's.

A glass clinked against his having switched to beer when he drained the last of the whiskey, bringing him back to the present.

"Cheers to that man," Tommy said.

Arnold laughed at the large, cheesy smile plastered to his face. Ann and Diana each raised their plastic cups, joining in.

"Now we can really see what mischief this one had in mind," Arnold teased, tickling Diana's side. She fell back into Arnold's arms and laughed.

chapter twenty-four

Diana

Arnold and Tommy were attempting to make a fire in what Ann called the "old school" fire pit. Diana had been about to ask if they just wanted to use the gas one, but Ann had shaken her head, flashing a devious smile. She had to admit, it was comical even from over here.

"Hey," Diana whispered to Ann. "Come closer. What do you think?"

Diana felt herself sway as she lifted her right leg to point toward the guys. Her whole body rocked like a small boat.

"What're you doing?" Ann's laugh was almost melodic.

"I'm being subtle. What do you think?" Diana said.

She waved her arm as she finally managed to kick off her shorts. "Of your coochie, or of them building a fire?" Ann asked.

She freed her shoulders from the straps of her romper. "No, not my *jewel*," Diana laughed. "Of Tommy!"

"Shhh!" Ann swatted her thigh. Even in the dim mood lighting surrounding the pool, Diana could see Ann blush. It was fun. Ann never took anything seriously, at least not with guys.

"Wait, is he the friend of your parents? The one from yesterday?"

Ann smacked her thigh again. The stinging sent a tickle through Diana's body. She erupted in laughter until Ann pulled her index finger to her lips.

"Shhh, Diana," she whispered to herself.

The light from the heat lamps reflected off the hot tub, but the area outside of the pool was pitch black. She wasn't 100% sure where Arnold and Tommy were in relation to her and Ann; she had lost track of them. But they were out there, somewhere.

Diana's tiger shirt had long since been taken off during an intense and messy game of flip cup, leaving her in her bikini top. Now that her right leg had been freed from her shorts, she thought she was ready to go. She stood up and looked down to see that her left leg had somehow gotten trapped. Before Ann could answer, Diana yanked her shorts from her left leg, causing her to fall back onto her butt.

"Oww!" Diana howled in between bursts of laughter. Ann rushed over to her side.

"Oh my god," she giggled. "Are you okay? How drunk are you?" She reached forward to help Diana off the grass; some-how, she had missed landing on the tiles. Diana was laughing so hard she snorted, causing Ann to lose her balance and land somewhat on top of her friend. Ann rolled off Diana and lay next to her on the ground until both girls had steadied their breathing.

"I am not drunk. I'm having fun," Diana answered indi-gently. "Now, how did you take your romper off?"

She was still light with laughter, and happiness danced in her voice. She could almost hear it.

"One body part at a time." Ann replied as she sat up. "Unlike you. Are you and Arnold okay? You must be out of serious prac-tice if you can't get your shorts off!"

Diana collapsed under the weight of her laughter. "It's your fault for not helping me!" She managed to sit up next to Ann.

"Horseshit!"

"No, it's true. A good friend would have helped me take my shorts off," Diana teased.

"Well, I would hate to be a bad friend," Ann said, as she began to smirk. "Let me help you with your top!"

Ann leaned forward and pulled the tie of Diana's American flag bikini top. Instead of covering up, Diana chuckled and undid the bottom tie.

"FREEDOM!"

Her war cry ended as she plunged into the pool.

chapter twenty-five

Arnold

Arnold looked over at Diana and Ann. They were laughing like two wild hyenas. He loved it. He looked back at the fire when movement caught his eye. He looked up just in time to see Diana cannonballing into the pool. From where he was sitting, it looked like she was already topless. He glanced at the clock on the side of the guest house. It read 12:15 AM. Early, but now the night was really beginning.

"Hey, Di," he heard Ann call, "I'm going to get some drinks for us!"

Diana swam to the side of the pool. "You're not coming in?" Her voice was impish, like a feral fairy.

"I am, but we are out of all the beverages. You know, alcohol, water, I'll be right back! I would bet Arnold's swimsuit you haven't been hydrating."

Arnold was surprised that Ann was walking toward the house, leaving his drunk girlfriend alone to swim. Currently, she was doing crooked laps across the pool.

"Hey," Arnold shouted to Ann. "You good?"

Ann paused and cast a long look over her shoulder in

Arnold's direction. It seemed she forgot that while she couldn't see him, he had a clear shot of her. A curt smile forced its way onto her face, and he could barely hear as she mumbled something.

"What?" he called back.

"Yeah, I'm running in for some water. Di's already half naked in the pool," she said loud and clear this time.

"You're leaving her all alone in there?" Arnold chuckled.

"Not alone, she's with you!" Ann turned toward the house, calling over her shoulder, "I also have a little surprise for the four of us inside."

Ann continued toward the house until the darkness ate her up. Arnold stared at where Ann had disappeared into the night for a few seconds before taking a glance over at Diana. She seemed to have taken a break from laps and was now floating on her back.

"If Ann's calling someone half naked in what she was wearing, I'm pretty excited to be hanging out," Tommy said, laughing.

They were both still working on the foundation of the fire, but the vision of Ann in her black tube top with a gold circle supporting the middle of the top and the sides of the bottom together was quite a sight. If Arnold didn't know Ann, he could see the appeal of her in that swimsuit.

"Don't draw too much attention to it," Arnold said. "Diana thinks everyone is entitled to their opinion until she's drinking. Then she thinks that everyone should be a nudist," he added with a laugh.

"And it doesn't bother you?" Tommy asked.

He kept his eyes glued to the newspaper and twigs in the fire pit, giving it as much care as a giant tower of cards.

"It does. I mean, what guy wants other people looking at his girl? Especially his friends, right?" Arnold replied, reaching over to hand Tommy the matches.

"Thanks, man."

"No problem," Arnold said, looking back over at Diana. "She's a good girl. She was running around naked when I met her. She's hot in a way that's different from most women—adds to the envy that I take her home. Everyone knows, or learns, I don't share."

Tommy held the match against a twig until it caught.

"Noted," Tommy laughed. "No issues here. I got my eyes on my own prize."

"Good man. So, how long have you known Ann?"

"Not too long. Mostly just casual," Tommy rattled off.

"Really? How did you end up here?" Arnold asked.

"My parents have known Ann's for a while. They weren't able to be here today, but the Hwangs are supposedly a great connection to have if I apply myself to being *more* than just a doctor. You know?"

"So they sent you here to make a good impression and hopefully score a job," Arnold said as he removed his shirt.

"Something like that. Ann had already invited me. I didn't realize it was the same party. She found it hysterical when we put the pieces together," Tommy added.

"Wow. . . She must really like you."

"When my parents had the Hwangs over, I had only met them. I knew they had a daughter around my age." Tommy paused and fiddled with the logs some more. "I just didn't realize that the Ann I knew was the daughter of my potential future employers."

"She's either gonna give you the best recommendation of your life or utterly destroy you."

"Guess we're gonna have to make it our best performance yet," Tommy said, looking down at his shorts.

Arnold howled and grabbed two more beers as Tommy moved a few more pieces of firewood.

"Ready?"

"Let's light 'em up," Tommy said, dropping a match into the fire pit.

They shotgunned their beers as the flames roared. Tommy ditched his polo shirt and khakis, and Arnold threw a mesh over the fire.

"And let 'em out," Arnold added, as the two men charged toward the pool, kicking off their boxer briefs and swim trunks as they ran.

chapter twenty-six

<u>Diana</u>

Diana felt the night air wrap around her skin. She heard Arnold and Ann off in the distance. Whatever they were saying was unintelligible, probably arguing over who was taking better care of her—another drink, another water. It didn't matter, though. Nothing mattered. The grass had begun to bleed into the water. The pool was flooding onto the patio. It seemed that nothing had mattered to Diana at that point. Nothing but her melting into the water.

She felt at peace. And then. . . the grass she was floating on violently shook and rumbled beneath her. It was an earthquake. The ground was eating her up. Swimming into her mouth. She gasped for air. It consumed her. Sadness overwhelmed her as she lost the struggle.

It was cold, and Diana felt confused.

A shape loomed above her. She tried to speak, but her words were lost in her throat. A familiar voice floated around her, muffled in the distance. She tried to speak again, to scream. There was a popping sound.

"I'm here, Dee." The voice was clear now.

"Arnold?"

"Diana, I'm here," Arnold said.

Someone was shining a light into her eyes and pressing their fingers into her neck.

"What the fuck happened?" Ann's voice cut through the bustle of noises swarming Diana's head.

"Tommy and I did cannonballs into the pool. Diana must've gotten thrown off balance and gone under. We pulled her up within seconds," Arnold said.

The light was near blinding. In her peripheral, she could see two tall figures talking. She assumed it was Arnold and Ann.

"Fuck. Fuck. FUCK!"

Ann came into focus and was stomping her feet, shaking her hands and head. Rage pulsed off her body in waves. Even from the ground, Diana could sense her wrath hovering.

"Arnold."

The word sounded foreign and raw in her throat. She tried to sit up but couldn't raise more than her head.

"Ann, relax. She's okay," said Tommy.

"Move," Ann snapped.

"Just relax," Tommy said, putting his hand gently on Ann's arm.

"She's a little shaken up. Let's give her what she wants, and then you can check on her, okay?" Tommy pulled Ann into an embrace. "Doctor's orders," he added.

"You're not even a doctor yet," she said. "And you two are the dumbest."

Diana heard Arnold clear his throat as he squatted down next to her.

"Hey, you okay?"

She heard him. Knew he was close, but it didn't make sense. Everything was still weaving and bobbing like she was floating. She moved her neck, looking around. She watched as he lowered himself onto the ground. His big arms wrapped around her. She could feel his calloused hands on her back.

"It's okay. It's all going to be okay."

After a few moments, Diana looked up at Arnold. His face was younger than ever, a slight blur against the swirling grass behind him. Diana leaned over, putting her head on his chest.

"It's cold," she whispered.

"Here," he said.

She felt him shift, and then the softest feeling wrapped around her skin.

"How cute," Tommy said.

"Kind of nauseating though," said Ann.

She couldn't see where Tommy and Ann were, but she recognized their voices. She seemed to be sitting upright now. Ann was walking toward her, drifting almost above the stone floor. Her friend stopped and lowered herself to the ground. Diana smiled.

"Here, Di," Ann said. "Take it. It's an apology. I shouldn't have left you alone with these two bozos."

Ann handed the water bottle to Diana, who took a few tries but managed to grab it and take it.

"Don't worry, I took a sip from it before, so it should be easy to open," Ann said.

The world seemed to clear up a little. It swayed less, and Diana's thoughts became more manageable. She could even open the bottle! Ann always remembered that Diana struggled with the caps. Always a joke, *you can move your own Christmas tree, but you can't handle a twist-off!* It was true. Sometimes Diana's dexterity failed her. Like tonight, apparently, she had almost drowned.

Diana sipped her water and watched as Ann spoke in a dramatic voice.

"*And* once Diana has finished her water, I have a secret surprise for all of us."

She laughed as Ann smirked in Arnold's direction. Arnold responded with a raised eyebrow, which Diana saw, and Ann seemed to ignore.

Elizabeth Scozzari

Diana tried to drink her water fast. Hoping the sooner this moment ended, the more they could get on with the party. The water was warm and tasted bitter, but she was determined. No matter how much she hated warm water. She was halfway through when the other three had started laughing again.

Arnold always teased her about her love for the cold—snow, ice water, ice in the bedroom, not that he'd ever been into trying much. Warm water tasted gross to her. This one especially. But she kept at it. They kept laughing. Diana tried, half-smiling and nodding along, but her eyes weren't connecting anywhere.

When she only had a few sips left, Ann pulled out four test tubes.

"Who's ready for a surprise?" Ann asked in a sing-song tone. While she spoke, she shook the test tubes loosely. Suddenly, the liquid began to light up into pretty neon colors.

"What are those?" One of the guys asked. Diana missed who had spoken.

"Sunshine," Diana exclaimed as she reached for the one with yellow liquid.

"Not quite." Ann opened her hand and put the mini flashlight she was holding down, the test tubes losing their neon glow. "They're shots, nothing too exciting without the blacklight."

"Tommy, the pink is for you. It was supposed to go with your shirt, but. . ." Ann trailed off as her eyes scrolled down Tommy's body. She raised an eyebrow when she reached his towel.

"Arnold, the blue is for you. Unfortunately, your swim trunks are also off, and that leaves the green and the yellow," Ann said, holding the last two test tubes. "Technically, both match you, Di, but since you seem to want the sunshine, here. Well, cheers, everyone," Ann said, lifting her test tube and shooting it back.

The other three raised theirs, each draining the liquid.

Diana felt her throat tighten. Her head shook from the zip. Bitterness filled her mouth. Not what she thought sunshine would have tasted like. Almost immediately, she finished the few sips of water she had left and smiled.

The bitterness was gone. She was happy to be here with such happy people. People she loved, surrounded by the water and grass. She missed the sunshine, but now the sunshine was inside her, and she felt instantly warmer.

"Speaking of missing shirts and swim trunks, Ann, you're the only fully clothed person here," Tommy said, smiling.

"You're all wrapped in towels, and Di still has her bottoms on," Ann replied.

"For now, at least."

Arnold laughed and pulled Diana in close to him. Diana looked up and kissed him. She began to laugh as she attempted to stand up.

"Not anymore," Diana said. She stood, wobbling from leg to leg, getting her bottoms off. She tossed them at the boys. "Hurry up, Ann!"

She jumped back into the pool as if nothing had happened. In an instant, Arnold and Tommy were up on their feet, towels cast to the side, heading toward the water. Ann's laugh floated over Diana's body.

The sunshine had left them, but now there were giant foods surrounding them. There was a red, white, and blue popsicle. Diana licked it, but it just tasted like the water. Arnold was fighting a lobster, and Ann was walking into the pool with the biggest bottle of champagne Diana had ever seen. Tommy seemed to be avoiding the food, staring hungrily at Ann.

Diana felt incredible. It was as though she were flying through the watery sky. She was the happiest she had been all day. She felt invincible and warm. She loved Ann for giving her sunshine; she felt warm and free.

"Ann! More sunshine!"

Before Ann could oblige, Diana was lifted into the sky, floating with Arnold tucked underneath her. His skin felt rough underneath hers. Not smooth. She moved her hands up to his hair. It was so sticky from the pomegranate he put in it; she would never fall. Ann sat on Tommy's shoulders, waving her arms at Diana. She giggled.

"You'll have to beat me," Ann teased.

The laughter sent pleasant tickles over all the places where her skin was touching Arnold's. She missed anyone being between her legs. Her sex life had become a rodeo, and she was always on top. Worse, like one of those animals outside the supermarket. Put a quarter in a ride.

"Where does the quarter go?" She wondered out loud.

"No quarters, Di. We're playing chicken."

They were playing chicken! She held on tighter as she laughed again.

"Remember, ladies, we want a fair fight. Any unnecessary roughness will result in kissing and making up," Tommy said. His voice sounded like that of a boxing announcer.

"Give us a minute, will you? We're not ready yet," Ann said, bopping Tommy on the top of his head. Leaning in, Ann whispered to Diana, "You sure you're okay to do this?"

"Yes! Flying and sunshine and ponies," Diana whispered back.

"Where are you seeing a pony, Di?" Diana lifted Arnold's hair up.

"Oh god," Ann groaned. "No ponies. You're good?"

She shook her head and watched as the world fell back into place. Ann tapped Tommy's head and said, "Okay, we're ready!"

"SET? FIGHT!" Arnold shouted as he and Tommy began walking toward each other.

Ann and Diana were reaching for each other in an attempt to knock the other one from her man's shoulders. Diana's knees tingled as Arnold held them, while goosebumps ran up her arms whenever Ann gripped them. She almost couldn't bear it. Suddenly, she felt herself soaring backward through the air. Diana opened her eyes underwater. After several blinks, Arnold's legs and butt came into focus. *Butt*, she thought. Diana swam closer to it and bit it underwater. When she broke the surface, he wrapped her in his arms.

"We lost, but you put up a good fight," Arnold said.

"I bit your butt," she said.

She slid her arm down from his hip onto his crotch. She smiled when she felt him ready for her.

"Yeah, let's go play that game," he said with a smile.

"Gross. Besides, you owe me a shot since you lost," Ann said. Swimming over to Diana, she snaked her arm around her middle and pulled her to the ladder. It tickled, causing Diana to giggle the whole way. "Come on," Ann said.

When they were out of the pool, Ann took hold of Diana's wrist. Fireworks erupted, and even the grass tickled as she tried to keep up with Ann.

"We'll be right back," Ann called over her shoulder.

They reached the chairs, and Ann grabbed a towel to drape over Diana before leading her up to the house. When they got to the back door, Ann reached into one of the hanging plants and removed something.

"What're you doing?"

"Do you remember last year that guy I had been on a few dates with had given me some pot brownies? And you loved them?"

"Yeah, but that's not a brownie," Diana said, a giggle already creeping up her throat.

"Good job," Ann said with a chuckle. "But it's close enough."

They sat cuddled together on the outdoor loveseat on the deck with the towel wrapped around both of them. Neither said much as they smoked, other than Ann's instructions for what to do: "Pinch it, pull in through your mouth, hold it. Good girl."

It was like a song. When there was only a little left, Ann stood up.

"Stay, finish that. I'll be right back with the shots!"

Before Diana could respond, Ann was gone. Diana watched the wind move through the plants. She imagined it dancing through the grass and the trees. Going to take a puff, she realized it was no longer lit. Diana sat fumbling with the lighter until Ann came back.

"I couldn't do it," Diana said softly, looking up at Ann.

Ann looked down at Diana, her head shaking back and forth. Her hair moved like the wind was playing tag with it.

"You're like a child sometimes." Her voice was soft as she put the joint in between Diana's lips.

"Inhale," Ann instructed, as she flicked the lighter. "Don't worry, I'll always take care of you," she added.

Warmth spread down over Diana's body as her friend kissed the top of her head.

"Thank you," Diana mumbled.

"Now let's go take these shots before you pass out, okay?"

Diana's body burst into goosebumps, each firing off more sensations throughout her body, as Ann guided her back down to the pool. Giggles filled the air with happiness. She could live her whole life being led by tingles.

"Finally," Tommy exclaimed. "They're back!"

Both men looked so happy. Diana clapped. She loved being this happy. The only thing missing was Tim. Tim was the best chicken partner and had smooth skin. His hair was never sticky.

"And we come bearing shots," Ann added. "Blue for the boys and green for the girls."

"Cheers," Arnold said.

"To new friends and nudism," Tommy declared. "Cheers!"

The foursome played another round of chicken until Ann fell into the water. Tommy embraced her in a consolation hug.

Diana giggled as Ann wrapped herself around Tommy's body, the water giving them funny-shaped limbs.

"Want to go inside?" Ann asked.

"Only since this afternoon," Tommy said.

The two separated. Tommy struggled over to the pool stairs, and Ann made her way over to Diana and Arnold.

"Tommy has to use the bathroom, and I'm going to show him

where it is, inside." Ann winked. "Try to contain yourselves until you get into the guest house, you two. Good night!"

"Good night," Arnold said.

Tommy turned around, unsteady on his feet, and nodded at Arnold, who nodded back. Ann took a veering Tommy by the hand, leading him up the slight hill. After they disappeared, Arnold lifted Diana up and began to kiss her.

Little fireworks erupted over Diana's body everywhere Arnold touched. His lips brought a moan to her own. Water caressed her skin as the cool air kissed it. They moved up and down through the night air. It was all too good, too much. She could barely wait, the sensations running wild over her body.

"Where're we going?" Diana asked, the cool breeze gliding across her skin.

"To bed," Arnold said.

She missed the water, but was met with a bed of clouds. Tingles rushed her body. The sheets were like little whispers on her skin.

Arnold's skin brushed against her; he felt so different from the clouds. He tasted like cinnamon candy. She couldn't get enough and wondered if his candy stick tasted the same. She ran her tongue across it, but it tasted salty. She felt herself pooling between her legs. With every pulse, she wanted him more. He guided her on top of him—she told Ann there were ponies here —his hands like fire across her skin. She looked down at him. She blinked, confused by the lack of freckles, the soft layer above the muscles.

Diana blinked, and Arnold's face came into focus. He was so hard, pressing against her. . . She inched up, feeling him settle between her butt.

"Wrap it."

He pushed up against her, his stiffness sliding across her. She shivered, dipping back into delirium.

"Shit," Arnold said.

"No glove—" The words clogged her throat.

"I didn't bring anything. . ."

The clouds around her grew harsh and angry.

"—no love," said Diana.

He pulled away from her, and coldness seeped into her skin. Still, the clouds and their soft texture caressed her.

"I'll be right back, MOD. Right back," Arnold said.

Then he floated away.

Diana was writhing against the clouds, floating along, feeling every whisper they left against her skin. Something sparkled in the corner. Water! Diana realized how thirsty she was. How warm the sunshine had been inside her, how the stinky weed had dried out her mouth. She had never before been so happy to see it.

She did the backstroke through the clouds until she could finally reach it. One of them had Diana's name across the front. Sliding herself to an upright position, she shuddered at the sensations of the clouds, the plastic, the cool water. She drained almost the entire bottle of water and returned it to the night-stand, and then Diana sank back into the clouds and waited for Arnold.

chapter twenty-seven

<u>Arnold</u>

Arnold was rock hard and ready for release. He just had to find those condoms, but first he had to find his truck. To do that, he had to find that fucking path. He scanned the light from his phone's flashlight across the grass. The grass and the stones kept crossing over each other.

His flashlight dinged. Looking down, Arnold saw a new text. The letters blurred in and out until finally he could make out the numbers from the other night, words too.

"Amber?"

A noise in the distance distracted Arnold. He shined the flashlight around but only saw trees and stones. *Condoms*, he thought, *truck, path*. He kept walking through damp grass. How late was it?

Condoms, truck, path. . . His foot landed on something extra cold. He adjusted the beam of light. His foot had landed on stone, then another one. Good! Now he needed to find the next one. Then he would find his truck, which would bring him to condoms for Amber. *But we don't use condoms*, Arnold thought.

Again, he heard a ding from his phone. Another message.

He had to find his truck and Amber. Continuing on the path, he heard the rustling of branches. Arnold stumbled backward, and the noise got closer.

Falling to the ground, Arnold's flashlight bounced away from him, landing face down.

"Amber," Arnold called out. "Amber?"

chapter twenty-eight

Diana

Diana inhaled sharply. The air had been still around her;
everything had gone to sleep, including herself. Heaviness
throbbed between her legs as something wet and hot traced the
inside of her thigh. In its wake, a trail of icy air. Within seconds,
warm air tickled the area. It was like the cloud was traveling
through the seasons.

She lifted her hips, hoping the wind would caress her aching
clit. Her breath caught in her throat as something ran against her
center. It felt better than she remembered.

"Aaah. . ."

She felt something incredible slide inside her. It filled the
hollow spaces inside her. She ebbed toward it. Her mouth
opened, taking in breath, and it moved deeper inside her,
making the space it needed. She felt herself tighten around it,
greedily take it in as much as she could.

"Aaahhh."

Diana saw mountains covered in snow, surrounded by
purple trees. She felt like she was floating. The movement

against her sent a quiver throughout her body. Soon she would become a body of water.

"Mmmhmm."

Diana felt pressure against her backside as she rocked herself against the cause of her pleasure. A longing shiver ran through her. Quick, sharp pinches scattered up the inside of her thigh. She arched herself, pushing her shoulders against the clouds, lifting herself up, like an offering.

"Arnold, Arnnoo—owww!"

Diana cried out. There was pain and then a sensation like she had never felt before. It brought her closer to the edge of the mountain top.

Diana felt her eyes roll further back into her already closed lids. She was weak with pleasure coursing through her body and felt herself float away. Release rushed from her. When her body stopped shaking, Diana rolled into a ball and curled up onto her side, the high walls of clouds surrounding her.

"Arnold?"

A sting ran through Diana's butt cheek. Before she could breathe another word, Diana was sleepless, dreaming.

chapter twenty-nine

Amber

Amber wasn't able to blink. She had been trying for several minutes to no avail.

It was like her eyes had been taped over, bound by a semi-clouded piece of black plastic. She felt the room spinning with every attempt to free her eyes. The spinning quickened with each try. A dull ache was starting to form across the bridge of her nose.

Amber lifted her arms to her face. She felt a piece of gauze taped over her eyes. Her heart began to pound. Her breath accelerated. She had no idea where she was; she tried feeling around her, but Amber seemed to be groping at air. Nothing was in her reach, other than the surface on which she was sitting.

She heard a strange sound, like something that would have come from a wounded animal. She turned her head in the direction from where the noise travelled and heard soft sobs. The animal-like noise rang out again; the sobs, now louder, she realized, were coming from her.

"Hello?"

Sitting in the dark, Amber waited for a reply.

chapter thirty

<u>Diana</u>

A blaring noise assaulted Diana's ears, reverberating throughout her brain. Her eyes fluttered. She wasn't awake enough to feel anything but exhaustion. After stirring under a sea of blankets for a few moments, she gained enough energy to reach out for Arnold to make that noise stop.

She only found more blankets. No Arnold. Diana tried to roll over to see if maybe he was on the far side of the bed, or maybe in the bathroom, not that she could see much from this vantage point—only if he was at the vanity, but it didn't seem like anyone was there. The sound stopped, and Diana lay still.

Before she could thank her lucky stars, the beeping resumed. Diana tried again, this time rolling toward the noise. She reached her arm over and found the phone that connected to the main house. Diana lifted it off the receiver, and the sound stopped immediately. She dropped it next to her ear, half rolling on top of it since her arms were too weak to hold it properly.

"Diana," Ann's voice came out loud and frantic, "are you awake?"

"Shhh."

Elizabeth Scozzari

It was all Diana could manage. Ann was too loud.

"Is Arnold with you?" Ann nearly screeched in her ear.

"What?"

"I'm coming down to the guest house. Something's not right."

Diana heard the phone click and tried to understand what Ann had been on about, but she felt drained. Her entire body was hurting, and her eyes wouldn't open all the way. She closed them and played the conversation back as best as she could. Ann was upset and looking for Arnold. Arnold was seemingly not in the guest house, and Ann was on her way down. Diana tried concentrating, and nearly wet herself when Ann came barging through the door, telling her to wake up.

"I must have dozed off," Diana said.

"Are you even awake now?"

"I don't know."

"Doesn't matter, you will be," Ann continued. "If you can sit up, drink this," she said, thrusting a mug in Diana's direction.

"I'll try," said Diana.

She attempted to scoot herself back toward and up against the headboard. She managed enough to be able to take the mug from Ann, who then pulled the blanket up over her legs. Diana futzed with the rest, tucking it under her chin.

"Here," Ann said.

Something landed on top of Diana's shoulder. She put the coffee cup onto the nightstand and grabbed the balled-up t-shirt.

"Not so much of a nudist this afternoon, are we?"

"It's a little different when everyone is shitfaced." Diana pulled the shirt over her head, struggling to get the blanket out from under it. "Did you say afternoon?"

"I wasn't shitfaced," Ann snapped back. "It's almost one."

"Well, shit. I must have been," Diana said.

She leaned forward, getting the t-shirt to slide further down her back. With effort, she managed to shift her legs around until she was in some sort of sitting position. She picked the mug back up, still warm from the coffee inside, and placed it on her knees. Her eyes struggled to keep up with where Ann was as she paced back and forth in front of the bed. She was still so out of it and afraid that all the commotion might make her throw up soon.

"Can you bring it down to a five, preferably a three? I'm struggling, and if you keep this up, I'm gonna puke on you."

Ann stopped mid-step and turned to face Diana full on. Ann beamed for a second. Diana couldn't fathom at what, but before she could ask, it was gone.

"I'll try," Ann began, "but there's a slight problem."

Diana took a sip of her coffee and looked over at Ann. She looked exceptionally pretty, especially in the dated guest house.

Everything in the Hwang home was exquisite. Modern and tasteful. Old-world, but with a reimagined new charm. Everything but the guest house. It was still a champion for late eighties/early nineties nostalgia.

"Can't be too much of a crisis since you did your makeup." Diana tried to chuckle until she felt the bile rising in the back of her throat. "Mmm," Diana moaned, as she swallowed hard. "Can you explain this to me over food?"

Diana winced at the glare Ann shot her.

"There's a platter of food on the side table. How asleep were you when I came in?"

Her eyes followed Ann's hand. Sure enough, a large platter of steaming food sat so close, and yet, Diana turned to put her coffee back down on the end table.

"Shit. . . my fault for thinking you were functional," Ann griped as she began putting half an egg sandwich, breakfast potatoes, and fresh fruit on a plate. "How drunk were you last night?"

"You were standing over me when I woke up. If you hadn't called me earlier, I would've woken up thinking I slept with you."

Ann cast her a stony glare. It was almost unfair how pretty her friend was when she was angry.

"Try eating some of this, and I'll fill you in, okay?"

"Thank you," she croaked. "You really do look extra pretty today."

"Diana, shut up," she snapped. "Please," Ann said, "I need you to listen."

She fumbled until the plate was flat on her knees. Diana lifted her eyes to Ann and nodded as best she could.

Ann sat down on the bed and began, "So, last night Tommy and I were in the kitchen making out." Diana tried to smile, and Ann looked really excited. "He picked me up and put me on the countertop and tried to go down on me. You know how I feel about that." Her smile faded, leaving behind the face of revulsion.

"Yeah, you should get over that," Diana mumbled as she picked up her egg sandwich.

"Not any time soon." Ann stood, mimed throwing up, and shuddered, before continuing, "I grabbed his face with one hand and his hand with my other. I kissed him some and guided his fingers inside me. All good." Diana winked at Ann as she rounded the corner of the bed and then bent down. "Is this your water, Di?"

Diana looked up. "Maybe?"

"It has an *A* on it, but since Asshole isn't here. . ." Ann shrugged and tossed the water bottle on the bed as she continued stomping her way through the bedroom. "Anyway, at some point we were lying on the kitchen counter about to bang when he realized that his wallet with his condoms was outside. So, he goes outside to get his condoms, and who knows how long later, I was still inside waiting for him. I ran up to my room to grab sweats and a tee, and I saw someone walking out of the gate."

Ann paced into the bathroom, checked herself out in the mirror, adjusted her hair, and left, continuing to pace. "I ran outside to get him. You know how easy it is to get lost on this property." She sighed. "But then, I saw Arnold. I nearly died.

Literally, imminent death. He was naked, mumbling some weird shit to himself, and—"

"What kind of weird shit?"

Diana asked through a mouthful of pineapple. "It's not important, Di," Ann said.

Ann's dismissal should have been enough to deter her, but something about the way Ann wasn't taking the opportunity to tear Arnold down caused her mild panic.

"The way you're avoiding it makes it seem important to me."

"He was calling out for Amber, that's all I really heard," Ann said.

Her tone was unusually solemn for reporting on Arnold being a fuck up. Instead of gloating, she rearranged the beach-themed figurines in the entertainment center.

"Oh."

Diana returned her sandwich to her plate, the taste of bile now mixing with yolky goodness.

"I'm sorry," Ann said.

"It's not your fault. It's his." She reached to her side and picked up her coffee, taking a small sip. "I love this mug," said Diana.

The oversized mug looked ginormous in her hands. It had her initials on it and was her mug when she was a guest at the Hwangs'. Ann gave her a small smile before she continued walking around the bed like a jungle cat.

"Continue, please?"

"I was going to see if he was okay, but when I got closer, he fell over," Ann said. Diana snorted, spat her coffee into her cup, and began laughing. "What?"

"Of course, he did. He won't admit it, but I think he's always been kind of terrified of you. He thinks you're the one who left a dead cat on his doorstep!"

"Oh, that's right. I sent Amber one too," Ann said. "The note sent with his said something about playing with someone else's pussy, and if I remember, hers was somewhat threatening. I don't remember the specifics," Ann said as she returned to the foot of the bed.

"Imagine being Arnold, running into *you* while thinking about Amber alone in the middle of the dark, dark night. . . You're terrifying, and I kind of love it," Diana said.

"It's not like I killed the cat." Ann shrugged and continued, "I got it from the animal hospital affiliated with my parents' medical center."

"We know that, but I'm one hundred percent sure that neither of them did."

"That's probably because I signed hers from Arnold." Ann smirked. "Anyway, ancient history aside, his phone flashlight thing shut off when he fell, but not before I saw his angry boner —I nearly threw up, by the way. How can something so small be so angry? He called out again for Amber. By that time, I saw Tommy in the backyard with his flashlight—much flashier than Arnold's by the way—so I grabbed him and went inside."

Ann sat on top of the light-green-and-pink flowered comforter and put her hand on top of Diana's covered foot. She squeezed it, moving further onto the bed.

"I didn't think he would drive off in the middle of the night, Di. I didn't even see his keys anywhere. I just assumed—"

"What do you mean, drive off?"

Ann remained silent. Diana looked at Ann. Her face was still as stone. She inhaled sharply as if bracing herself.

"Tommy and I went and rolled a blunt before we went back inside and were smoking. Mr. Pre-Med has a pretty good stash, by the way. Anyway, we started going at it again, so we went to his car, the white one that had been next to Arnold's truck, and it was gone. Arnold's truck was gone."

Ann stood up from the bed and started pacing again, moving decorative knick-knacks from one spot to another, only to move them back the next go-around.

"I assumed that if he was naked, outside, calling for Amber, that he was drunk and stupid. At worst, she was picking him up.

Trust me, I was already planning on addressing that on a personal level. Then I realized that his truck was gone." Ann turned to face Diana. "He was already gone. I figured he'd be back before you woke up. If you're going to do something stupid, you should at least do it right. But earlier, when I walked Tommy out, his truck still wasn't back."

Diana sat in silence, tightly holding her coffee up, wishing her breakfast would settle down.

"Maybe he's out with Mark?"

"Diana, I don't know how your boyfriend's mind works; for that matter, I'm having doubts about yours right now too. I know I'm not the president of the Arnold fan club. I'm not even a registered member. But if Arnold met Mark, butt naked with his mighty-mini hard-on at God knows what time in the middle of the night after calling out for his sidepiece, I'm going to need to buy a lottery ticket and a Bible because I will have seen it all."

Ann sat back down on the bed next to Diana. Taking the coffee mug, she placed it back on the nightstand before she took each of Diana's shoulders in her hands.

"I'm sorry, Di. I'm sure it's not what you want to hear. And you're right, there's a possibility, albeit a very small, microscopic possibility, that he's with Mark or even Tim. I'll get your phone, and you can start with Arnold first."

Diana raised her head, looking into her friend's deep, dark eyes. Their hard edges were softening. A pang rang through her gut. In all the time they had known each other, the years Diana and Arnold had been off and on, Ann had never shown sympathy toward Diana when it came to Arnold's transgressions. The fact that she was starting today made her stomach twist.

"It's okay. He made his own track record, but I chose to forgive him. Let's give him the benefit of the doubt until we have all the facts." Diana forced a smile. "All the detective novels have to pay off for something, right? When was this. . . when you didn't see his truck outside?"

Elizabeth Scozzari

"Tommy left around nine-thirty. It still wasn't back on my walk down here." Ann's face was deadpan.

"So, Arnold, assuming what you're telling me is—"

"I wouldn't lie about this. I wouldn't lie to you," Ann said. Her tone brought the temperature down several degrees.

"Ann, I know you wouldn't. I just—" Diana's voice faded. Exhaling, Diana searched Ann's eyes. "This isn't the first time he's done this." Diana cleared her throat. "Cheated. If that's what he's run off and done—seems like the obvious answer. But there's something else. Something you're not saying. I can see it. I just can't figure out what it could be."

Diana picked up the coffee mug, turning it around in her hands. Standing up, Ann resumed her pacing. Diana thought about what she was doing to the rug. Ann stopped at the foot of the bed. Her eyes weren't reaching Diana's; a stillness settled over her. As Ann spoke, the weight of her words crushed her.

"Her sister had a baby on Thursday. There were complications, but everyone thought things were okay. The baby took a turn for the worse this morning. Whatever it was wasn't fatal, but far enough outside of the norm that both my mother and father got called in—"

"That's terrible," Diana said. "But why both of your parents? Your mom is General Counsel, and your father, well, he definitely wasn't the obstetrician."

Ann resumed her lap around the guest house. She stopped next to Diana, her hand resting on Diana's knee.

"The police are apparently involved," said Ann.

"They're saying that someone *tried* to hurt the baby?!"

"Well, this would be the second Storm baby in less than a year who's died. Last October, Amber went into premature labor. The baby was born, but it died within hours. From what I've overheard, there was some suspicion about Amber's premature labor. Of course, there was some strong arming on the part of Daddy Storm, but with two daughters, one dead and one *almost*

206

dead grandbaby. . ." Ann's voice trailed off as she sat on the corner of the bed.

The mug almost slipped from Diana's hands. She fumbled, sloshing a little over the lip. Ann popped up, rushed over, and took the mug, putting it on the nightstand. Sitting back down next to Diana, she wrapped her arms around her. Diana couldn't move.

October.

Her eyes closed as she leaned against Ann.

"I can't," she started to say. "I don't understand."

Ann pulled back, running her hand over Diana's hair. "You don't have to," she said, shaking her head. "It's against HIPAA and a million other laws, but I called Becky, the girl I met when I was a candy striper. She's a perinatal nurse now. I asked her to check for me. Arnold's listed as the father of Amber's baby."

Ann let the sentence hang between them.

"But. But he never said anything." Diana's breath hitched as she continued to ramble, "He still wants kids. He knows that I don't, but he, uh. I. . ."

Ann grabbed Diana tighter, rubbing her back.

"I'm going to find your phone. You can try calling him yourself if you still want to. And we'll go from there, okay?"

Diana nodded. As slow as she moved, the room still spun. She felt even worse than when she had woken up. Ann got off the bed in search of Diana's phone. She watched as Ann looked at Arnold's duffel bag, still there from the night before. Her stuff was right next to it. Diana shook her head, and Ann reached into her beach bag first. She stood with Diana's phone in hand.

"You'll have to plug it in. Let me see if there's a cord in the other room." Ann came and went faster than Diana could collect her thoughts. "I'm going to run up to the house and get you some more coffee. I'll be back in a little bit, okay?"

"Yeah, thanks."

A weak smile flashed across her face.

Diana waited until her phone turned back on to unlock it.

Dozens of texts and missed-call notifications popped up. Ignoring them, Diana tried calling Arnold's phone. There was a single ring before his voicemail picked up. She tried two more times, all with the same results. Opening her texts, she was about to try Arnold when the last message from Tim caught her eye.

> 911 Dame, CALL ME ASAP.

She pressed call. Tim answered on the first ring.

"Are you okay?"

"My phone died. I'm still at Ann's."

"Have you heard anything or. . ." His voice trailed off.

"I've heard a lot this morning. Ranging from cheating boyfriends as baby daddies to Amber's sister almost losing her newborn. Is this what your 911 was about?"

Tim coughed on the other end of the phone.

"Wow, um." She heard Tim exhale. "You said you're still at Ann's?"

"I am. And I'm stranded here. Since, according to an eyewitness, Arnold left butt naked with his tiny hard-on raging for the world to see, calling out for Amber in the middle of the night. I'm hungover, and I feel like death. And Ann is taking pity on me."

Tim groaned, which did nothing to make her feel better.

"That's a lot," he said. "I'll be there as soon as I can, okay? It's been a weird morning."

"You're telling me," Diana said.

"I'll call you when I'm on my way. Okay?"

"Sure," Diana said. "Thanks, Mister. You said it was an emergency; is everything okay?"

"It's shitty, Dame. The whole thing, but you're okay and I'm here."

"I know."

"Catch ya later, kid."

"See ya, chief."

Diana looked at her texts. The majority of them had been from the Pretty Little Liars group chat—someone had changed the name of the group to "A SHOULD HAVE WON"— and from Tim. There were eight from Arnold, and two were from an unknown number. She hadn't opened the ones from Arnold. The preview of the last message was clear enough.

> I want the wife, the status, the children. I want Amber. . . Not you. . .

The other text was a photo; the words "Attachment: 1 image" were in the preview. Diana opened it. Her heart dropped from her throat to her knees. It was a sonogram. The message read:

> We lost our first one. Stay away from Arnold. Stay away from us. We're together now, and we're going to move on, start a new life, and a new family.

Diana couldn't finish reading it. She closed her texts and put her phone on silent, dropping it onto the bed. With her knees pulled up to her chest, she rested her forehead on her arms as she sat there waiting for anything to make sense.

chapter thirty-one

Arnold

Arnold groped for his phone. His eyelids were heavy and being pushed closed by the hammering throughout his head. *What the fuck had happened last night?*

The ground didn't feel familiar. He'd drunkenly ended up on his own floor too many times to know what it felt like. Diana was too much of a neat freak, and Ann's parents paid big money to keep their mini-castle clean. Unless he was in the driveway? But it was freezing. It didn't matter the time, nowhere on asphalt in the middle of summer on Long Island was the ground going to be *freezing*.

Meanwhile, his head was on fire. It felt like someone had beaten the living shit out of him. Not that he had been beaten up since he was a kid. He'd been in fights, Lord knew he had been in some real shitshows, but his ass hadn't been kicked since he was a tween. Between workouts, sports games, and benders, Arnold had put himself through a lot on more than one occasion. He couldn't recall feeling this awful. The pain was too much. It seized his thoughts the longer he was awake. The last thing he felt before he succumbed to the agony was the rough texture of the cold, cold floor against his cheek.

chapter thirty-two

Diana

Ann got Diana her coffee and gave her a Beverly Hills 9OH2O water bottle.

"You could have just gotten me another plastic one your parents got for the party."

Diana wasn't sure if it was more or less weird having Ann fawning over her with sympathy, punctuating her every move. It could be overbearing when it was her regular amount of caring.

"I could have, but why?"

"Because it's normal?"

"Diana, I hate to tell you this, but we are way past normal. Your now-ex-boyfriend is with a girl whom he knocked up and whose parents are now being questioned in her niece's death."

The color drained from Diana's face, and a wave of nausea turned in her stomach. She tried to swallow, but her throat constricted.

"Ahh," Ann said. "What I should have said was that it's the least I can do."

"Probably," said Diana.

Her voice fought through the hurt bubbling in her chest. Ann

Elizabeth Scozzari

nodded and walked over to where the clicker was, along with a water bottle from Diana's bag.

"Just in case the other one tastes too fresh and clean for you."

Diana tried to smile. There was something endearing about Ann trying to do normal. She left both waters in front of her, clinging to her coffee mug for dear life. Ann crawled across the bed alongside her friend. Wrapping one arm around Diana, she used her other arm to turn on the television. The flipping of the channels was soothing, even if she wasn't paying any attention to what was on. She shifted her weight, leaning into Ann's armpit. There were people laughing, but it seemed hollow. They were acting. It didn't count. It was pretend.

What had happened last night? In the few months? He had been with her in this bed hours ago. She could still feel traces of him on her. Diana shuddered.

"You okay, honey?" Ann asked.

"Yeah, just got a chill."

A cell phone pinged. Since Diana had shut her sound off after hanging up with Tim, it had to be Ann's.

"It's Tommy!"

"What?"

"It's Tommy," Ann said, waving her phone in Diana's face. "The text I got was from Tommy."

"Nice," Diana said.

"Right?!" Ann laughed at her. "He wants to come over in an hour." Diana smiled.

"That's great. I'm not sure when Tim will get here, but I'll be fine in here. Unless you were planning on. . ."

"No, well, actually, with my parents. . . but listen, you camp out in my room. Or the library, you do love the house library!"

"I do," said Diana.

It was true. Their library was the stuff of Beauty and the Beast, but it wouldn't be the same today. Diana wasn't sure if anything would be.

216

"Let me call Tim and see if he has an ETA. I'm going to pee and brush my teeth anyway. Try to feel a little more human."

Finishing what was left of her open water bottle, Diana opened the fancy one.

"Huh," Diana said, "there is a difference."

Ann stared up at her in disbelief. For the first time in too long, Diana laughed so hard she could barely catch her breath. Then she began to cry. She felt Ann's weight shift on the bed.

"No, no," Diana said, straightening herself up. "I'm good. I just. After all this time, you were right about Arnold and the water."

"I would say I told you so, but—"

"Please, all of your pity is weird."

Sitting up straighter, Ann flipped the end of her ponytail over her shoulder.

"I don't know why you don't listen to me. Tap water is just as terrible for you as your ex, Di. The bottled water you buy is subpar, the fact that you refill it with tap is almost as offensive as you ever taking *Assclown* back—again."

Ann winked as Diana leaned forward, leaving the cozy nest she had made in the bed.

"Now, morphing back into a human is a fantastic idea! Up you go," Ann said, smacking Diana's butt as she tumbled out of bed. "I'll hang out until you get ready. You look like you stumbled off the struggle bus."

"Thanks," Diana said. A small chuckle escaped her.

She felt like she was wading through dense fog on her way to the bathroom. Half falling, half sitting, she situated herself on the toilet and picked up the phone to call Tim. The phone was still ringing when she looked down at her legs. There, on the inner part of her thigh, was a bite mark.

The sensation of someone caressing her replayed in her thoughts. The circular motion of a finger or a tongue. Diana felt the bathroom swirl around her. Arnold had never bitten her before; he hadn't gone down on her in what, years? Diana felt the goosebumps on her arms and legs rise; last night had been absolutely incredible. She closed her eyes, fighting the spinning room. She felt like she was falling. Good or not, Arnold had left to get condoms and hadn't come back. He had gone. Gone to be with. . .

Coldness spread across her body, and everything faded away. "DIANA!"

Diana opened her eyes. Ann was standing over her. There was a fan swirling behind her head. Her eyes fluttered before closing.

"NO," Ann shouted. "Diana, wake up!"

She opened her eyes again. The fan was still there. Taking a deep breath in, she looked around the room. It seemed that she was lying on the bathroom floor.

"What happened?" Diana asked.

"I don't know!" Ann exclaimed. "You tell me!"

"Um."

Ann scoffed and walked away. From Diana's vantage point on the ground, she looked like a real-life Giantess. Ann ran the water and snapped the faucet off. She returned with a washcloth in hand, now looking like an angry giant.

"You went to pee and to call Tim. Apparently, he picked up and heard you doing some weird moaning mumbling thing before he heard a boom." Ann said, as she wrung out the water and walked back to Diana, laying the cold washcloth on her forehead. Diana shivered. "The same boom I heard that brought me in here to find you on the floor," she added.

Diana felt like she was in slow motion. Ann was upset, and Tim was on the phone. And she was on the floor, again.

"I'm sorry," Diana said. Her voice was small, even to her.

"Don't be sorry," Ann said. "It's just scary. And I don't know if you hit your head."

She looked up at Ann, the washcloth obscuring her vision.

"I'm not mad, Di," she said, looking down at her friend. "If this wasn't the thousandth time you fainted this week, I wouldn't care. I'm never letting you drink again. At least not until you control whatever this is."

She tried to move the cloth over.

"Oh no you don't," Ann said, putting her arm on Diana's shoulder. "Tim is coming to get you. He was already on his way to get food before heading over here. Which, BT Dubs, you should explain that food gets cold between Syosset and West Islip. And knowing what you two eat, it can't be good cold. I'll spare you the lecture today, but really, Diana, we need to talk about your takeout consumption."

The words were landing on Diana in a wash. She didn't have Consumption. The last known case was in the 50s. But she was exhausted. Her body hurt. She wasn't sure if she was mostly tired, hungover, disappointed, or just in a weird dream-like universe surrounded by green and pink bathroom tiles. At least she was going home with her best friend in the world. That was something to look forward to.

chapter thirty-three

Arnold

The lights burned through Arnold's eyelids, forcing him awake. Once again, he ran his hands across the floor surrounding him.

Nothing, not his phone or furniture, was within reach. Maybe if he could move, but everything hurt too much. It wasn't as cold as when he passed out, but he was still lying on the floor. Which floor, he still had no idea.

After what felt like an hour's worth of effort, Arnold sat up. There was a wall behind him. He could feel it with his arms reaching backward. The area surrounding him was still dark. He couldn't make out anything close to him. His eyes began to adjust, despite the stabbing pain from the brightness. The lights were coming from another room! A room he could see through a window. Why would he be anywhere where there would be inside windows?

Arnold tried not to blink. It made it harder for his eyes to adjust. A small person took form under the bright light. Her blonde hair, half pulled back, held by something that seemed to be a medical instrument, looked almost yellow under the light. Amber?

He strained his eyes, trying to lean forward through the searing pain. Was she wearing his jersey? He had never seen her in another one. Her back was perfectly straight. It seemed like her legs were stretched out ahead of her. There were patches of what appeared to be dried blood clashing against the white of the jersey. Arnold's stomach pulled, and he tried to swallow. He was afraid he was going to be sick.

Arnold scrambled to get up. Pain pawed at his back, and he hit the floor again. He had to see if Amber was okay. If she were even alive. He pushed off the floor, rushing forward like he was a linebacker. Fire rained down on him. He landed with a crash on the floor. His back felt warm and wet. His hands shook as they touched the sticky metal point, following its rough exterior to his pierced skin. He was chained to the wall with at least one meat hook. Arnold gagged and coughed as hot, foamy puke splashed off the floor and onto his face.

What the fuck had happened?

chapter thirty-four

Diana

Diana had insisted that she was fine to get up after lying still for almost a whole fifteen minutes. Begrudgingly, Ann agreed. As good as her housekeepers were, it would skeeve her out to be on a bathroom floor for that long as well.

"Besides," Diana had pointed out, "not sure I really want to be giving out a free show of my jewel to everyone today."

"Tommy is just leaving now," she said. "Won't be here for a solid 20 minutes, I'm sure."

Diana watched as Ann's legs jittered as Ann watched her sit on the bed to put her shorts on. Her lucky Mets shirt had been out on the bathroom counter when she had gotten out of the shower.

Thankfully, it was blue with orange writing, instead of white. Diana didn't know where her bra was, and it was hard enough getting her outer layers on. The last thing she felt like having was her nipples on display for everyone to see.

"Are you not putting anything on underneath? No bra? No panties?"

"Ann, are you judging me for going commando, because—"

"No, no. It's just. Those are the same ones you wore yesterday, no? I could have lent you a pair or something."

"It'll just be until I'm home."

"You stress me out, girl. You think Tim is almost here?" Ann asked.

Diana walked back into the bathroom and unwrapped her hair from the towel. She usually would have shaken it out, but one glare from Ann had made her reconsider.

"Probably, you're like 20 minutes from me, and Tim had already left."

"It's 27 minutes door to door from your townhouse to here, but only 26 back," Ann stated.

"Why?" Diana asked.

"I think it's the traffic light on Higbie." Even after a shower, she didn't have it in her to explain to Ann that that wasn't what she had meant. "Just trying to make sure you're covered before Tim gets here." Ann flashed an impatient smile. "You're single now, you know. Need to make sure you're not leading anybody on with those perky nipples you got since your DDs really do warrant a bra."

"Ann, you're killing me."

Ann stood up and walked over to Diana. She tugged at the bottom of her shirt and then pressed the front part in, creating a perfect French tuck.

"I can't fault you for your ex," Ann spoke sternly. "But you didn't *have* to drink so much." Her eyes squinted at something outside. "Tim's here!"

Diana had never heard her so happy about Tim's existence since she had met him.

"Great timing. Because if that wasn't, I would crash back into bed and ruin your hook-up session with. . ." Diana's voice trailed off. She followed Ann's gaze, still focused outside. "Is he—"

"—bleeding?"

They looked at each other. Ann ran to the bathroom, grabbing a towel from under the sink. Diana tried to rush to the door. As Tim's sneaker touched the pavers surrounding the pool, he was greeted by Ann, who was shoving a towel at him. Before she could say anything, Tim raised his one arm up in surrender. He laughed as he spoke, "Don't worry, I only bled on the grass."

"Thank Baby Jesus," Ann said.

Diana and Tim passed a silent look between them as he cleaned up his arm with the towel.

"And are you okay?" she said, looking sideways at Ann.

"Oh, yes," Ann said. "Are you okay? What happened?"

Tim looked past Diana and Ann, almost as though he was looking at the wall behind them through the space between them. Diana's stomach dropped.

"Tim?" she prompted.

"Nothing important," Tim said, shrugging. "More importantly, how are you feeling?"

Ann's phone went off, interrupting the conversation. This time, it sounded like her phone was ringing.

"Excuse me," Ann said to Diana.

Tim watched Ann as she skirted around him and back toward the main house.

"What happened?" Diana said, reaching out for Tim's bleeding arm.

Tim looked over his shoulder to where Ann was pacing on the deck.

"I'll tell you in the car," Tim said. A look of unease came across his face. "I know she's harmless, but. . ." Tim's voice trailed off. "Besides, I have my Dame to look after. What is coming with us?"

A smile broke the strain on Tim's face, making Diana feel better than she had all day.

"Come on," she answered, waving him along with her into the guest house.

Everything Diana had brought with her was in a neat pile close to the door. She did a quick sweep of the room. If she did leave anything, she could always come back or pick it up at the office.

"These two bags?" Tim asked.

"Yup, just my beach bag and my clothes bag."

"What're you doing with Arnold's stuff?"

"I'll have the housekeepers take it out with the trash," Ann said, stepping into the room. "Tommy is stopping for coffee and pastries on his way over." A smile crossed her face as she pocketed her phone. "Thanks for coming to get her," Ann said, putting her hand on Diana's shoulder.

"Anytime," Tim said. He looked down at his arm, gesturing it up as an offering, and raised his eyebrow, "Do you, uh. . ."

"Mm, no," Ann said quickly. "Just leave it on the duffel bag. It shouldn't be the worst housekeeping has ever seen."

Tim nodded and pulled his lips in. It was a terrible face, one that the two of them had spent years laughing over. But somehow it worked for him, Diana thought, especially when he felt uncomfortable enough to be extra reserved.

"Thank you so much, Ann," Diana said, hugging her friend. "You take such good care of me!"

"You're very welcome," Ann said, giving her tiny friend a squeeze. "I told you last night, not that you probably remember anymore, I always will."

"Well, we're gonna go. Good luck with Tommy," Diana said.

She gave her friend one last hug. The birds chirped as the pool filter kicked on in the backyard.

"I'll keep you posted. Let me know when you get home, and if you need me, call me! Oh, and wait," Ann said, shouting. "Hold on." Diana watched as she darted over to the other side of the guest house and returned with two large bags. "Don't forget these," she said, proffering the goodies to Tim. "Just the favors from last night. One for you and Tim. I threw in a pair of red and a pair of white sneakers for each of you. I guesstimated your shoe size," she said, casting a glance down at Tim's feet. "Plus, I threw in some leftovers for you, Di. Don't worry, they're all in separate bags."

"Thank you," Tim said. "Thanks, Ann."

Diana forced a smile as she and Tim waved goodbye and made their way back up the stone path. Each step felt like she was dragging the weight of the world behind her.

"So," Tim said when they reached the guest parking lot, "where do we start?"

"Want to start with what happened to your arm?"

"I'd rather start with why Ann is giving me sneakers instead of restraining orders."

"You came to the rescue. She can now get laid without worrying about me." Diana laughed. "And if I had to venture a guess, Arnold dropping the bar oh-so-low that she can probably appreciate the lesser of two evils. For now, at least."

chapter thirty-five

Tim

He looked at Diana for a moment before throwing the stuff in the back of the car. Then he went to her side and helped her in. She hadn't said anything about Arnold yet. He knew most of what happened, at least from Arnold's perspective. The piece of shit had sent a near play-by-play to the guys' group text. With each new blue message bubble, Tim felt a vein throb or muscle tighten that he hadn't been aware of before. He was so angry that he kept deleting all new messages as they came in. When Mark had called him, Tim had already thrown the phone across the room twice.

He could barely stomach the voicemail from Mark. "Dude, he's lost his mind. Did you know? I thought the other day had been a one-off—" Tim had hung up, erasing the message almost immediately. He gripped his steering wheel, thinking of all the things he knew that she didn't. That she shouldn't know but would be crushed to know he kept it from her.

"Tim?"

"Hmm," Tim said. He looked over at Diana, then back to the road.

Elizabeth Scozzari

"Thank you," she said. Her voice was quiet, but strong. He relaxed his grip at hearing it. "Thank you for everything."

As her hand touched the top of his arm, he felt his knuckles release.

"Of course," he said.

The sound of the engine stirred throughout the trees surrounding the parking lot. Clearing his throat and nodding toward the back seat, Tim added, "Now, about food—"

"I thought you were getting it on the way here? At least that's what Ann said."

"I asked her if she had something for you to snack on in the car or if I should stop to get you something." Tim rolled his eyes. "But yes, we can and will get lunch. I'll stop by the sandwich place, but only after you tell me what is going on."

"Good thing we have a long drive ahead of us," Diana said.

Tim could hear the strain in her voice. She talked through everything as if she were stuck in molasses. He listened, taking in each new piece of information, trying to help make sense of the timeline. She would be halfway through one part and then remember a bit more about something else. It sounded like she had barely remembered most of the night, with the exception of shots and the sensation of water and bursts of sunshine.

She had started hooking up with Arnold, something he had most certainly left out of his narrative, but then only vaguely recalled the bite on her thigh. They had been five minutes from her townhouse when she had finally told him about the sono-gram. Tim felt the weight of her words in his heart. It was worse than hearing it from Arnold. At least then he could be angry, lean into the rage. Driving, he couldn't even hold her. His grip tightened around the wheel again.

"I saw the preview of the last text Arnold sent," Diana said, the words thick in her throat, "but I didn't open it. No idea what he said or didn't. Right now, I don't want to know; what I saw was enough."

It wasn't until his car was parked that he looked over at her.

Without speaking, Tim reached out and took her hand. He could feel her hurt, the betrayal, and disappointment. She had given up so much for Arnold—they both had in their own ways.

"I'm not stupid," Diana said, holding her gaze out the window behind him, "It's over. Obviously, he's moved on, but I'm done. I have always been honest with him, and if he knew. . . Look, I said it to you the other day, right? It's been clear that we wanted two different things. Unlike him, I haven't been looking for someone else to make my dreams happen with. We gave it another shot to see if things were going to work." She turned to face him. Her features, usually warm and inviting, were distorted. She looked like a nightmare version of herself. A raging storm of emotions beneath a broken exterior. "So why not just call it quits? Fix their relationship, make more babies, or whatever. It might have been weird, but we probably could have been amicable about it. You know? Adults!"

Diana's face started turning a shade of red that Tim equated with the Mets losing the World Series.

"Diana?" he asked. "Are you okay?"

She blinked once. Tim realized it was a stupid question and braced himself for whatever he unleashed.

"Of course I'm okay. I'm fainting like a hysterical woman from the eighteen hundreds, I'm hungover, covered in bruises and a fucking bite mark, and oh yeah, I was finally figuring out who I was and what I wanted, only to be the butt of a joke. A joke, that by the way, could be sponsored by Babies R' Us. I'm great. I'm just fucking great."

Diana's breath grew choppy, and suddenly, large tears fell from her eyes. He watched as she pulled her feet onto the seat, drawing her knees up to her chest, and cried deeply.

Tim reached over and rubbed Diana's back in slow, soft circles—the same way she had when his mother died. He waited as her sobs slowed down.

"Hey, Dame," he said.

"Yeah?"

She sniffed, looking up into the street. "Whatever you need, I'm here."

"Thank you," said Diana. His heart sank as more tears formed in her eyes. "This dame is exhausted, dirty, hungry, and just wants to watch the Mets v the Phillies with her best friend while completely denying that the rest of the world exists. Is that too much to ask?"

"Diana, they're planning the Nationals—"

"Today, at six. I have yesterday's game recorded."

Tim looked up into Diana's eyes. While they were usually a bright, radiating green, they were now a light gray. He had only seen her eyes turn that color twice before, and one of them had been when her grandmother passed away. Tim pulled Diana into his arms and gave her a big squeeze.

"You can rest, do whatever you want. I will get food. Then we will eat, watch both games with no spoilers, and after, we'll tackle endless hours of the Cooking Channel, or a black and white. If you want to cry or scream, you do whatever you want. I'll even let you massacre me in any board game of your choice, just say the word."

"Is it really letting me, if I'd win anyway?"

Her face crumpled into something like a broken smile. Diana lifted her head and kissed Tim on the cheek.

"Thank you," she said again, her voice barely above a whisper.

"Always," he whispered back. "Now move your ass. There's baseball to watch."

chapter thirty-six

Amber

Amber heard the horrific noise again; this time, it was louder and followed by a loud whoosh and a clank.

"Hello?"

Panic ran through her words as she tried again for a reply. She shifted her weight, crossed her legs underneath her, and sat up straighter. She was a Storm; things like this didn't happen to her. Or they didn't before last year. A pang of sadness ripped through the fear in her chest.

"Hello, Amber." The unfamiliar voice crawled over her skin like bugs. It wasn't just the even tone of the voice that unnerved Amber; it was how the voice came out. Distorted, decidedly *not* human. She couldn't tell if it was male or female. Maybe there was an accident? The room felt cool, and there were those stiff blankets, like the kind from her lady doctor's office, on the bed. She wasn't wearing any jewelry. Her shoes had been removed, as had her jeans. All the things they removed from the victim at an emergency scene. It tracked, since she couldn't recall how she got here.

The last thing she remembered was Arnold texting her that

he had done it—he had broken up with that cold-hearted shell of a woman. He wanted to start their life together. Get married, make another baby *with her*.

Amber tried opening her eyes again. Only pain and blackness responded.

"We're starting now."

"Who are you? Starting what?" Whoever it was, they ignored her cries. "Hello?"

"Today's breaking news headline."

"PLEASE! Help me." Amber tried to move.

"Stormy seas ahead for a prominent Long Island family. An investigation into the near-death of Molly Storm's newborn baby. . ."

Amber screamed. "MOLLY! ROSELYNN!"

The metallic taste of blood filled her mouth. The voice chuckled. Unnatural and evil, like Caleb from Buffy. His eyes had scared her the most. Her own felt dry, on fire almost, and swollen.

"If you don't stop screaming, it won't be near death. It will be fatal."

Amber pressed her teeth together, pushing her tongue against them until they pinched the muscle. It was distracting, but not as painful as the gut-wrenching ache of her heart.

"That's a good girl. The patriarchy doesn't like it when two women from the same family can't breed properly. Too bad you couldn't have done a better job carrying yours. It does seem fitting, though. Have you ever learned from a mistake in your life?"

Acid rose up her throat, overpowering the bitter taste of blood. She hadn't been in an accident. And her niece, her baby niece, threatened for what? Her body jerked forward.

"No, no, swallow it down. We all know you can take it." There was another attempt at a chuckle. "To be fair, I don't really blame you. I think you're honestly too dumb to know any better. But it'll all be over soon."

"Over?" Amber spoke through clenched teeth. "What is happening? Why can't I see? What about my sister, my niece? Where is Arnold?"

Her voice broke like her spirit. The sound of liquid splashing onto the floor echoed her tears. There was a loud clanking sound and a whoosh. The draft pulled in air from the hallway. The smell of gasoline filled Amber's nostrils.

"Oh god, oh god," she whimpered.

chapter thirty-seven

<u>Tim</u>

"We lost," Diana groaned.

Her head pressed against the inside of his shoulder. They had both snuggled up to watch the Mets play the Phillies. Before they got cozy, Tim had grabbed some extra napkins from the kitchen; at least a handful were from Mojo's and a few were from Wendy's, just in case. Diana seemed to be holding up after her outburst in the car. He didn't want her to hold it in, but he hated seeing her hurt.

"We did," Tim chimed in.

Tim muted the post-game conference. Diana sat up and turned so her body faced him. She leaned forward to grab her water bottle from the table. The plastic was worn and crinkled as she uncapped it.

"Please tell me you're not reusing that again after tonight?" Her cheeks grew pink.

"Okay," he continued, "let's confirm we're recycling that bottle when we're done with the water, right?"

He nodded his head as he spoke. Diana's guilty smile broke

into a broader one. She finished the water and handed over the bottle.

"Yes, yes," she said. "I had one from my purse—was it this morning or yesterday? I can't remember, but it tasted like ass."

Tim laughed lightly; his Diana was sitting in front of him. She looked like she had been through the ringer, but the brightness that lived inside her was still there. Arnold has hurt her, not broken her.

"So, you're familiar with the delicacy of derrière, eh?" Diana just shook her head and laughed, tension cut her smooth skin, and tears pooled in her eyes. She rocked forward onto her knees and threw herself over him like a blanket.

"I'm sorry that we had to lose today," he said.

She sniffled against his chest. He shifted them around, her weight falling dead against his body, until he was able to free his arms. He made soft circles on her back, a reminder that she wasn't wearing a bra. He closed his eyes, annoyed at himself for noticing, again. Her body sank further so that she had now become more of a rugby ball than a person. Tim didn't know much about the sport, but he'd pick this ball up and carry her as long as she needed.

"I mean, the Mets losing isn't quite unheard of," she said. "Even if we've been kicking butt lately."

He looked down; her eyes, more green than gray, were looking up at him over her knees. Streaks of tears were drying on her face, the wetness still visible in her eyelashes, but there was laughter in her smile.

"That's fair. Not optimistic, but fair," Tim said.

"At least we scored a run?"

"See what you're going for there," said Tim. "Would food make it better?"

"I'm not really hungry," Diana said, sitting upright.

"Understood."

"But if you want to—"

"Don't even offer. I'm staying put all night. We both knew that one day you would have to be the emotionally vulnerable one, and that I would have to step up to the plate."

"I was going to say we could order something. Buuutttt, since you're invested in being the strong one, cookie dough is my go-to when emotional," Diana said.

"Thought you weren't hungry?"

"I said not *really* hungry." She smiled up at him. "Plus, if you're going to be here all night—"

"You're stuck with me by your side."

"—you would have seen it eventually."

"Do you turn into the Cookie Monster or something?"

She laughed. The full belly kind, and for a minute, Tim felt his heart relax.

"I'll run out, stop by my house for some things, and you pick the movie?"

"Sounds good, but after the game, right?"

"Yes, Dame," Tim said. "You women and your sports!"

A buzzing on the table killed the happiness in the air like a sniper. He wasn't sure where Diana had put her phone, or if it was even on, but his was. Even on silent, he made sure of that before they started the game; it sounded like a train barreling through at midnight. Maybe it was because there was the possibility of who would be on the other end. Tim grabbed his phone and saw Mark's name across the screen.

"Everything okay?"

"Uh, yeah," Tim said.

He pressed the side button twice, silencing the call. He returned it face down on the table.

It was about Arnold, he was sure. It was one thing to leave Diana for Amber. If everyone was being truthful, they were a better match. They would have been the perfect Greek Life couple, but Arnold had been with Diana. How he handled it was trash. No matter how much he loved his brother, it was a fact.

What Tim had a harder time understanding was how he *couldn't* have loved Diana, no matter how perfect he and Amber were. She wasn't cold-hearted or uncaring. She loved quietly, fiercely, and Arnold had fucked that up. Tim warned him that Diana would build a wall. Protect herself. Arnold hadn't listened and, instead of fixing it like he had said he wanted to, he ran off the deep end into another woman. Tim didn't have to listen to any of the bullshit now.

"You sure?" Diana asked.

She scooted backwards and pulled her knees up to her chest. "I don't know how your knees don't need WD40 or something when you go to walk. They're either pulled up to your chin like Urkel's pants or you sit cross-legged."

Her head cocked to the side.

"Yes, Diana, everything is okay. And I'm kidding about your knees."

Diana straightened her head, and her features softened. "Kidding? Or are you jealous of my flexibility?"

"You found me out. And now, with my head hung in shame, I am going to pick up provisions, like cookie dough, and anything else I've ever seen girls do in a rom-com. Has anyone ever told you, you're such a girl?"

"Maybe once or twice," she said. "The audacity, right?"

Tim rolled his eyes.

"I'm also going to pick up something quick from the diner for dinner. I should be back in an hour or so. Does that work?"

"Thank you so much." Leaning forward, Diana crashed back into Tim and squeezed him tight. "Don't let anyone tell you that you don't make the best gal pal."

He squeezed her back.

"Gee, thanks."

Diana pulled back, now sitting on her knees; he had a feeling one day he was going to have to actually worry about those too.

"You know what I meant, I just. . ."

"I know, Dame." Tim patted her shoulder before grabbing his phone and keys. "It's hard when the guy with the biggest dick in the room is a girl," he said, lightly punching her shoulder.

"Hey," she said, sitting back, "at least I don't swing it around!"

chapter thirty-eight

Arnold

Arnold had managed to get one meat hook out before he blacked out. Blood and skin had caked beneath his nails and between his fingers. Now that it was dry, it was itchy.

Pain had begun to spread throughout his face. It reminded him of having his wisdom teeth extracted. His jawbone ached; worse than the time some biker had cracked him in the face with a bat. Somehow, it hurt more than the torn flesh of his back. Neither compared to watching what was happening across the way.

He blinked, each time trying to picture something other than what he was seeing. Someone was talking to Amber. It seemed like they were reading her something off a screen. Black clothing covered their neck and head. Dark coveralls made it impossible to size them up. They had surgical gloves and a mask on, and some type of goggles covering their eyes. When they finished, tucking the electronic device into their pocket, they sprinkled a can of something around the room. He couldn't see what, just drops of liquid rising and falling through the air. It didn't matter though—if they touched her, he would kill them.

Somehow, he would.

He tried to scream, to let her know he was there, but his mouth wouldn't work. She needed to know that he would save her. He didn't know why she wasn't moving—if maybe she knew who this person was. Arnold pushed through the burning agony, but no words came. Only a ghastly noise escaped him. If he didn't know the sound had been coming from him, he would have thought a wild animal was on the loose. It didn't matter; he had to try to warn her. They would eventually have to open the door. Her head turned toward him. Her eyes were bandaged. *Fuck*, he thought. The door opened, but she didn't move. Her head turned further in the direction as it closed.

He screamed again, the metallic tang of blood flooding his senses. More animalistic noises. He touched his face, repulsed by the stench of rotting flesh. His mouth hung open, his jaw slack to the side. The feel of his fingers was like daggers. He kept prodding. He felt his teeth, but not his tongue. Where his tongue should have been was a nub.

Arnold wailed, confused and, for the first time, scared. Not just for Amber, but also for himself. The sounds he made were more mutilated than his broken jaw.

chapter thirty-nine

Diana

They laughed as Diana walked Tim to the door. Once he was outside, she headed upstairs for a quick shower and to change into her pajamas for their proper girls' night. She hadn't heard from Ann in a while, which she hoped meant the girl was at least enjoying herself. Diana thought about reaching out. She thought of her phone tucked away in her room. The same place she had been since they got home.

If Ann were really worried, she'd pop over. It wouldn't be the first time, but at least this time she didn't have a key. Diana had spent hours looking for her set—the ones Ann had found in her room, along with Diana's phone. It had been a nightmare for both of them. Decidedly not worse than the following months of random house calls made by Ann, "just looking out for her bestie!"

She glanced over at her phone. Frustration and anger seized her, followed by the chilling loneliness of sadness. No, she wouldn't be able to handle it. At least not today. Thankfully, she didn't have to do anything right now. She was off tomorrow, it would be her very own Independence Day and the anniversary of her newfound freedom. Her phone, Ann, whatever drama Arnold had said in his text could wait until then.

Diana looked around her room, confusion buzzing through her body. She had left her waffle shirt, the one with the small red and pink flowers, on the floor with her shorts. It had been yesterday, before—her stomach flipped—Ann's party. Hadn't she? She sat on her bed, breathing against the urge to freak out. There was a lot going on, and it was easy to forget when she wore something.

She closed her eyes. Tim had been here; he helped her unstick herself from the sleeve. It had to be before. Taking a breath in, Diana stood and walked to her closet. She exhaled, opening the door and looking down at her laundry basket. It was starting to overflow. Piece by piece, she emptied it; everything *but* the shirt she was looking for was there. The shorts were the same ones she was wearing. At least, she was pretty sure; there was no real way to tell. All of her shorts were the same brand, size, color, and cut—same as her jeans, not that it would help her now. A noise interrupted her thoughts.

Diana stood up and tiptoed toward the stairs. Her ears strained against the silence. Nothing. She crouched down, trying to keep her footsteps light and even on the stairs. Her cell phone was still in her room. Stopping about one-third of the way down, she tried to peek over the small bit of wall before the railing. Still, nothing. The back door was at the bottom of the stairs in case she needed an emergency exit. It was bolted as far as she could tell from where she was.

She kept going. No noises, no dark or shadowy figure looming ahead waiting for her. Further down into the living room, everything seemed as she had left it. The television was showing a still from the Mets' game, asking her if she wanted to delete the recording. The clicker was where Tim had left it. She walked around the dining table and into the kitchen. Nothing. When she got to the front door, she noticed it was unlocked.

Her body shook, and paranoia rattled her down to the core.

Everything is normal, she thought. *No sudden movements, no dead giveaways. Everything is normal until you grab your damn phone.* She locked the door, turning in what felt like slow motion, and began making her way upstairs. *Everything is normal,* she repeated. Tapping each syllable out as she touched each fingertip one after the other against her thumb.

Diana felt the weight of the quiet. It was heavy and uncomfortable, managing to amplify her every step, each creak and moan the 29-year-old building made. Was it the building, or was there someone else there? She didn't check the basement, and she hadn't looked in either of the spare rooms upstairs. Not that anyone could hide in her gym room. She and Tim had taken the closet door off and made it a reading nook, but there was always the second bedroom. She swallowed, trying her best to choke back her own fear. *Everything is normal.*

The second she stepped inside her bedroom, she lunged for her phone. Grabbing it and her baseball bat, she shuffled into her gym room. Her yoga mat was laid out on the floor, and all of her assorted Pilates blocks and resistance bands were stacked in a wicker basket. She burrowed into the accent chair in the corner.

She tucked in, crossing her legs underneath her and gripping her bat one-handed, Diana called Tim. From here, she had a full view of anyone coming into the room.

After three rings, it went to voicemail. Diana picked up a water bottle from the end table and tried to focus on her breathing. She was struggling to keep herself calm. There wasn't anyone in her home. She was stressed and tired, and it was her mind playing tricks on her. She looked down at her phone, contemplating calling Tim again or maybe throwing on some music. The last thing she needed to do was to look at any of her texts or, worse, social media. Amber had an online presence.

Ann had found it when Arnold had first been caught with his hand in someone else's cookie jar. With all her campus involvement and Greek Life, Amber routinely updated every aspect of her life on all the social media platforms. The last thing Diana needed was to see pictures of the perfect philanthropic socialite sorority, Amber, next to All-American athlete turned gym teacher, Arnold. She would have been happy for them if he had just ended it before they started dating. Before, he told her that he was choosing her.

Diana felt her heartbeat in her throat. She tried to swallow it down, tried to manipulate her breathing between small sips of water. She counted all of the blue things in the room, then the yellow, and then the green, including all the leaves of her fake pothos plant. She had just about finished her water, and her breathing, while forced, was even. Diana had to do something other than sit here.

She stood, tucking her phone under her armpit. Diana held the bat like a shovel; the common misconception was to swing at an intruder, but the real trick was to jab. Aim for the ribs, brace yourself for the sounds of impact, and run like hell when something cracked.

Back in her bedroom, she angled herself toward the door as she tried to straighten out the mess she had made looking for her waffle shirt. From her drawer, she grabbed a white t-shirt with an orange on it and her boxers with bananas on them. She looked down at her pajamas, *Orange ya glad I didn't die?* She squeaked out a small laugh. Even to her ears, she sounded manic.

Crazy, maybe, but at least she was okay. The noises, the door, all just little things discolored by her breakup with Arnold or her sporadic fainting, which seemed to be worse under stress. She would go back downstairs and pick out a movie for when Tim got back.

Diana took off her jersey, adding it to the pile of washing. Then she unbuttoned her shorts and stood up, letting them fall to the floor. Her phone started vibrating in her hand. She tried to look at it. Her arm felt unattached to her body as she lifted it to see the screen. Instead, the room swayed left to right as her ceiling came into view.

chapter forty

Arnold

A sound pierced Arnold's ears, causing him to wake up. His jaw was on fire, and he was painfully aware of the smell coming off him and the sliminess of his back. The sound of a wailing banshee echoed through the space, feeling like an icepick digging through his ears.

Amber!

Arnold wretched himself forward, heaving as he felt the piece of metal ripping through his back. He wondered about the person who stuck him like a pig. Did they pinch his skin with clamps before piercing it? Had they caught his muscle? Arnold hadn't felt it right away, not like this. He knew it was infected. His body alternated between cold, hot, and passed out.

After he got the first two out, he couldn't find the strength to figure out how many were left, but he knew they were there. At the very least, there was one left keeping him tethered, but the pain spiderwebbed across his whole back. If there was one hook left or seven, Arnold wouldn't have been able to tell the difference. He just knew that he wasn't strong enough to free himself. Wasn't strong enough to get to—the sound blared again. This time, Arnold could make out three beeps synced to red and white flashing lights, and then an announcement began.

"Attention. Disposal will begin in ten seconds. Attention. Disposal will begin in ten seconds." The bass pulsed against his skin.

He tried to steady his breathing, but something was very fucking wrong. He wasn't in a horror movie; things like this didn't happen in real life. Certainly not in bougie places like Long Island. Even back home in Chicago, they just shot each other up.

Arnold heard a door open and then close. This had to be some sick joke. A really bad acid trip. Tommy had been talking to him about his small-time drug dealings. The good shit he got from his Pharma connections. He wouldn't have put it past Ann to ask him to spike their drinks for fun. A light turned on in the room next to his, Amber's room, pulling Arnold further into darkness. *NO*, he groaned. Looking straight ahead, he could see Amber still sitting on the table. Were her eyes still bandaged? She was disheveled and groping around her. Her hands were free!

Why isn't she ripping the bindings from her eyes and running? Amber!

He scrambled forward, forcing a howl from his lips. He felt his skin split and separate from his body. His vision blurred, but he kept his eyes locked on the girl he'd loved. Behind her, a burst of flames erupted. He heard Amber scream. She could make it to the door. It was behind where she had been sitting. She only had to calm down. She was stumbling. The smoke would only get worse. Arnold dragged himself forward. He could feel the blood, hot, running over his body. If he could just get to her, get her to calm down, she would see that the door was right behind her.

Amber's screams began to fade. He was losing her in the smoke and the flames. A loud thud crashed into the window separating their rooms. Amber's raw hands pressed against the glass. Her body jolted forward; her face, badly burnt, pressed flat on the glass between her hands. Black holes had taken the spot where her baby blue eyes had once been. Arnold's stomach tightened. His mouth pooled with saliva. She never knew he was here, wanting to—trying to help her, warn her. He howled again from the depths of his soul. The sound of crackling filled the air. Wafts of scorched hair and flesh penetrated Arnold's nose. His soul numbed as he doubled over and vomited.

chapter forty-one

<u>Mark</u>

Mark's thumb hovered above the answer button. Tim had been radio silent for a few hours and had even hit the f-you button earlier. After the shit Arnold had been texting them, Mark wasn't sure exactly what was waiting for him on the other end of the line.

Bro code wasn't something he had ever taken lightly, and had only depended once he joined a fraternity all about making a better world with better men. Both Arnold and Tim were his brothers. Not that he was sure their friendship would survive this. The phone vibrated in his hand.

"Hey," Mark answered. "Sorry I missed your call," Tim said.

"You declined my call," Mark corrected. "Not taking it personally, there's a lot of shit happening right now."

"I don't even know where to start," Tim said.

There was a rustling in the background.

"Have you seen the texts? Because there are a lot of places we can start."

"I've been deleting them throughout the day without opening them."

"Something's not right, man," he said. It wasn't often that he was concerned about Arnold's—or anyone's—behavior, least of all his own. But this was a level he'd never seen a person hit before. "He's lost it."

"No shit," Tim said.

"It was one thing for him to bail on Diana, but there's a full-on money shot of Amber sitting in your phone right now if you haven't cleaned house in the past 45 minutes."

Air blew through the phone, followed by a clanking sound that was an assault on Mark's ears. Metal rattled, and then Tim grunted, "Fuck!"

"You okay, bro?"

"Why wouldn't I be?" Tim said. "I'm at the store and these carts won't separate."

He laughed.

"What're you doing at the store on the Fourth of July?"

"Just getting a few things," Tim said. "What're you doing?"

"Well, I was going to have a couple of guys over," Mark said, "but one of them is waist deep in sorority pussy and the other is at a grocery store."

"Dude," Tim groaned. "You're probably not wrong, but. . ."

"I know it's weird for you." Pausing, Mark added, "She's your best friend, and Arnold is your Big. Look, I know I can be a piece of shit, but what they're both doing to her right now is completely fucked."

"What do you mean? Tim asked.

"Have you seen the shit on social?"

"No," Tim said.

Mark stood up, put the phone on speaker, and walked into the kitchen. If no one was coming over, he'd make his own party.

"So, then you missed Amber in Diana's shirt?"

"What!" Tim's yells were followed by a series of bangs and bumps that echoed in Mark's freezer, where he'd left it to take out a pint of Ben and Jerry's Chunky Monkey. "Sorry, ma'am. Mark, hold on."

Mark snickered. He could only imagine Tim, flustered and still trying to help old ladies cross the street or some small-town hero shit. Mark went to the cabinet while he waited and grabbed a microwave bag of popcorn and some M&Ms. It wouldn't be some kind of bender, not like whatever Arnold was on, but if his friend was going to force them to watch front row as he self-detonated, at least he'd have snacks.

"Shit," Tim muttered under his breath.

"What?"

"I forgot there's still blood on my shirt," Tim said.

"Um, okay," Mark said.

"It's a long story, but I fell and cut my arm earlier. As if it wasn't bad enough that I almost knocked some poor old lady over, I apologized covered in blood!"

"Am I worrying about the wrong friend?"

"No, I've been a tad distracted the past few hours. It's less than when you two dumbasses head butted each other and you knocked his tooth out." Tim sighed. "Do I even want to know about this shirt?"

"Do you *want* to know? Probably not, but dude, it's a side by side. The right side is her—definitely Amber—lying down, no pants, no visible panties, just the shirt. It's white with little flowers on it."

Mark heard the change in Tim's breathing through the phone. Hopefully, that old lady he scared was far away and hadn't gone to get security. He wasn't sure how Tim was going to take the rest of the post.

"You're sure it's Diana's? I didn't think you paid that much attention."

"I don't. In this case, I didn't have to. The left side has Diana facing away from the camera in the same shirt. The caption? 'She WHORE it first, I wear it better,' but she put *whore* all in caps. It's on her page, but he's tagged in it."

"Is it long-sleeved?"

He could feel Tim's emotions rising through the phone. *Dude's gonna long-distance melt my ice cream.*

"Yeah," Mark said.

"Diana's grandmother made her that shirt."

"Nana Rosa?" Mark said.

"*That* you remember?"

"That woman was a saint. And she made a mean eggplant parm. One she taught Diana to make even better. I told him he'd better get the recipe before he ever broke up with her."

"What the f—excuse me. Sorry!"

Mark started the popcorn and laughed into the phone.

"It was months, years maybe, before Nana Rosa passed." Mark swallowed and shook his head. He had only met the woman a handful of times, but she was the kind of grandmother everyone wished they had. The shirt post had been bad before. "I didn't think it could have gotten worse."

"Yeah," he said, his voice cracking, "he knows it too. That her grandmother. . . We literally just talked about getting her to see my mom's doctor two days ago. How could he do this to her?"

The corn started popping. If anyone pulled this kind of shit on his sister, he'd kill them. Mark was certain Tim liked Diana more than a sister or a best friend, not that he was sure his friend knew it; he could imagine how angry he was.

"She's going to be okay," Mark said. "He's my best friend, but he cheated on her for what? Two years? One of them after swearing up and down that it was over. Obviously, it was never really over. You know about the stuff with the baby, right?"

"Yeah," Tim said.

"We all know Arnold grew up rough, and it put a chip on his shoulder. He likes the easy way. Diana was always going to be too good for him, too much for him, but I always figured that unless she broke it off, he wouldn't have gotten rid of a sure thing. I love the guy to death, but. . . Well, my point is she'll bounce back. She's a good girl, and has the best guy I know taking care of her. . ."

Mark's voice trailed off. He grabbed some pretzel sticks and peanuts from the cabinet. He hated them, but his sister loved them in her popcorn. Once he hung up with Tim, he would call her and see if she wanted to come over for a movie night or something.

Maybe bring her new boyfriend around. He'd have to pick another movie since "American History XXX" wasn't really a family film, and not one he wanted to watch in the vicinity of his sister.

Tim cleared his throat.

"Thanks, man." To Mark, Tim sounded surprised. Then he continued, "But seriously, why are there a hundred kinds of cookie dough?"

"Get the one in the yellow container," Mark said.

"What?"

"When that little shit James broke my sister's heart—"

"That kid was the worst," Tim said.

"—that's all she would eat for days. The cookie dough in the yellow container. My mom thought she was going to make herself sick, and eventually threw it out and reused the container.

My sister was hysterical when she opened it up to find red sauce instead of raw dough."

Mark heard Tim shuffle the phone around. He watched as the countdown on his popcorn reached single digits. He'd have to make at least two bags if his sister was coming by. He still had to text her.

"Again, thanks. When did you get a soft side?" Tim asked.

"Don't tell anyone, okay? And don't expect me to be the fifth wheel when we go out. Not that I can really see Arnold and Amber sitting across from you and Diana. Though, I'd put my money on Diana to rock Amber in a fight."

"You have a problem, and as a history teacher—Wait, is all this shit on her private page or her sorority page? If anyone from the school board or a pissed-off parent sees that? Burning his bridge with Diana is one thing, but his career?"

"I know, man. I'm not sure if it's public or just mutual friends. The fact that she's a fucking Storm and *her* parents were being questioned by police. I have no idea how these things work. I've tried to get ahold of him. But he's unreachable."

"Keep trying him. Someone has to be the voice of reason. It can't be me, not this time, man," Tim said.

"He's really fucked if it's me. Tell Diana I said, 'sup,' and don't forget to work in the head nod. Peace, brother."

Mark dropped the call and dialed his sister. He'd try Arnold again right after. It'd been a minute since he saw anything else come in from him. Maybe someone else got through to him. Someone other than Amber, at this rate, Mark was sure she'd be the death of him.

* * *

Four bags of popcorn and an order of two pizzas later, Mark was ready for his sister and her new boyfriend to come by. They'd been dating for two months, and it was about time he properly vetted the kid. He was not having another James situation.

Now he was just waiting for them to get there. Mark had already eaten half of his ice cream and had thrown the rest in the freezer, but if they or the pizza didn't arrive soon, he might just polish it off. Anyone could have an out-of-control cheat day, right?

His phone beeped, distracting him from the thoughts of Chunky Monkey. Mark looked at the screen, surprised to see a new message from Diana. His eyes almost fell out of his head when he opened the screen to see a side of Diana he hadn't imagined. *Not her too.* He groaned.

"Have these people lost their fucking minds?"

Maybe Tim had done too good a job passing along his head nod the right way.

For the second time in his life, Mark opted out of an easy score. The last chick had been crazy. Tall, athletic, with red hair— one his sister swore was a wig from the one picture he had of her face. It was a profile shot. She seemed familiar, but exotic. Safe but dangerous. He didn't care if the hair was real or fake; her nudes were very real and very vulgar. But her type of crazy was too much for him.

He typed back.

> You're hot, so this pains me to say, but not in this lifetime, sister. We'll pretend it never happened, Diana.

Mark saved the image, *nothing wrong with looking*, and deleted the text.

Had it not come from Diana's number, he wasn't sure he would have recognized her. The parts of her body that were visible were on point. He hadn't been lying about her being hot, but the picture itself was dark. Nothing identifiable was visible. Unless, Mark guessed, you had seen it before. It definitely was not one she took with her cell phone by herself.

There was a knock on his door, Mark pocketed his phone and went to answer it. His sister and some shaggy-haired kid were standing there with two pizza boxes and two 2L bottles of soda. A rogue cheat day for sure. He had just turned down something, but what exactly, he wasn't sure. Who knew how far a heart-broken woman would go with her ex's best friend? It didn't matter. The picture hadn't said anything, and he hadn't engaged. For that, he could allow himself the rest of the Chunky Monkey, even after all this crap.

chapter forty-two

Arnold

The door to his prison made a whoosh as it opened. Anger coursed through his body as a laugh track filled the room. Whoever had opened the door would be dead. It didn't matter if it killed him in the process. He would rush them and bash their head into the wall.

Movement caught his eye. Arnold's fingers scraped against the hard floor as he tried for purchase. He felt agony, worse than seeing Amber burned alive, as he lunged forward. He made it two steps when the light flipped on. It shocked him, knocking him to the ground. He could feel the brightness burn through his eyelids. The laugh track stopped, and a real laugh echoed off the walls.

Arnold lay on the floor, blood dripping down his back. He had been caged like a rabid animal and was now retreating like a punished one. He was spent and fading into the darkness.

* * *

When Arnold woke up, he was lying on his back in the dark with a heavy weight on top of him. He could barely open his eyes from the pain. A raw grunt came from him as he tried to free himself.

His hands felt as though they were heavily bandaged. They felt strange and sore. It was hard to concentrate. His entire body was in pain. His shoulders slumped down. His arms dropped to his side. He was at a loss.

"Giving up?" The voice was distorted. Arnold couldn't recognize it. "That's a shame. We all know how much you like to play games."

As Arnold's brain started to race, the smell of gasoline wafted up toward him. He had already seen how this had played out with Amber. Someone had to be looking for him, had to miss him. Diana had to be worried about him, or Mark, or Tim.

He was breathing too fast, but he couldn't stop. He felt dizzy and hurt. Everywhere hurt beyond words or comprehension. His mouth was dry. He couldn't swallow. The more he tried to move, the more disoriented he was. He couldn't see anything except darkness, and yet the room felt uneven. He wasn't sure if he was moving or if he had lost his mind.

His face was wet. The noxious fumes of gasoline burned his nose. He tried to breathe out whatever had spilled in his mouth, burning his gums. It was no use. He clamped his mouth shut, choking on the pain. Arnold lifted his hands to his face. There were too many layers of gauze. He couldn't feel his hands. If there was a blindfold, he couldn't get it off.

"Let me give you a hint: They say thumbs separate us from the animals."

A chortled growl rumbled in his throat. He sounded like Mark's old bulldog, Marky.

"Cat got your tongue?" More animal noises filled the room.

"Don't worry," the voice said. "No animals involved. It was me."

The tone shifted from playful to something else. A predator that had grown bored with its prey.

"I took your tongue, and your hands, and your whore."

Arnold couldn't see, but he could hear the sound of empty plastic bouncing onto the floor. He kept swatting at his eyes. If he could just take the blindfold off. Maybe he wouldn't make it out, but he would know who did this to him, to Amber.

"Oh, and there's no blindfold, so you can stop waving your stumps around," the voice said. "I took your eyes. I assumed you would have figured that out after seeing Amber. Not that she could see you."

Even to himself, Arnold sounded like nothing more than a wounded animal. A mist landed over him, shocking him into silence. The sting settled into his open wounds. Over the blood, a different smell—a familiar smell, one that stood out against the fumes—filled his nose. Arnold tried to focus on the smell, pushing everything else away. Something light and beachy. As a face began to take shape in his mind. It vanished with the strike of a match and the slam of the door. The blast of heat brushed against Arnold's body.

A voice came over the speakers again. This time without the alarm.

"Breaking news adds to the *Storm* of the century. A formal investigation has been launched by police into Amber Storm for the first-degree murder of her fetus last October."

Flames licked Arnold's wounds. He was barely conscious. Images of the sonogram, his baby girl, filled his mind as the fire consumed him.

The announcement continued, "Amber Storm is now missing. Her sister, Molly Storm, has no comment on whether she believes Amber could have been involved in the fatal attempt made against her baby."

chapter forty-three

Tim

Everything had taken Tim longer than expected. He had been gone close to two hours and still didn't have everything he needed.

He debated not stopping at home at all. Tim looked at the blood on his shirt and thought of the old lady. He needed a quick shower, and at the very least, some clean jeans and boxer briefs for tomorrow. He would just wear his sweats and a t-shirt over tonight.

The shower had helped, and the wound on his arm had needed a washing. He had done a thorough job cleaning it, so he doubted it would get infected. One EMT training and one semester of anatomy had done more than just inspire him to work in finance or business. He had cleaned his cut. Tim rolled his eyes at himself as he pulled out of his driveway. It had been an extra forty minutes between bringing the groceries in, getting ready, and lugging the groceries back out. But he was on his way back to Diana's, the sounds of piano, sax, trumpet, and trombones playing through his speakers, soothing his soul. It was a quick drive, but still relaxing.

Parking his car in front of her townhouse, he threw on his flashers, got out, and unloaded the groceries and his overnight bag by the front door. He reached for his phone to let Diana know that he was just parking his car. It wasn't in his pockets. He went back to the car, not on the seat or the cup holder.

Shit. Had he left it at home? He ran his hand under the seat, relieved to have found it. There were a few missed calls and texts, mostly messages from the guys' group he was avoiding. The missed call from Diana caught his eye. Tim ignored the texts and immediately called her back.

"Hello?"

Her voice sounded wrong.

"Dame, are you okay?"

"I'm alright," Diana said.

"I'm walking up to your door now."

"Okay, just come upstairs when you get here," Diana said.

Tim hadn't read through her texts before calling her back. A tightness ran through his stomach.

"Will do."

The front and back doors were locked. Tim ran back to his car for his key, but it was gone. He went to call Diana. Standing at her front door, he noticed something was wrong with the plant she kept outside. It was fake, like all of Diana's plants, but it wasn't sitting in the pot the right way. Tim lifted it and heard the soft clink of metal running across ceramic. He frowned and lifted the plant: a small silver key.

Tim returned the pot to the table, lifted the key, and slid it into the lock.

"Fucking-a," he said to himself.

Unlocking the door, Tim put the key and the plant back to rights. He managed to get everything inside in a few trips with what he hoped was not too much noise. Tim locked the door before heading upstairs.

"Diana?" he called as he walked further into her house. "It's just me! Tim!"

"I'm up here."

She sounded so far away; her voice so small. He walked up the stairs, unease following close behind him.

"You're in your room?"

"Mhmm."

Tim rounded the corner to her bedroom. Diana was sitting on her bed, looking exhausted and scared. Something wasn't right. Tim walked over to her the same way he was taught to approach an injured animal. He sat on the edge of her bed, close but not in striking distance.

"Diana."

"At first I thought it was you forgetting something—"

"I would have called," Tim interjected.

"—my next guess was Arnold, but that was stupid. The front door. It wasn't locked."

"It was."

"I locked it," she said. "I walked around the downstairs, and everything looked like it should, but the front door was unlocked. I flipped it and ran upstairs. I tried to call you—" Tim opened his mouth, but she continued. "So I waited. In the reading nook, until I got myself together. When I went to stand up, well, I woke up naked on my back.

"Was someone here? Did they—?"

"No," Diana said, shaking her head. "I was changing over there," she pointed to the closet. He could see her clothes hanging off the laundry basket. "When I stood back up and put my boxers on, I saw it."

"Saw what?" Tim's eyes followed Diana's. There was a purple and black bruise the size of a half dollar on Diana's inner thigh. "What the fuck is that? What happened?"

"And I remembered," she said. Her voice shook.

"It's okay. I'm here, I'm listening. You're safe." Tim swallowed. "Take your time and tell me what you remember."

"I told him condoms, I always did. He left to get them, I

thought. When he came back, he went down on me like he actually liked it."

Tim fought the urge to interrupt her. *But he doesn't. Mark doesn't bother unless he likes a girl, but even he sees my point that it's like Heaven on earth, but Arnold? He hates it.*

Diana's eyes snapped up at him. "Harsh, but—"

"I said that out loud." He groaned. "I'm sorry—"

"It doesn't matter," she cut him off. "He left. Not just for condoms. Ann told me this morning that Arnold had left in the middle of the night. Tim, he never came back. So this—" She took a deep breath in and gestured to her thigh. "This happened after he left. It looks like a bite mark." She sniffled, and her voice strained as she continued, "I don't think it was him."

The rest of her thought was lost to tears. Long, ragged tears.

Tim leaned forward. He didn't have a chance to say anything before she fell into his arms. He held her as she cried.

*　　　* *　　　* *　　　*

Tim took an icepack from the freezer.

"Here, it's going to be cold," he said.

It wasn't just a bruise. The muscle underneath was hard and raised. Like someone had managed to bite into her adductor muscle.

"Thanks," she said.

She sucked in through her teeth as she rested the icepack against her thigh. Tim placed his hand on Diana's back and guided her around the wall toward the living room.

"I'm restarting the game," he said. "We can watch that, or if you prefer, a movie. Either way, I will be making us some Mama Ames Magic Eight-Cheese Mac and Cheese."

"Damn," Diana said. "I must be in a bad way."

He turned to see her attempting a smile. She strongly believed that if one didn't laugh, they would cry. He just wasn't sure it was going to be enough this time. No matter how strong he believed she was.

"Thank you," Diana said.

Her eyes looked tired and like inverted olives. The whites had gone red from crying. It looked like someone had dimmed the sparkle.

"You're welcome," he said. "Think about what you want, and I'm going to get some snacks. Just remember that dinner is coming."

"Yes, sir." Diana gave what looked like a half-hearted smile. "One thing though," she called as he started walking away.

"What's up?"

"You have the clicker in your hand."

"Oh shit," he laughed. "What channel do you want? The game, a movie, what?"

"Channel 45."

Sports filled the TV screen. Tim put the clicker on the coffee table and grabbed his phone. He had one new text from Mark.

Bro's officially gone too far. Sent me a text about being a hero. Diana's shirt is here. There was a picture underneath of Nana Rosa's tombstone.

Tim felt his nostrils flaring up at the ends. Tension raked through his brain and across his shoulders. If throwing his phone would fix anything, he would have whipped it into Route 27 by now, hopefully just in time for a truck to completely destroy it.

"You okay?" he heard Diana ask.

Tim's eyes met hers. It sucked. If Arnold wanted to destroy her, that was his bag, but why bring Mark into it, and why did Tim have to keep being the bearer of bad news? He shook his head back and forth and cleared his throat before speaking.

"Yeah, I'm—no. There is something you should know. I'd rather you hear it from me than the fucking internet."

Diana sat back and looked up at Tim. She patted the arm of the couch. Slowly, he walked closer, perching there.

"Your white thermal, the one with the small red-and-pink flowers—"

"The one Nana Rosa made me! I was looking for it earlier when I was upstairs. When you were gone, and I heard the noise."

"Yeah. Apparently, Amber has it."

"What?" He watched her jaw drop. The little color she had gotten into her face drained. Every time she started picking herself back up, she ended up on the ground. At least this time it wasn't physical, though he wasn't sure that was actually better. "Are you sure?" she continued. Her voice was barely above a whisper.

"There's a picture on her Facebook page that has Arnold tagged, and it's her in your shirt. Mark told me about it earlier. I talked to him while I was at the store. I didn't check the post, but the caption makes it pretty clear."

Her body swayed. Tim moved closer, ready to catch her if she fell.

"She's buried in her own one, you know?"

Tim nodded. He did know. He remembered her excitement over their matching shirts, and then the way only she could have accepted that it was her grandmother's outfit of choice for death. He could have taken anything from her; he had already taken so much, but he took her thermal. The last thing her grandmother made for her. For them. *Piece of shit*, Tim thought to himself.

"Diana," Tim said, resting his hand on her head. "You okay?"

"I don't know. I don't think so," her voice cracked, taking a piece of Tim's heart with it. "It's the one she made for me so I could, we could. And it's on. . ."

Her tears fell like a hot summer's rain. Tim didn't move.

"I know it won't be the same, but Mark's going to get it back for you. Arnold made it clear where he could find it." She didn't need to know that Arnold had sent a picture of the deposited shirt on top of Nana Rosa's grave. *Dog shit would be too good of an adjective for him.* "It won't make it better, but I'll have it dry cleaned, as many times as you need."

Tim's left hand made a fist so tight his knuckles went white.

"Tim. Hey, Tim," Diana said, shaking his knee. "It's okay."

Tim looked down at his hand. The plastic whined underneath his force. Relaxing his fist, he gave Diana the clicker.

Standing, he started to walk back into the kitchen. He stopped and turned to face her again.

"I'm sorry. I'm sorry that this whole thing has been happening to you. I'm sorry for letting it get to me, to the point where you're asking if I'm okay—"

"Don't be," Diana said, cutting him off. "None of this is your fault. There are two people to blame. Neither of them are here now. The relationship ending is one thing. It's probably for the best, but my shirt? I can only imagine what he's been posting or saying in—"

"If it's an indication, Mark thinks he's out of control. Probably better that he's grabbing your shirt instead of me."

"My point exactly. That's terrifying on its own. I don't know what's going on anymore. With me, with them, but I know that I have you. And Ann, when her head is out of that guy's ass—"

"She does it and doesn't even know what it's called."

"—I have a job, with health insurance, and a beautiful home. So many memories of Nana Rosa." Diana stopped to sniffle and laugh. "Metaphor my dear, messed-up friend. You saw her practically throw me at you yesterday. I can only imagine the man is hung like a Greek God or something, because I haven't checked my phone, and she hasn't just shown up. I'm going to be okay.

Maybe not today, and maybe not when I see the picture you're referencing, but one day." Diana lifted her face up to him, resting her hands on his knee. "Besides the point," she continued, waving her hand off to the side. "You're going to make me your mom's mac and cheese. There's nothing that can't cure, right?"

"Almost nothing," Tim's voice grew solemn.

He was happy to see Diana finding the bright side, but he couldn't let her ignore what's been happening to her health. He took a deep breath, sitting next to her, before he recommended the doctor his parents had gone to, the one who had gotten them to the right specialists and who had stuck by them until the end.

Tim's mom had been diagnosed with Lewy body dementia, but it was Tim's dad who truly suffered watching his wife disintegrate, seeing things that weren't there, forgetting the people around her, losing her ability to take care of herself. Before he had fought his own battle with a brain tumor. It was better that his mom wasn't *around* for that. In the end, his parents went within months of each other.

"I'll call and see if they can get you in this week, okay?" She nodded. It was slight, but it was clear.

"I didn't even think," she started to say.

"Why would you? You're young and should be healthy. She didn't either, Diana. She didn't until it was too late. My dad and I didn't think either. I'm not doing that with you."

"You won't have to," she said. Her hand felt chilly against his knee.

"Good," he said. "Because you are going to sit here wrapped in your blanket, and I'm going to make you Mama Ames' cure almost-all. It probably won't do anything for your social issues. Look at how you sit!"

"Hey," Diana said, playfully smacking Tim's thigh. "I don't have social issues. I just prefer to be social with a *select* group, and there's nothing wrong with sitting like this."

"Fictional characters and a few leftovers from college aren't really a *select* group, Dame."

"You love it that we have nicknames from books our friends would never read!" Diana shouted into the kitchen.

"Speaking of the illiterate, Mark says, 'sup,'" Tim said, nodding his chin at her.

Diana roared with laughter.

"Is that why he texted me earlier? I saw his name come up before banishing my phone out of sight."

"Show me later, woman. I'm trying to cook."

For the first time in what felt like hours, Tim could breathe easy—well, easier.

chapter forty-four

Diana

Diana stayed on the couch while Tim made their dinner. Before he had started the magic of Mama Ames' recipe, he had brought enough snacks to pacify their old frat house, including a double shot glass of cookie dough topped with a dollop of whipped cream.

"Thanks! Is this for presentation or portion control?" she said, accepting the treat.

"Yes," Tim answered. "I'm making dinner. I realize we're sad, but I'm not enabling your cookie dough problem."

Diana laughed to herself.

"Sad, huh?"

He wasn't wrong. Diana was sad, scared, and hurt. There was a lesson here, probably a dozen of them, that if Nana Rosa were still alive, she would have pointed out while making her own magical recipes, like her homemade pizzelles. She wasn't here, wasn't whipping up something in the kitchen—she was only here in spirit, which meant Diana would have to start figuring things out for herself.

She flipped through the channels, oblivious to what was on

the screen, thinking about what her grandmother would say, more importantly, what Diana would tell her.

"Hey, Tim," Diana said, unfurling herself from the couch.

"Yeah?"

"I'm going to run upstairs real quick." His face popped out from the kitchen.

"Anything I can do for you?"

"Nope, I'm just going to grab my journal."

"Okay," he said, "if you need anything. I'm right here." She flashed a thumbs-up and started walking around the couch.

"You got it, Chief, or is that chef now?"

"You're hysterical."

Diana walked up the stairs at a pace that under different circumstances would have driven her batty. While she was feeling okay, she wasn't trying to test out how okay she was. She flipped on the hallway light and walked right over to her reading nook.

Stacked on top of her "to be read" list was her journal. Most of the time, Diana chose a pen color at random; she had a color for each of her energy centers, letting the universe connect her to what she needed. After the past few hours, her heart chakra was in dire need of attention. With intention, she grabbed her green pen and her journal.

"Huh," Diana said out loud.

The book underneath her journal should have been *If We Were Villains* by M. L. Rio. The plot centered around a group of Shakespearean actors, and Diana had been planning on reading King Lear before diving in. Instead, *Gone Girl* by Gillian Flynn was on top. Diana shrugged. *Just another tick in the 'Diana is losing her shit' column.* With her journal and pen in hand, she shut the lights off and made her way back to the living room.

"Got everything you needed?"

"Yup," Diana said.

She crossed through the living room and took a seat at the dining room table.

"My journal, my pen, and a nice view of some sexy cook in the kitchen. Though for hired help, he is wearing far too much."

"Dame," Tim said, turning away from the stove. "That's sexual harassment in the workplace."

"It's a good thing you're not getting paid then," Diana teased back. She pulled her legs up onto the chair into a crisscross position.

"Before you start," Tim said. He had crossed into the living room and was standing on the opposite end of the table. "All joking aside, I heard what you said. Earlier. About someone else being the person who bit you. I believe you. And, we don't have to do this now, or ever, but if you want to talk to someone, I'm always here."

Diana swallowed the lump that had formed in her throat. "Thank you, Tim," Diana said.

Tim gave her a small smile. Standing under the lighting from the mini chandelier, his tiny, almost invisible freckles could be seen scattered across both sides of his nose. She and Nana Rosa had picked the fixture out together. Diana had almost managed to hang the damn thing by herself too, but thankfully, Tim had been around to help, or it might not have been as secure.

She opened her journal, thumbing through the pages, surprised by all of the red and black. It had been a while, but her journal tended to be blue, green, or yellow. Sometimes purple. Very rarely did she end up with orange or red, and never black. The handwriting looked like hers, but the words were angry, violent even.

"Tim," she croaked out. "Tim!"

"What's wrong?"

Diana looked up at him, lines etched across his face. "This, this isn't mine."

Tim dipped back into the kitchen, and she could hear him move the pot to another burner and listened to the clicks of the gas as it shut off. He was back, by her side, thrusting Big Yellow into her hands.

"Drink this," he said. Leaning closer to the book, he added, "The handwriting, it looks like it could be yours, but—"

"It's uncanny."

"—the words."

She looked up at him and then back down at the book. He looked confused, concerned. He had believed her every step of the way; she needed him to still believe her.

"It doesn't sound like you at all. You might not have felt the same way you used to about your relationship with Arnold, but this is hateful."

"It's terrifying," she said. "It looks like my journal. It was in the same place as my journal. Except the book it was sitting on top of was wrong, but—"

"Wrong?" Tim pulled out the chair next to her and sat down. "What do you mean?" he asked.

"Not wrong. It wasn't what I thought I had there. It was supposed to be *If We Were Villains*, but instead it was *Gone Girl*."

"Okay, and you're sure?"

"Yes! I wanted to read it, I bought it with the intention of reading it, but Arnold dragged me to the movie before I had a chance. Every time I start it, I still see what's his name from the movie, and it interferes with my reading. It's been holed up on my bookshelf since then." Diana took a deep breath. "Do you suppose it's Arnold? Just breaking into my home and making me think I'm going nuts? Who else would move shit around and swap out my journals and whatever else the fuck they're doing?"

"The kid has been my friend for years, but that sounds advanced even for him. The social media stuff would be a stretch if it wasn't mostly her."

"Do we call the police?" Diana asked.

She stared at Tim as he took a breath. "Well, Arnold has a key, right?"

"He's never had one. As my locationally closest and most responsible friend, you're it."

"Hmm," Tim said, turning around to face Diana. "So then what's the spare key in the plant for?"

Diana paled. "What key?"

"Under your plant," Tim looked over his shoulder toward the door.

"Out front. That's how I got in earlier. I went to grab my key from the car, but it wasn't there. It's probably at home, but..."

She pushed herself up and out of her seat, swallowing hard; she felt like she might throw up. She stopped between the bathroom and the living room.

"Diana?"

"There's no spare key. If there is a key outside that works—"

The whites of Diana's eyes flashed behind her eyelids as she fell backwards onto the floor.

* * *

Diana opened her eyes. Tim's face was hovering above her. "Better than the usual view," she mumbled.

"I'm assuming you mean my face," Tim said. "Let's not call it the usual view, okay? No need to encourage you."

He moved out of her line of sight.

"Hello ceiling, my old friend," Diana sang.

"Come on, Simon, let's get you up."

"First of all, I was singing the Disturbed version, and everybody knows Garfunkel has the better voice."

"Yes, but Simon had the better career."

"I would roll my eyes at you, but I'm really tired of seeing everything spinning."

Diana let out a small laugh, one that quickly dissolved into tears. Sitting up, she sniffled, wiping her nose on the back of her hand. She went to speak, to say anything, but her voice cracked. Only little squeaks escaped her as she cried.

chapter forty-five

<u>Tim</u>

Reaching out, Tim put his arm around Diana's back. Before he could even give her a reassuring squeeze, she rolled right into him. He stroked the hair sprawled across her back. He didn't think Diana had written those journal entries, but he also had seen his mother, the same one who made their house a home filled with love and food, write a letter to the president accusing him of murdering thousands of men by drafting them to Vietnam.

Including his father.

When his dad got back from his business trip, Tim explained what happened. The handwriting looked like hers, but didn't. It was the last time his dad went anywhere without her by his side.

Tim's heart sank as her tears soaked through his shirt. He hadn't looked at the dates in the journal, but she had been like this for months. With all the shit Arnold put her through when he cheated the first go around, it was possible things like this had slipped under the radar. He lifted Diana up and walked them over to the couch. At some point, he would have to talk to her about it. He looked down, following the slope of her nose, the tips of her nostrils fluttering as she breathed. Tomorrow he would talk to her, but not now. They stayed like that long after they both had fallen asleep.

* * *

"Good morning," Tim said, looking down at Diana's profile. "Hi," she said. Sleep was still woven in her voice. "What time is it?"

"It's a little after seven," Tim said.

"I woke up before the sun," Diana said. She began to yawn, "but then you trapped me here."

Her body reached out as she yawned, and she pulled her body into a ball after she stretched.

She shivered against him. He had seen her do it a million times, like a bulldog after a good stretch. A little shimmy to shake off the sleep. It had been longer than a dog's age since he had been close enough to her to feel it. Diana's back was slightly arched as she snuggled deeper in between Tim and her couch. It was already morning, and he didn't need any encouragement. Tim's thoughts stopped short, but not short enough. His body was very awake, and maybe she wasn't aware of the extent, but she would be if he didn't get up soon.

"While this is surprisingly comfortable, I'm starving," he said.

He tried twisting himself onto his back, but the couch wasn't that deep, and without a blanket, it made his predicament more obvious. Thankfully, she was still facing the back of the couch.

"Breakfast?"

She rolled and slid back so she was sitting on the arm, her legs in a tangle next to Tim's face. The smell of the coconut oil she used as lotion was faint in the air.

"You can cook?"

"You're a dumbass," Diana said.

She took the decorative pillow that had been underneath her

head and hit him with it. He tugged it away using it as a partial shield, just in case. Sweatpants, unlike jeans, weren't painful and were more like advertising.

"I think you mean, I'm dumbfounded," Tim said.

"I've cooked for you before," Diana said.

She stretched again. Tim looked down as her white t-shirt inched up. From this angle, he could see too much of her. He had ignored her physical attributes for months, years, and all of a sudden, he found himself painfully aware of all of her. Like how amazing her punny boxers made her butt look as she walked into the kitchen.

"You've baked stuff. You've reheated leftovers, and nobody, I mean *nobody*, can order takeout or delivery like you can."

"Please." She laughed. "You just give me thirty, maybe forty minutes or so."

"So you can go grab bagels?" Tim shouted into the kitchen.

"Hope you like bleach in your tea!"

Tim looked down. Shaking his head at himself, he waited until he heard an array of clicks, clanks, and swearing before he got up. Walking to the bathroom, Tim played back the night before. After Diana had cried herself to sleep, he couldn't move her.

Instead, he let her be and turned on her favorite movie. He eventually dozed off himself. He had been expecting her to wake up before him, but was pleasantly surprised, if not a little confused, to wake up to her still asleep in his arms.

He let her sleep. No matter how she felt about it, after all she had been through, she needed rest. Tim turned the television on to the news and kept the sound low. He had been reviewing the past few days and the past few months before she woke up. He turned the shower on in the bathroom. Just a quickie to wash up.

The past few days felt like a whirlwind, too much to process for him; he could only imagine how she felt. His thoughts instead traveled back to when they were in college together. While he was pledging, she had opted for a double minor. He had already introduced Diana to Arnold when he realized the extent of the feelings he had started to have for her.

There was a time after graduation when Tim had been hopeful that it would end. No more hooking up, no more on-again, off-again bologna, but both Arnold and Mark were in the teaching program, so they stuck around in an apartment near frat row. Diana seemed happy with Arnold. The longer they went together, the more serious it became. Her happiness was more important to Tim than whatever crush he had been developing.

One night, after a truly horrendous movie, Tim and Diana stopped at the bar for a few drinks. It was nothing different from what they used to do when she and Arnold were together.

Except, she wasn't with Arnold. There had been a fight, a fall-out, the first appearance of Amber, even if Diana didn't know it at the time.

Tim and Diana had a lot of drinks and a lot of laughs.

Sure, there was shitty stuff in life, as Diana put it, but the celebration must continue: the movie was the worst they had seen, and Tim was buying a house. Not far from where he grew up, but close enough. He wouldn't have seen it if he hadn't been visiting Diana the day they were putting the "For Sale" sign in the front yard. It was perfect for him. Diana was excited that they would now be living seven minutes apart. Tim was, too.

They had gotten back to her townhouse that night. Both very drunk and opened some random bottle of champagne they found in Diana's fridge. The bubbles. Her hair. It was all a blur. He could remember the feel of her lips. They were like nothing he had ever tasted before. Passing out in her spare bedroom, Tim had spent the morning realizing the room wasn't spinning, the ceiling fan was just switched on and wobbly.

The next day, they hadn't talked about it, but they hadn't ignored it either. Nana Rosa made eyes at the two of them over breakfast. She didn't say anything, but for the first time since she met him, she pinched his cheek instead of his butt.

Tim had felt the potential. He thought Diana had too. After a few hungover hours watching home repair shows together, they attempted to fix her wobbly fan themselves. He held her hips as she stood on the bed, insisting on cleaning the fan before he was allowed to touch it. Her grandmother would not forgive a dusty fan if a handsome man were fixing it. As old as she was, Nana Rosa was a terrible flirt with everyone. He had never picked up his tools from that day.

Then Monday rolled around. Arnold called Diana after work but before the game as though he hadn't hooked up with another girl. Of course, he was sorry, would never do anything like it again, but he had. Within a few months, it was clear exactly how little Arnold had kept his word. Before she had the chance to confront him, Nana Rosa had passed. It hit Diana hard, and Arnold swore this time he would do better. Barely a year later, Arnold had already blown it.

Tim thought about that kiss. Thought about Diana's body in a way he had never let himself before. The way she snuggled against his chest, the way she fit in his arms, his body. The way her chest moved against him as her breath ran across his skin. It was too soon. Way too soon with all that was going on, but still, Tim thought of her at the pond, not the creepy picture, but the actual memory of seeing her in the pond in person. Her eyes were bright, almost glowing.

"It's ready when you are!" Diana shouted outside the door. He stifled a grunt.

"Coming," Tim said.

He grabbed the bar of soap, gave himself a second wash, and rinsed off under cold water.

When he stepped out of the kitchen and into the makeshift dining room, Diana was putting a jug of orange juice on the table. She bit her lip like she was holding back a laugh. He wondered if she somehow knew what he had done in the shower. Tim looked at the rest of the table.

"Holy shit! You weren't kidding about breakfast though,

were you?" He pulled out his chair and sat down. She smiled and joined him.

"I never kid about breakfast," she said. Pointing to each item, she elaborated, "I made chocolate chip pancakes, eggs over easy, toast, bacon, breakfast potatoes with my own handcrafted original recipe, and sliced avocados."

Beaming as she moved from item to item, she waved her hands from the plates toward Tim.

"Oh, and I forgot," Diana said, gesturing to the pitcher of juice. "Mimosas!"

"You're too much." He laughed and filled up his plate. "Thank you! I'll be sure to do the dishes before we get through that pitcher, just in case."

"Perfect," Diana said. "Now, pass the potatoes, please."

The two ate mostly in silence. It was good to see Diana smiling, even if it was at her potatoes. Tim cleared his throat.

"Not to ruin the moment, Dame," Tim said. He rested his fork on his plate. "How're you holding up?"

"Wobbly," she said. She moved her potatoes back and forth like a hockey player with a puck. "It sucks. All of it sucks. But I keep reminding myself that I have you, plus Ann, the girls from Book Club—"

"The same ones you just watched a whole TV show with?"

"Okay, yes, it was also a series, but Pretty Little Liars started as books." She rolled her eyes and continued, "I love my job and am doing well for myself. In the grand scheme of things, it's really not so bad. At least, that's what I keep telling myself. It's a kick in the balls, but again I'm doing pretty alright!"

Tim understood what Diana was saying. It was a black-out pain, quick and devastating. Pain that stopped the breath but haunted the body long after the initial blow. And then, as quickly as it came, it would stop. The memory of the trauma lasts longer than the trauma itself. The pain seemed to have leaked out of Diana last night. Now she was focused on letting go of its hold.

"I'm never taking him back again," Diana said. "Not that I think he's planning on coming back this time. And I'm also not beating myself up for wasting so much time with him. It's done now, so onward and upward."

"And physically? How're you feeling?"

"Good, but that could be the mimosas talking," she smiled. "I'm tired, but okay. By the end of the week, we'll have a doctor's appointment and hopefully answers. It's just like we talked about, one thing at a time."

Diana grabbed the last piece of bacon, leaving a handful of crumbled pieces.

"She says as she eats the last piece of bacon. Please tell me we didn't eat a pound of bacon."

"I can't tell you that if you don't want to know."

"Have them check your cholesterol when you're there," Tim said, flinging a potato at her.

"Rude!" Diana picked the piece of potato off her plate and popped it into her mouth. "We do not waste spuds in this house."

"You're a spud," he said. Her laughter lightened the heaviness from their early conversation. "I love that we're on one day at a time, but I would like to make a today item. Something I will take care of so you don't have to."

"Proceed," Diana said.

She spread her arms as if to invite a party into the room.

"We should secure your home." He began combining leftovers and piling plates as he continued, "It's cheaper than hiring me as a full-time bodyguard, and it will give everyone peace of mind."

Diana scoffed. "Have you been talking to Ann?" she asked.

Tim laughed, nearly dropping the plate he was scraping into the garbage.

"I forgot about that! She doesn't have a key, does she?"

"God no. I love her and she's great. But she would deem the

leftover mac and cheese in the fridge a hazard and come in just to throw it out."

"Because kale is just as comforting as cheese," he said.

He felt her eyes on him as he moved back and forth between the kitchen and the dining room. Each time, he gave her a look and held up a hand in an attempt to remind her that she had cooked, so now he would clean.

"In the light of day, *Amber* makes more sense than Arnold; you said it's her social media stuff? Maybe she just wanted to make a point. Idk, bitches be crazy!"

Tim looked at Diana, who sat with her elbow propped up on the table and laughed so hard he farted. Which set her off into a fit of hysterical giggles. When he caught her from falling off the chair, they were both in tears and on the floor.

"I was saving—Mark's text—for this kind of comic relief," she said. Small hiccups punctuated her sentence. "But now—I'm afraid—you might—poop, if we open it."

"Low blow, Dame," he said.

Tim tickled her, dodging her flying elbows and feet, until she ended up cradled between his abdomen and his legs, on top of him. His arm was wrapped around her chest, and he could feel her heartbeat pounding.

"If you—don't stop—pee!" She squeaked another hiccup. "I'll pee on you."

"It might be worth it," he said.

Rolling over, he kept his grip on Diana. His body molded around hers as he stood them up. He walked her to the bathroom and left her on the toilet. He turned and headed out of the bathroom. He had cleared the last of the table and was in the kitchen when she came out.

"Hey!"

"Yes," he said, turning around.

He shivered as her finger traced along his arm.

"You never told me what happened here," Diana said.

"That," Tim said. He chuckled and grabbed a Tupperware

from the cabinet. "Well, after you fainted and I was still on the phone, I heard a commotion." Diana walked by him and returned with Big Yellow in hand. She leaned against the counter, snuggling the lemon-colored water bottle. "Not knowing what happened, I hung up and called you back. Ann answered, spat out that now wasn't a good time. Before she could hang up, I told her I was on my way. I ended up on the cul-de-sac."

"You mean the one past Ann's house? Through the property that butts up against the Hwangs'?"

"Yes," Tim said, looking at his feet. "That's the one."

"But you've been to her house before!"

"Not when something's been wrong with you!"

He felt his voice crack and hoped she didn't notice how scared he had been.

"Okay, but what does that have to do with your arm bleeding?"

"I figured it was closer to her backyard anyway. So I ran across—"

"Wait," Diana said. He watched her almost drop the yellow reusable bottle. "You ran through the neighbor's backyard into Ann's?" Tim nodded his head. "But their whole property is fenced in," Diana said.

"I know," Tim said, "because right as I got to the top of the fence, I snagged myself on a piece of barbed wire and fell off the damn thing."

"Oh god!" Diana shrieked, choking back her laughter. "Do you know how lucky you are?"

"Lucky?"

"I think one of the neighbors has an electric fence or something. But seriously, you fell off a fence trying to get into Ann's yard?"

"I'm fine," Tim said, rolling his eyes. "Thank you so much for asking."

"Mister," Diana said. "You okay?"

"Yeah, I was fine then, and I'm fine now," Tim said. "Better without you patronizing me. Annoyed at myself and at Ann, I ran back through the neighbor's yard, hopped into my car, and backtracked until I found the right street. Thankfully, the gate had been left ajar."

"And you didn't want to tell Ann because. . ."

"Because I figured you'd take the piss out of me enough for both of you," Tim said.

"I'm glad you're alright, Mister. And I'm especially thankful that you came to my rescue."

"Anytime, Dame! Just maybe not when you're at the Hwangs'."

Diana stuck her tongue out at him.

"Serious question though, what were you planning on doing after you rescued me? Were you going to carry me over the fence?"

Tim started the faucet and turned to face her. "You know, I hadn't thought about that."

"Are you going to be okay tackling these by yourself?"

"Of course," Tim said.

"You sure?" Diana asked again. "I don't mind helping."

"Yes," Tim said. "I'm an excellent cleaner-upper. Mrs. Danvers taught me well."

"Ugh, I realize she's a fictional character, but she still creeps me out," Diana said, pushing in her chair. "Also, your mother was a sweetheart, one of the cleanest, kindest, least Mrs. Danvers-y person I've ever met. She definitely taught you how to clean! Which is good, because while I don't need shower supervising yet, I figure while you're here. . ."

"Go, go, go," Tim said, waving her on. "I'll just be here scrubbing away. If I hear any thuds, I'll be up in a jiffy, ready to laugh at *you* this time."

From the kitchen, Tim heard her go upstairs and the countless trips back and forth from her bedroom to her bathroom. He thought about the first time she had stayed over at his parents' house. She had been so nervous about leaving the bathroom as neat as his mother had prepared it that Diana had turned the water on, made two or three trips from the guest room to the bathroom, and shut the water off, having never actually gotten in the shower.

Laughing to himself as he took off his watch, Tim started the dishes.

chapter forty-six

Diana

Diana was still smiling when she walked into her bedroom. She grabbed her phone, intent on only listening to music. Her Bluetooth speaker had just connected when Diana looked behind her door.

Her towel was there, no robe, but she wasn't going to spend the day hanging out like a bum. Or at least not dressed like one. As Nana Rosa used to remind her, "If you look good, you feel good." And right now, she needed something to feel good about.

She turned the water, twisting the hot as far as it would go, making sure to only half twist the cold. There had been so much going on in her life, too much over the past few days, she hoped a lava-like shower would help to scald away some of the ickiness.

Arnold was gone.

It hurt, but it also meant she could live her life for herself. It seemed stupid that she had ever forgotten that. There was nothing she could do about her health until she talked to a doctor and got real answers, no matter how much she dreaded the thought. As the water seeped into her thick hair and ran down her body, Diana felt her muscles relax.

Feeling her body unwind, Diana grabbed the shampoo and started washing her hair. Letting it sit to soak in, she washed her face. Turning back around so the hot water was at her back, she massaged away the shampoo and the tension in her neck. Leaving her face wash on, Diana loaded her hair with conditioner. Her thoughts, which usually wandered, had stayed in the moment. She absorbed as much of the hot water as she could take while following her silly shower routine.

She had just finished rinsing off her face when her song stopped playing. Feeling a twinge of panic, Diana peeled back the curtain. Relief washed over her when her ringtone blasted through the speakers. Whoever it was could wait. As the ringing stopped and her music resumed, Diana had rinsed most of the conditioner out of her hair and was washing her body. The suds from the soap tickled her neck as she scrubbed herself from shoulders to tippy toes. If there had been a trace of anyone on her, they were now floating down the drain with the soap scum.

Her breath caught in her throat. There was the possibility that someone else had touched her, tasted her, over the weekend. Pain zipped through her leg as she pressed her finger into the bruise. She had been so messed up. From what she had heard from Tim, it sounded like Arnold didn't do that for anyone, not just Diana, but there was no proof. If she wasn't entirely sure, or couldn't sound fully sure, a policeman wouldn't believe her. A defense attorney would have a field day with her, and for what?

She would face it, take things as they came, but for right now, she was home and safe and clean. She'd book an appointment with her gyno to cover her bases. It was the only doctor Diana had been good about seeing routinely. Dr. Jacobson had been so kind when Diana disclosed that her partner had been cheating. No judgments, just medical facts and best practices to keep *herself* safe. If anything was wrong, she could deal with it then.

Diana killed the water, wrapped herself in her towel, and got out of the shower. Before she started to embark on her after-shower routine of hair care, coconut oil, dental hygiene, and dancing her heart out, her phone rang again. This time, she answered.

"Hello?" Diana said.

"Hi." Ann's voice boomed through the speakers.

"Hi, Ann, hold on one second," Diana said, grabbing the speaker and lowering it a few notches. "Hey, what's up?"

"Nothing much," Ann sang into the phone. "What's up with you?"

"Just got out of the shower."

"Good," Ann said. "At least you didn't know it was me when you didn't answer before."

"Yeah, I've been avoiding my phone since yesterday. . ."

"And rightfully so; some of the things have just been, well, let's say anyone covering the story of a socialite turned slut will have a hard time not making it seem like they write for TMZ. Glad you're showered, though. What are you doing for lunch?"

"Lunch," Diana said. "Isn't it still ridiculously early for you to be thinking of lunch?"

"Yes, Di," Ann replied haughtily, "but who knows you better than me?"

Diana laughed into the phone. "Yeah, I can do lunch."

"Terrific. I'll pick you up at one-thirty?"

"Sounds good to me," Diana said. "Looking forward to hearing about yesterday."

"You know how I feel about kissing and telling," Ann said. "Hope you're ready for all of the gory details. See you later, boo!"

Diana heard three beeps. Ann swept in and out like a rainstorm in Central America when she wanted to. She sounded excited. Diana was happy for her. Sometimes she felt like Ann spent so much time on superficial things or hating on Arnold, not that she'd have to anymore, or worrying about Diana, that she didn't have enough fun.

She went to press play when a text from Mark caught her eye: Not you too, Diana. Whatever it was couldn't be good. She would look at it later, like the rest of her messages. She resumed her music and her routine.

* * *

"For someone so tiny, you make more noise than an elephant," Tim said.

He was sitting on the couch in the living room. Diana ruffled his hair as she passed by, looping around the couch.

"For someone so smart, you're kind of a dipshit," Diana teased back.

"How was your shower?" Tim asked. "Wet?"

"Yes," Diana said through a snort. "You're never going to let that go, huh?"

"You took a shower without actually taking a shower." Tim laughed. "So no, I'm never letting it go." Diana plopped down on the couch next to him. Flecks of water flew off the tips of her hair, landing on his face. She laughed as he brushed them off. "But I do have to head out for a little bit."

"Ohhh," Diana said, lifting an eyebrow. "Anything fun? Top secret mission? Not that I figured you'd want to spend all day here."

"Few things sound better than spending the day with your best friend, but I have a few errands to run, including getting your shirt back."

"Ahh," Diana said. "What time are you heading out to meet him? Because if you're not leaving for a little bit, I'll make him thank you cookies or something. They won't be homemade, but if we keep all that cookie dough here, I'm going to eat it. I just hope it doesn't cause a rift between him and Arnold."

"Don't worry about that. Arnold is doing enough damage on his own. I'll head out around 11 or so. I have to take 27 to head back here anyway, so I can stop at Home Depot and get you a new lock for the front door. If you want? Can even see about one of those hidden cameras for the table?"

Diana leaned over and hugged Tim.

"I would love that. I'll give you my credit card before you head out," she said, making sure to get as much of her wet hair on him as possible. "You're the best!"

"And you're like a wet dog," Tim said, shooing her away.

She sat back on the couch and looked over at him. Tim was staring at her, a small crease stationed between his eyes.

"I'm okay, Tim," she said. "You're still here, and until Ann beckons me for lunch, I'll probably just read on the deck with the front door locked. Not sure how long I'll be after that, but I guess we'll find out?"

"You won't consider staying inside, right? That would be crazy town?" He asked. She glared at him. "Fine, but I'm taking the key out from under the plant. Probably should have done that sooner," Tim said. He shook his head and started for the door. "Maybe Ann'll actually have worked up an appetite this time?"

Diana laughed. "I don't know how she functions. Hydration, healthy foods, and an obsessive skin care routine."

"Avoiding anything that might make her happy."

"Ugh, one of the perks of having Arnold dump me was that I didn't have to have two people in my life that couldn't stand each other—"

"And you still don't. I'll mind my p's and q's. And I'll never dump coffee on her."

Diana burst into giggles and made her way to the kitchen to prep cookies for Mark.

"We can watch the game if you want," Diana called out.

Her face was in the fridge, looking for the container of the cookie dough. The amount of snacks and food Tim had gotten for them was jarring. She was almost out of room for water bottle collection.

"Um," a voice said behind her. Diana jumped. Turning

around, she threw a blind punch. Tim moved to avoid the connection. "We'll work on that, Dame. But the key is gone."

She stared at him. "What?"

"The key I used last night. It's gone."

Diana felt her body go clammy. She picked up Big Yellow and took several gulps.

"Tim," she said. His face swam in and out of focus. "What the fuck is going on?"

His hands gripped her body as she started to fall. She kept her eyes closed as he led her over to the couch. Her eyes locked on the clicker while he propped her up with pillows.

"Can you please not become some fainting woman of the 1800s. I don't know if they make smelling salts the way they used to!"

"Ah, yes," Diana groaned. "How dare you ruin my Victorian Era with practical thought?" She could see the fear in his eyes and wondered what hers looked like. "We're really not funny, huh?"

"I think we're hysterical. I'm also calling the doctor now. Watch TV, or don't, just don't move. Please."

She smiled as best she could. Tim's voice was somewhere between a mumble and a growl as he stormed back and forth through the kitchen. When he came out, he handed her a spoonful of cookie dough.

"They're going to see you the day after tomorrow," he said. "I preheated the oven. Eat this, rest, please, and then we'll hang out. I can always get your shirt—"

"Today," Diana said. She took the spoon from him. "I have the appointment. You should see Mark, I'm so grateful. But you can't be my bodyguard every second. Plus, Ann and I have lunch plans. It'll be like a changing of the guards or something."

"Fine," Tim grumbled.

She found something for them to watch, an old black and white Hitchcock film, while Tim threw some cookies in the oven. They hung out, snuggled on the couch, picking at a few of the drastically underdone cookies, just the way she liked them, until Tim got up to go.

They were standing in the hallway by the front door. Diana handed Tim a tin of cookies for Mark and a plastic baggie with a few for him.

"Thank you for everything," Diana said, embracing Tim in another hug. "You're really the best, Mister."

"You're not so bad yourself, Dame," Tim said, breaking away.

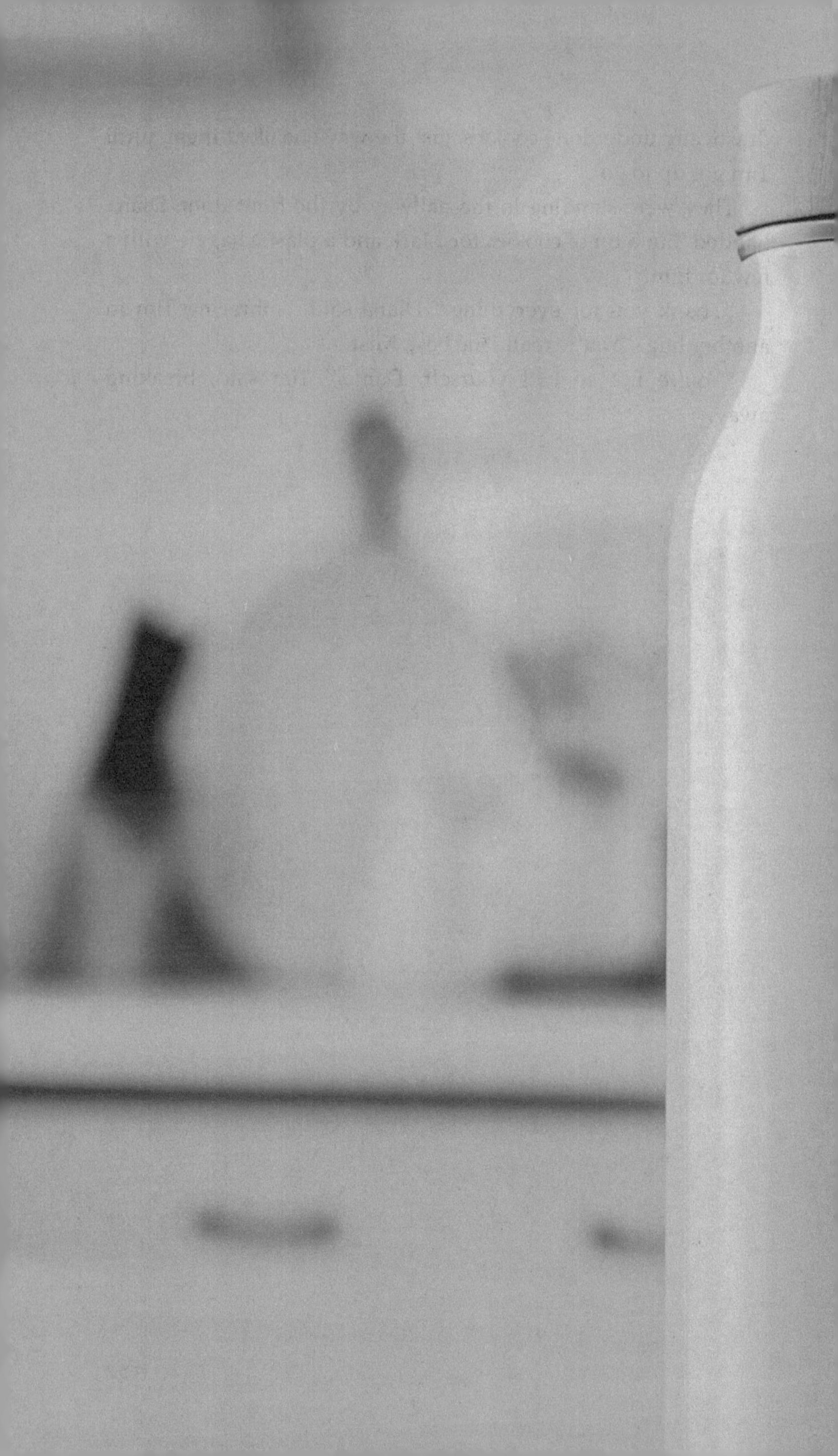

chapter forty-seven

<u>Diana</u>

Diana closed the door, locking it behind Tim. She grabbed two half-drank bottles of water from the fridge and combined them into one, making sure to throw the empty bottle into the recycle bin.

Better habits were starting today! She took her water bottle and the book from Judith and stared outside her back door.

The sun was shining, and the trees were so green. Tim had suggested she stay inside, but it was gorgeous out. If she had her phone and her baseball bat, it would be the same as sitting on the couch. She ran upstairs to get both. Her phone was at 2%, *crap*. She plugged it in next to her bed and texted Tim.

> Phone is charging. I'll be downstairs for a bit. Don't worry, be happy. You think that would make a catchy song???

Diana laughed at her joke, grabbed her weapon of self-defense, and headed back to the living room.

Outside on the deck, the sun, the wind, and the temperature were all up high and felt reinvigorating. Sitting with her eyes closed, soaking in the sun, she thought about cancelling on Ann. She laughed with her head tilted back, causing her to choke on her spit. She reached for her water bottle and polished off most of it. Returning her head to the chair, Diana stretched, sinking further in. This is what she needed.

Her mind drifted. She saw herself walking down the beach. Arnold had been away for the weekend; hindsight suggested he was visiting Amber, but at the time, he said he was going back to Chicago. It wasn't often that Arnold visited them.

He wasn't from a great part of the city, and outside of his one aunt and uncle, along with their children, Arnold didn't have strong familial ties. It was something that Diana had believed connected them. While on his own vacation, Diana hopped in her car and went for a drive. She decided on a whim to stop at a beach further out and further east. She had been walking alone. There were a few people scattered way out, but as far as she was concerned, it was just her. The wind was coming off the water. It was too cold to truly be at the beach. She wrapped her long hair around her hand, twisting it lightly and pulling it through itself.

The warmth from the sun wasn't much, but she had been able to find solace.

Diana had stayed there for what felt like hours, watching the great ball of burning light move throughout the sky. The sunlight and clouds shook off their sleep, getting ready for another day. She had been at peace. She went back the next day, and every day, until Arnold had come back. She tried to tell him about the peace and the calm, but it wasn't the same.

She had suggested they go; she drove—which Arnold hated—and at the last minute, she pulled off at a different beach. Something inside her didn't want to share *her* beach with him just yet. There was still hardly anyone out there, but she felt cramped and crowded. He grumbled about the cold and pointed out how rough the landscape was. It wasn't like Robert Moses. Maybe she should have taken note, but sitting on her porch now, sponging up the sun, reading one of her favorite books, Diana felt that same peace. It had taken a shitty path, but things had irrevocably changed now. Her life was going to be her own.

Diana opened her eyes and laughed as circles of color exploded in front of her. Looking up at the sun, even with closed eyes, was never good for anyone. Like a kid, Diana reached forward, trying to grab the spots of color. She lifted her water bottle to her lips, disappointed that she was all out. Her stomach growled. Diana looked around for her phone, remembering it was upstairs. Ann might be looking for her. She should have remembered to bring it out. She put the bat on her chair and laid her book on top of it. It wasn't the best bookmark, but she'd be right back.

She closed the screen door, turned around, and watched in amazement as the walls slid into the floor. They melted like crayons, streaks of colors bleeding into the hardwood. Diana's body began to fade away. She was too familiar with this feeling. She only wished she could make it to the couch before—

chapter forty-eight

Tim

According to the clock on the radio, it was already a quarter to four. Tim pulled out his cell phone. He hadn't heard from Diana since she said she was charging her phone. Knowing her, she probably got lost in her book and nearly shit herself when Ann came knocking for their lunch date.

He could imagine the new asshole Ann would have ripped Diana for not having her phone embedded into her flesh before whisking her off for a day of whatever Ann had planned for them. Which certainly wouldn't include Tim.

But she hadn't answered his last text.

> Hey! Hope you two are having fun. Switched plans. Stopping for a security system now. Then Mark's. I'll start changing the locks when I get there, if that works? Leftovers and a side of catchup for dinner?

She was probably fine.

But—flashes of Diana fainting the past few days, the look of fear in her eyes, the journal that she said wasn't hers—there was a chance she wasn't okay. A vibration ran through Tim's pocket.

Pulling out his phone, Tim checked his texts. Diana had finally answered him.

> Tim, last night was a mistake. I'm really disappointed in you. We're not getting dinner or ketchup anything. In fact, it's probably better if I take time for myself right now. Don't reach out again, or right now will turn into forever.

Tim squeezed his phone, wanting to throw it across the parking lot. He knew Diana wasn't in the best place, but this was a complete one-eighty and then some from where she had been this morning. Ann could be jealous and possessive, but there was no way she would be able to talk Diana into pushing him away. As Tim sat staring past his steering wheel into the distance, his phone beeped again. Fumbling around, he finally managed to pick it up. It was Mark.

> "You okay, bro?"

His heart was shaking like a leaf in a hurricane. His blood pumped through his ears; his jaw clamped shut. His heart reared against his chest. Tim took a sharp breath in and called Mark.

"Hey, man," Mark said.

"I'm not okay," Tim said. He rolled his shoulders and breathed out slowly. "You home?"

"Will be in the next half hour, and you're coming over. We need to have a talk about the level of crazy going on out here."

"I don't want to know what that means."

"No, you don't. But you're gonna. See you at my place soon." The line dropped, and Tim's phone buzzed again.

Mark had sent him a screenshot of a new group text, this one named "Team All American," not including him. He would give it a few days. Maybe after a week, it would all blow over. Tim zoomed in on the picture Arnold had used to create the group chat. It was hard to say for certain, but one thing was clear—whoever's face was inside the thick red circle with the slash across it was not invited to the conversation. He texted Mark.

Is that a picture of me?

Mark's response came back before Tim could close the message.

You are public enemy number one.

"Someone should tell Flavor Flav," he muttered to himself.

He was walking toward his car. He had a new set of locks and a home security system that did him no good. Tim turned and made his way back to the store. What did he need them for? He would just return them and be done.

Thankfully, he had left without taking her credit card. He didn't think he could bear mailing it back to her. *It's going to be okay, just relax, man.* Tim sighed and changed direction again. If things did change, he'd want her to be safe. Not in a few days, safe immediately. He thought of those journals again. Of his mother. A pang radiated in his chest. It didn't matter that she had just kicked him out of her life; he needed her to be safe.

Out of the corner of his eye, he noticed a truck idling nearby. He could have sworn it was Arnold's truck; the driver was impossible to make out under a black baseball cap. It was hard to tell if it had silver lettering or not, but it did look like the letters of their fraternity.

He kept his cool but picked up the pace. It seemed to have driven off. A loud revving sound caught his attention. He looked around. The truck was coming straight for him. The driver gunned it. Tim ran between a section of cars. The sound of crunching metal filled the air. Tim felt the jolt as a nearby car bumped into the one he was behind.

The truck revved its engine again and drove off. Tim stayed low between the cars until it passed. The giant White Sox logo on the back solidified it. That was Arnold's truck, but who had been driving it?

Tim dialed 911 and reported the accident. A truck had just driven into a row of cars in the Home Depot parking lot. No, he wasn't injured or involved. A twinge of guilt filled him. It was probably personal, and while Tim hadn't committed the hit, he was going to run. If that was Amber—there was no reason for her to attack him. No logical one he could think of, at least, other than Arnold being mad at him. What did it mean for Diana?

He looped back around, getting into his Infinity, and called Mark.

"Hey, Mr. 305."

"What? I don't know who that is."

"Pitbull?"

"I have a full head of hair and I'm Greek and English, neither of which is at all close to Cuban."

"It's more because Arnold is saying you stole his girl."

"So someone tried to hit me with his truck?"

"What?!"

Tim replayed the events of the last ten minutes to him.

"That sounds oddly similar to what I was going to tell you when you got here."

"What do you mean?"

As Tim drove down the highway, he listened as Mark told him about picking up the shirt from the cemetery. A woman, with hair like Diana's, had been watching him for a while.

"Why were you there that long?"

"I wasn't going to pick up something from the woman's grave and not say hi."

"Dude, who are you?" Tim asked. "Maybe we should all be worried about you."

"We've spent years worrying about me; I'm enjoying the vacation."

"I'll bet."

"Anyway, when I got out to my car, that same woman was waiting in a white Honda."

"Same car as Diana," Tim said.

"No caption needed for this one. I'm pretty good with cars," said Mark.

"I know you are, buddy."

Tim took the exit for Mark's place and slowed around the bend only to get stuck at the right light.

"So, this bitch, with hair like Diana's, in a car like hers too, hits the gas coming right for me. I dove under my truck and watched as she peeled around the corner. Before she could get a second attempt, I hopped in and booked it outta there."

"You're okay, though?"

"I'm pissed!"

"I meant physically."

"Well, she didn't get me, but she clipped my truck."

"Why would you think it was Diana?" Mark coughed, and silence filled the line. "What did you text her yesterday?"

"What did I text her?" Mark sounded appalled. "Did she say that?"

"Dude, no one said shit to me. Is there a reason this fucking light by your house is red for so long?"

"Calm down, hot pants. I'll see you in a few and we can go over it in person."

The rest of the drive, which should've been the easiest, was the most stressful for Tim. By the time he made it to Mark's front door, his friend was waiting for him.

"Diana isn't the only person who drives a white Honda," Mark said as Tim walked through the front door, straight back through the hallway, and into the kitchen. Mark continued speaking, "Hey buddy, how you doing? You okay? Rough day at the office?"

"Next, you'll offer me coffee and cake," Tim said.

"I only have tea." Tim turned around. Mark shrugged and

went to the cabinet, taking out two mugs. "Hopefully some chamomile. You are stressed as fuck."

"And you're being a Suzy homemaker."

"More like a Hardy Boy, but sure," Mark said.

"So what mystery did you solve, Joe? Or is it Frank?" Tim asked.

"Jeff, duh." Mark shot Tim a weird look over his shoulder before putting on the kettle. *And this kid teaches history to teenagers?* Tim thought to himself.

"Anyway, look," said Mark, holding out his phone.

Tim walked over and stared at the screen. Amber was standing in front of a white Honda. It was six months before Diana bought hers.

"Scroll down to the comments."

Tim scanned down the list of various forms of congratulations until he saw it. RedHotRedHead__commented: You know who else just got this car? SMH I'd rather the car than the man!

"Who is red hot redhead?"

Mark grabbed his phone, walked to the table, and put down two mugs of tea. He sat down and gestured for Tim to do the same.

He had just pulled his chair in when Mark slid the cell over. Tim looked at it, a familiar profile of a girl with red hair. How many times had Mark shown them that picture? The endless debate as to whether or not it was a wig—which it totally was.

"That's the same redhead psycho that stalked you for how long?"

"Too long," Mark said. He sipped his tea and smiled, taking his phone back. "But that was also probably my fault. She was hot, and I got a lot of spank bank material from her."

"Please tell me you didn't reach out to her," Tim said.

He picked up his tea and took a sip. *Not coffee*, he thought.

"I didn't," said Mark. "But I did go back to the photos she sent me."

Mark pushed the device back toward Tim. A whole lot of everything filled the screen.

"Are these in chronological order?"

"Uh," Mark said. "Yeah? The newest are on the bottom. Why?"

"You said you didn't reach out to her, but she sent you the same picture twice."

"Bro," Mark said. He put down his mug of tea and stood over Tim's shoulder. Using his thumb, Tim pointed between two photos. "That's the one Diana sent me last night!"

Tim slid his chair back into Mark, pushing his friend backwards.

"Cool it, hot rod," Mark said, fixing himself. "I told her no."

He picked up his phone and switched over to his text. Tim didn't want to see it, but there was the picture from "Diana" and Mark turning her down.

"Wait," Tim said. "Go back to the other one."

Mark snatched the phone and handed it back to Tim with the earlier picture. He clicked through the settings on both photographs. The information from the picture was the same, but one said 'shared by "Diana,"' the other was from a phone number. Tim took out his own phone and searched it.

"The same number that your redhead used last year is the same number that texted Diana a candid shot of herself naked."

Tim fell back into his chair. Mark took both phones, looking back and forth between the two.

"Drink your tea, you look like shit," Mark said. "How'd you do that?"

"The info button."

"You remembered the number from the other day. More tea, let's go fucker."

"I'm good with numbers. It's why I gave up on PT and work in a bank."

"Well, shit."

The mug was still warm. Tim was surprised by how soothing

Elizabeth Scozzari

the tea was, even if it wasn't coffee. Maybe he should try that for Diana.

"This is chamomile, you said?"

"Mhmm," Mark said. "With honey."

"Cool." Tim drank more of his tea. "This isn't making sense. Someone, or ones I guess, tries to run both of us over, and your stalker tries to seduce you as Diana?"

"But how'd she send it from Diana's phone? The number's right. We have previous texts. Granted, I think it's happy birthday or something."

"Let's check," Tim suggested. "Shit, speaking of, we made you thank you cookies for getting her shirt back."

"Homemade? She makes the best—"

"I said, 'we.' And no, I used the cookie dough from last night."

"Fair." Mark picked up his mug and cell. "Go grab the cookies, bro."

Stepping outside, Tim felt like he was in a time machine. Inside, it was cool and dark, and the conversation with Mark had been bleak. Outside, it was still hot, still sunny, and too nice for all the shit going on.

He went to adjust his watch. It wasn't there. The last time he had it was this morning at Diana's when they were playing house and he was doing the dishes. Now she apparently hated him as she had so clearly texted. *Unless* Tim stopped at his car door. The pictures from social… Arnold had been sending them in the group chat.

Tim grabbed the cookies and ran back inside. Sweat was already dripping off of him by the time he stood in the doorway looking at Mark.

"We're going to need a pen, paper, and more tea," Tim said.

Mark raised his eyebrow.

"Let's fucking go!"

His friend pumped his fist in the air, standing up to get what they needed. The two of them made a list of the geographical info from Arnold's pictures, images that Tim would have preferred not to see.

The number was definitely Arnold's, so they were coming from his phone, but the images themselves all seemed to be from Amber, who knew Mark's redheaded stalker.

That was one possibility at least.

The shirt picture nagged him the most. In the group text, it was all one screenshot, but when Mark logged into his Facebook, it was actually two separate pictures. The one featuring Amber had a different location than the rest of them. Tim plugged it into Google Maps. The others had been up and down 27, but this one returned a building. He clicked on it, zooming in.

"Wait," Mark said. "Did you hear about this?"

Tim tilted his head and looked at Mark.

"The building?" Tim asked.

"Yeah. Massive structure fire," Mark said. Cookie crumbs sprinkled out of his mouth and onto the table. He shrugged, swept them into his palm, and tossed them back in. "They haven't said where it is exactly or who owns it."

Mark gulped his tea and belched.

"Gross," he said to himself. "Let's call Nate."

Tim exhaled and looked at his friend.

"Why?"

"'Cause he does real estate now," Mark said.

"I thought he did security."

"Semi-retired, just on weekends. He's making a killing, though."

"Mark, I've had a lot going on." Tim tried to take a breath, "Can you just tell me what the fuck you're thinking?"

"Oh, we can see if he knows who owns the building. Might be helpful."

"That's a great idea!" Tim's eyes widened. "I'll reach out to him."

"See, we're making progress. And I've made a dent in these cookies," Mark said. Tim looked at the empty tin, surprised to see most of the cookies gone. "When you go, I'm probably going to jerk off after all the pictures we just combed through."

Tim scrubbed his face with his hands. It was shit like that that made it easy to forget Mark had a brain that worked well sometimes.

"Dude, the fuck is wrong with you?"

His friend shrugged again. "I'll grab Diana's shirt, and then I'm kicking you out."

"Thank you," Tim said.

He looked back at the building as it was before it burned down. On a whim, he texted Nate.

> Long time no talk, brother. Mark said you might be able to help me. The building that caught fire, do you know who owns it? Lmk if you're around for drinks next weekend. We'll have a mini frat reunion.

Mark walked into the room holding Diana's shirt.

"Dude, seriously," Tim said, his voice cracking ever so slightly, "you have no idea."

They locked hands and patted each other on the back. After they pulled away, Mark handed him the thermal. How different it looked when he was holding it versus when she was wearing it. He remembered the other day, how cute she looked, flustered and stuck. How he had helped her free her arm before he stepped out, giving her privacy. Was that really only a few days ago? Tim's phone beeped, derailing his train of thought. Nate's name popped up with two new messages.

"Holy shit," he said.

"What?"

"I texted Nate—"

"Like I said to," Mark said.

"Well, I owe you both drinks then. Look at who owns the building."

Mark tilted his head, and Tim watched as his eyes skimmed the words.

"The burnt down one?" Mark asked.

"And the one where that last picture was taken." Tim texted Nate back. "That can't be a coincidence, can it?"

"Unless you want to discuss Jung's Synchronicity—"

"You hooked up with a psych major once," Tim said.

"I also teach history."

Tim sighed, his thoughts spiraling in circles. He closed his eyes. How would he process them if they were numbers? He'd start with true and false statements.

"Diana is supposed to be with Ann for lunch."

"Probably why she texted you that she hates you," said Mark.

"Not helpful." Tim looked back at his phone. "I'm sending you all of this. Go to the police station. I don't think Arnold or Amber tried to run us over."

"If you're wrong, are we still reporting it?"

Tim's heart pounded in his chest.

"I'm not wrong about it. And I don't think Diana's been imagining this shit either. I'm headed over to her place now. It all comes back to this."

He waved the text from Nate in the air highlighting where Tim had been shortsighted. Not anymore. He fired off his texts to Mark and made his way to his car. Things were becoming clearer every step of the way.

chapter forty-nine

Last Fall

I had been shopping for Christmas gifts despite it being October —never too early to shop for the ones you love. I hadn't been looking for anything other than some fall-themed gifts for my spooky friends when I saw Arnold's cinderblock-like head leaning over a dazzling sales case at Zales.

Interesting choice, since last I knew, he was most definitely as unfaithful as they come. I slowed my pace down, wanting to see what he was looking at. It wasn't until a hand slid down Arnold's coat and stopped right above his butt that I realized he wasn't alone.

The lights bounced off the rhinestones of the girl's studded burgundy beret, emphasizing how damaged her platinum blonde hair was. *Ugh, blondes.* She smiled, leaning in closer to him. They embraced.

My eyes traced the burgundy scarf wrapped loosely around her neck, matching her burgundy leggings; hadn't anyone told the Platinum Princess that it was a winter color? Sharpness bit into my skin. I winced and looked down at my hands. Blooms of blood raised from the half moons I made from clenching my fists. My tongue ran over the cuts, the metallic tang filling my mouth.

Tweedle Dick and Tweedle Twat grabbed my attention again. The girl's face was tilted toward the ground. Arnold was leaning over her, his chest puffed. The sales assistant had begun walking toward them. The woman's arms unfolded, and her head snapped up. Her cheeks were as red as the logo on Arnold's dumb baseball hat. Spit flew from her mouth as she spoke. Arnold shook his head and turned, heading toward the sales associate. The blonde stormed off. A woman who had been nearby ran after her.

"Interesting," I mused.

Intrigued, I stalked closer to the store. The sales assistant was with Arnold now. In his hand was a tray with a ring. Either it was diamondless or the diamond was pathetically small. The lack of glitz was a disappointment. There was something next to it that I couldn't see. The associate walked back to a different case and returned with another option. No visible diamond, but the associate had gone to the "Engagement" section.

The blonde wasn't Saint Diana, but she certainly had enough sense to tell him to fuck off for picking out such a small gem. At least that's what I thought at the time. Arnold and men like him and Mark are no strangers to me. Having not spoken to him, it only ruined my shopping trip, and not my whole day. I walked to my car, but before I could find it, a gut-wrenching wail caught my attention, bringing me back to the present. Who doesn't slip between moments, right?

I looked around, noticing the woman from the jewelry store standing outside of a minivan holding onto the Platinum Princess as she sobbed.

"It's okay," the woman said.

I walked by, catching the eye of the woman. I offered a sympathetic smile and a soft nod. Gag me. The woman dipped her head in appreciation. Once I was out of sight, I tucked into a row of cars waiting to hear what was happening.

"What do you mean okay? How is it fucking okay? He won't even listen to me."

Sobs chewed up the younger woman's words.

"Language. And he has a girlfriend, Amber. One he very clearly told you he was stay—"

Pardon the fuck out of me—this was Amber? The other woman, the sidepiece, the "I'll break it off with her", *Amber*? I wish I could say I was surprised by Arnold's tacky taste. But I wasn't.

"I'm pregnant, Molly. We're pregnant."

"Does he know?"

"I told him I wasn't sure I wanted it—" Now Molly was crying just as much as Amber. "He wants kids, and a wife, and—"

"You don't?"

"I do, but he's with someone else. We started out on a lie, and I don't want him to pick me because of this. I still have school to finish, things I want to do."

Her voice caught.

"And you're sure it's his?" Amber's face must have been something out of nightmares since Molly started backpedaling before I could truly marinate in the insult. "As your sister, I will always believe you, but you brought that other guy around.

Flaunted him, actually. The one from Daddy's country club. You seemed happy. . ."

"I was trying to move on. I was being petty and stupid. I was hurt. But I never slept with him. I've only ever been with Arnold. He's my only. My everything." Her voice broke again. "What am I going to do?"

"Well then," Molly said, her voice regaining its strength. "We'll figure it out. Whatever you want. When are you due?"

"I don't know. I didn't notice until the end of last month, and then the earliest appointment I could make is for next week. I only have the sticks you pee on at home."

Curiosity got the better of me, and I looked up. Her out-of-season outfit was probably picked to hide the minuscule baby bump. The way the fabric was tangled from her sister's embrace, I could see she was definitely pregnant. *Whore*, I thought to myself.

"Oh, Amber." Molly's voice rippled with emotion. "We've been trying for so long. Are you sure you won't consider keep—"

"I don't, I don't know anything," she said.

The drama was just too much. I rolled my eyes, almost wanting a box of Cookie Dough Bites from the movie theater.

"When is your appointment?"

"Thursday, 4 pm."

"With Dr. Belle?"

"No, I didn't want anyone to know, so I found a different doctor."

"Who then?"

"Dr. Jacobson. I've heard great things about her," Amber said.

She blew her nose and spoke clearly; apparently, her tears had come and gone. I clutched my imaginary pearls. Dr. Jacobson was one of the best on the island. I would know, she was my lady doctor. And it had only been a few weeks ago that I had run into Saint Diana in the waiting room. How divine would it be for them to run into each other there? I hold back the laughter bubbling in my chest.

Obviously, Amber is an idiot for thinking Arnold would support her aborting their baby. Having never had the conversation with Arnold directly, it was pretty clear that he had loved hooking up with Diana in the first place because she didn't want kids.

Something she and I have in common, though that's really

the extent of the similarities—unless you count an interest in fraternity brothers.

From everything I was told, Arnold wanted the whole picket fence bullshit. That was the last thing he deserved. By the time I started my car, a plan had formed. As the end of the week rolled in, Amber's pregnancy was confirmed. Too bad for her, she was too far along to terminate. Legally, at least.

I was happy to help, off the record, of course. Men like Arnold are trash; anything made by the likes of him should be in the composting program, not growing up loved. Amber's schedule had been easier to track than Diana's: Starbucks every Monday, Wednesday, and Friday morning. Tuesday and Thursday, it was something from the gym juice bar. That's where I saw my window.

A week after her doctor's appointment, I signed up for the same gym. My red hair, meticulously styled, popped against my all-black outfit. Paying in cash as Diane A. Diego, I signed up for six training classes.

"I just want to see if I can take you." I giggled, looking at his crotch. "I mean it."

The nineteen-year-old behind the register had pitched the training classes and told me his age, how much he could lift, and what other colleges had recruited him for sports before he chose Wherever University before I finished the waiver paperwork. Eye roll. He had slipped me his schedule after giving me the grand tour.

It was like the world wanted me to help Amber out.

On Wednesdays and Thursdays, he was the gym's best bartender, and he worked the desk on Mondays and Fridays.

"Maybe you can meet me later tonight?" I didn't even have to bat an eye before he agreed.

I got to the bar early, ordering us drinks. For almost two hours, I kept him eating out of the palm of my hand. It was almost so pathetic that I thought of finding a different target. But I wasn't going to look a gift horse in the mouth.

"I have to get home," I told him, my hand resting on his thigh. "But maybe next week. Well," I took a breath, making sure my breasts heaved right under his nose. "Maybe after my session, I can come see you by the bar?"

He looked like a sad puppy as he agreed. I wanted to laugh at the disappointment.

I expected him to be a little mopey, but he lit up like a Christmas tree when he saw me walk up to the juice bar. I wondered if I could get him to drool by the end of the conversation, not that it had been very long.

"I was thinking behind the bar." Leaning over the polished surface, I whispered into his ear, "It would be my pleasure to taste your juice."

He held up a finger and turned. I watched him start to clean the tops of the machines with a rag. I almost applauded when he accidentally moved the camera in the opposite direction. Once I was under the counter, I got to work teasing him, taunting him, waiting for that annoying voice. And then—

"Skinny special, please, Peter."

I had thought his name was Josh? I shrugged to myself, still working the head of his cock with my tongue.

"No problem, Amber."

As *Peter* charged her account, I slipped out and dumped a handful of pills into the blender. When he came back, I stood up and led him into the bathroom. He had lasted less than a minute, and I had the unappetizing taste of victory. It was a nice gym, and there were mini toothbrushes, the kind with the mouthwash in the middle, on the counter. I rinsed away Peter's taste and headed home.

The rest of my plans unfolded as I drove.

I shut the car off; that was then. I'm still in the car, but it's been ages since I've planned anything. These days, I'm all about the execution. I open the car door, leaving the past behind. *The future is now*, I smile to myself.

chapter fifty

<u>Diana</u>

Miraculously, she somehow managed to land partially on the carpet. Diana tried to sit up.

"Oh no, no, no," a voice projected into the room. "Let me help you."

Diana blinked a few times. A dark shape loomed over her; maybe she had hit her head on the way down. The form was a blur of shadows. The room came into focus, and hovering above her was Ann. She was dressed in a black jumpsuit, accessorized with diamond jewelry. She stood back a little ways. Diana's head rolled to the side. Ann's bright pink heels were next to her face. She was dressed more for some high-stakes made-for-TV business lunch than Diana had the wardrobe for.

"Take a minute, I'll go get you a wet rag and then we'll move you over to the couch."

She sounded pissed. The click of Ann's heels on the floor reverberated through her body. She was home. She had been outside reading. Diana couldn't remember why she had come inside. She tried to roll her head to see if either door was open. Otherwise, how else would Ann have gotten in?

"Put your eyebrows down, Nancy Drew. The screen door was open, and you hadn't answered any of my earlier texts. I was worried. I got tangled up, but I'm not *that* late."

Diana did her best to process what Ann had just said. The back door had been opened. She was getting something. Maybe it was her phone. Is that why she hadn't answered Ann?

"You okay, Di?" Ann snapped, tapping her foot.

"Yeah, I think so," Diana answered. "Just a little off, I think."

"I did find you on the floor," Ann said. "I'm assuming you weren't there on purpose?"

"No, I, uh," Diana said, "I think I fainted."

"Probably," Ann snipped.

Their conversation sounded like melted pudding to Diana. It seemed like Ann was mad at her, but it didn't make sense. Something was off.

"Is it because I didn't answer you? I don't know where my phone is."

"What?"

"You seem upset, or maybe I'm out of it, but I just wanted to check."

"I'm not upset. I'm disappointed."

"Because I fainted again?"

"No, Diana. Because I went out of my way for you."

Diana tried to sit up. The couch was probably a better place for her than the floor.

"Stay down, bitch."

Her tone was harsh. Her face was set like a stone. Diana knew this girl well, and even she wasn't positive Ann wasn't actually mad at her. Concerned, sure, but also upset? Ann was always a little touchy if Diana didn't put her first. She just said she wasn't mad. She was—what had she said?

Diana attempted a smile as she tried to stand up again. "I said. Stay. Down. Bitch," Ann said. She dug her heel into Diana's shoulders.

"Ow," Diana yelped. "What the fuck, Ann?"

Ann pierced her shoulder until Diana's back was flat on the floor. She could say what she wanted, but Diana was positive that something was bothering her. The room spun; she wasn't sure if it was from pain or being pushed back down. Diana closed her eyes, hoping to steady herself. A cold weight landed on her ribs under her breasts. Ann's heel left Diana's shoulder, landing with a loud smack against the floor.

"Don't you want to check out your surprise?"

Diana angled her head just enough to see something on her chest. She picked up the hefty item, realizing it was a watch. She looked up at Ann.

"Is it because I was late? We had lunch plans, right? I didn't mean to—"

"What are you doing with Tim's watch?"

She turned the watch over, bringing it closer to her face. The back of the watch was inscribed: *TEA*.

"Timothy Emrys Ames," Diana mumbled.

"Yes, Tim's watch," Ann repeated. "And what the fuck is Tim's watch doing here, Diana?"

"He must have left it here," Diana said. "I'll tell him to be more careful. I feel like shit, can't we talk about this on the couch?"

A laugh on the border of screeching startled her. In all their years as friends, Diana had never heard Ann laugh like that.

"He's not the one who needs to be careful, Diana," Ann said. She grabbed the watch and threw it across the room. "It's you!"

In an instant, the point of Ann's heel was pressing into Diana's cheek, pushing her face flat against the floor. The tip of Ann's black ponytail swung back and forth in front of Diana's face, dragging across her eyes.

Diana tried to move, but Ann was holding her down. It was hard to get her bearings. Something hard and bony, maybe Ann's knee, replaced her shoe. Drops of liquid hit the corner of her mouth and trickled into her mouth, filling it with an awful, bitter taste. It brought back the terrible taste of the shots from the party.

Ann's hand closed around Diana's mouth and squeezed, the metal of her rings cold against Diana's lips. She tried to scream, tried not to swallow, but Ann shook her head until she couldn't help it. A familiar sensation of tingles swept through Diana's body. Her muscles relaxed despite the panic she still felt.

"I didn't want it to come to this, you know. I just wanted you to listen. To make the *right* choices. I told you that I would always take care of you. You should have listened. At least now you don't have a choice."

* * *

Diana felt the sound of her phone going off throughout her body. It sounded like it was still connected to the Bluetooth speaker and someone had raised the volume to a million. Pain radiated in her jaw. Her whole body felt like she had fallen down the stairs on repeat. Diana went to rub the back of her neck in an effort to relieve some of the pain. Her arm wouldn't move.

With a pounding heart, Diana did her best to lift her head and look around. She was in her spare bedroom. The television was turned on to the news, but there was no sound. A burning building filled the screen. She blinked, but she still couldn't read the captions.

Her arms and legs were chained to the wrought iron posts of the bed. Her legs were bare. Her bra was off, and she was wearing her shirt with the orange pun. Her hands felt wet and clammy with sweat. Her phone dinged again. Diana looked around. Was it closer than she thought? Or was it still in her bedroom charging? A shadow moved over the light coming in from the window.

Standing above her was Ann.

"You're not going to get that?" Ann asked. "Let me help you," she said. Her phone was in Ann's hand. "In another example of being more careful, you shouldn't use your house number as your passcode for your phone. Especially when it's one digit repeated four times," Ann quipped, unlocking Diana's cell phone. "Really, Diana? 8888."

Diana watched in frozen horror as Ann's eyes widened, her one eyebrow slightly raised. She had transformed into a different Ann. As scary as she was, she had never looked more beautiful.

"You hate ketchup," Ann said, sitting down on the bed. "Unless you've also been keeping your love for *condiments* a secret, too?"

"What are you talking about?"

"You, Diana. We're talking about you. You and your secrets," Ann said.

"I hate ketchup. I don't have any secrets." She felt her chest constrict. "Ann, what the fuck? What is happening?"

"Really?" Ann snipped. "Okay, we're going to play a game—*my* game. I'm going to ask you a question. You're going to answer honestly. Meaning truthfully, without deceit or semantics."

"That's it? That's the whole game?"

"Oh no, honey," Ann said. She waved her finger in the air like she was hailing a cab. In her other hand, she still had Diana's phone. "It'll just determine *which* game we play next."

Ann stood up, typing something on Diana's phone. The sounds of the keyboard, followed by the familiar swoosh sound of a text being sent, were too sharp for Diana's ears. Ann walked a few feet away from the bed. Her whole body looked sharp and deadly.

"Now that we've cancelled on Tim for the rest of ever, we're not going to need this anymore."

Then she dropped Diana's phone and shattered it with her heel. Ann repeated the stomping long after the light from the screen died.

"Please, Ann." Diana started pleading. She hadn't meant to, but she didn't know what was happening.

"Enough, Di. Fucking enough," Ann snarled. Pulling her bottom lip in, she began to pick off pieces of the inside with her teeth instead. "Now let's start unearthing the truth, shall we?"

Diana had exhaled as Ann walked out of the room, the click of her heels getting further away. Until then, she hadn't realized that she was holding her breath. This was insane. Diana pulled on her chains. They weren't the handcuffs Diana kept for bedroom games in her Girl Scout bag in the closet. Those were real too, but had a safety in case someone lost a key. These didn't seem to have anything like that.

The more she struggled looking for a hidden latch or something, the more they cut into her. Thoughts raced through Diana's mind: ketchup, Tim's watch, her phone. It was like they had pieces from the same puzzle, but Ann had assembled hers all wrong. That, or Diana was missing a major piece. Her chest tightened as she tried to breathe. Diana's stomach flipped as she heard the click-clack coming closer.

Focus, Diana thought. Breathing in, she touched the tip of her thumb to each finger on her left hand. Exhaling, she reversed the order.

"So, are you ready?"

She sounded like her friend; she was even more beautiful than usual, but there was a sharpness to Ann that Diana was unfamiliar with. She nodded her head, still trying to control her breathing over her rising panic and the aching of her body.

"Not quite, I see," Ann said. Her eyes were lasered in. Diana tried to follow her sight but couldn't. "That's part of your problem, Di. You have no willpower. No control. You're scared and nervous, so you tap, tap, tap, tap your fingers trying to get a grip —" Ann's hand wrapped around Diana's pinky, squeezing tight enough that the tip of her finger began to throb. "And then lie to *me*, and say that you're fine when clearly, you're not, not, not, not." The edge in Ann's voice cut almost as deep as her words.

Ann dug in, applying pressure against her nail bed. "But I can help. Need to figure out how to breathe? It's simple."

The sound of Diana's bone snapping was audible over her scream. Diana saw a flash of white, for a moment she saw her pinky perpendicular to her hand, and then came the hurt. Her breath was ragged, and particles of snot and spit danced with her fast, rhythmic breathing.

"Much better, isn't it, dear?" Ann walked back toward the foot of the bed. "In, out. In, out. You're doing great."

Ann walked around the bed, her eyes locked on Diana's until she arrived at the side of the bed next to Diana's ribcage. Ann leaned forward and adjusted Diana's hair. "First question," she said, swirling the remaining water in the bottle. "What was Tim's watch doing here?"

Diana stared back at Ann.

"He left it." Tears and snot dripped down her face, leaking into her open mouth. "Dishes. He did the dishes."

Her words were forced, pushed through her clenched teeth.

"Did he do the dishes last night after he took you home?"

"No." Diana tried to slow her breathing. "This morning. After breakfast."

"Did he sleep here?"

Diana felt the sharp sting run through her face before she realized Ann had backhanded her. Ann rubbed a diamond on Diana's shirt. She looked down to see blood. The metallic tang reached her lips along with the salt from her tears.

"Focus," Ann said.

She repeated the question. Diana nodded her head, the movement shaking her arm, causing more pain.

"Don't withhold things, Diana. It makes me upset."

"We, we fell asleep. On the couch. As friends."

"Little Timmy is such a good friend, huh? He's a better friend than you, right?"

Diana's face was wet. Blood, tears, and snot were everywhere. She tried to snort it back, to make it easier to breathe. Her finger was on fire. She didn't know if it was the fear or the pain that made it harder to breathe.

"I don't understand."

"Have you read any of your texts from yesterday?"

Diana shook her head. A wet groan escaped her as her body jostled her hand.

"Of course you didn't." Ann sighed, the familiar look of disappointment mixed with the hatred Ann seemed to be holding on to. "Because you're not a good friend. I tell you I'm going to hook up with a man I've met once, maybe twice, and you don't even check to see if I'm alive. Nor do you tell me that your shitty boyfriend, who I openly hate, is flaunting his whore."

Ann stood up. The bed shifted, sending a wave of nausea through Diana's body. Even if Ann noticed, she continued her lecture.

"I'll give it to you that you didn't know at first. But when you did find out. When you saw their dead baby's sonogram, heard all about their plans for a happily ever after, what did you do? You didn't even call me to confide in. Why would you? You were so wrapped up in your *best friend's arms*, you didn't think you needed me."

Lifting one knee up onto the bed, Ann swung her other leg over Diana's body and hovered above her, holding Diana's right hand in hers.

"Not even a text of gratitude."

Blind panic numbed the pain Diana was currently in. "I haven't been looking at my phone—"

"You have, sweetie," Ann said. "I've seen you with your phone in your hand. Running scared. Running a fucking muck. Instead of calling me."

"Ann, what are you—"

Her grip tightened. Diana's heart raced. "Why are yo—"

A second snapping sound filled the air. Diana's scream lodged in her throat as Ann's weight dropped onto her chest.

Diana's right hand throbbed, the pain running rampant. "It's not your fucking game, Diana."

Water splashed into Diana's mouth before Ann forced her jaw closed. She shook her head. Diana tried to keep the liquid from going down her throat. She choked a little, but eventually it all slid down her throat. She tried to focus on the television screen behind Ann, to will herself to fight whatever Ann had given her.

"It's mine. Do you know there was a time I wanted to *be* you?" Ann said, shifting her weight back to her knees. "How stupid, right? You're nothing like I thought you were. Not since your grandmother kicked it; your mommy hurt your feelings, and you picked a piece of shit human as a boyfriend.

"I thought I could help you, guide you back to the strong woman I thought you were. Or at least forge you into something. But you're weak. Just like they were. You are more fun, though. Arnold had no idea what he was missing."

Diana choked on Ann's words as her hand touched the top of Diana's neck behind her ear. Slowly, she traced her finger down until she had knocked the t-shirt off Diana's shoulder.

"It is true he left you, Diana, correct?"

"Yes."

Her heart rate was racing—too fast. She felt too energized to be sitting so still. There was pain, but it was distant behind a buzzing wall. Diana coughed again, and familiar tingles danced across her back.

"Here, take a sip," Ann said. "It's just water, Di."

Ann slid her hand up Diana's throat, tilting her head back. Sparks erupted where Ann's fingers pressed into her jaw, opening it as she poured a few sips of water into her mouth.

"Better?" Diana nodded.

Ann saddled herself on top of Diana's hips. She trailed her fingers up Diana's bound arms. Each one taking its own turn roving over Diana's exposed skin. They traveled up and over the handcuff, locking themselves into Diana's hands. Ann leaned in closer, her body rocking against Diana's. A small voice told her to be still, but she couldn't control her hips as they rose to meet Ann's. Everything tickled, including her hands.

"Swallow."

Even whispering, Ann's words were a command. The bitter taste had taken over her mouth, and she wanted to throw up. Diana forced the liquid down her throat. Planting a soft kiss on her cheek, Ann latched onto Diana's thumbs. As she sat up straight, Ann pulled until Diana could no longer scream.

"You didn't know I was trying to teach you before, so now we're playing for fun," Ann said. She jammed her fingers into Diana's mouth, holding it open as she dumped the rest of the water bottle down her throat. Diana felt small sparks as Ann moved her hand out of her mouth and over it. Diana's lips squished against Ann's palm as she jerked it back. She was so thirsty, it didn't matter to Diana what Ann was giving her anymore.

"Good girl," Ann said. "You ready to keep playing?"

Diana couldn't move; her body felt like a hunk of lead being kicked around a thunderstorm. A shiny, sharp raincloud danced on top of her. She blinked, seeing Ann's face come into focus.

"Years of riding him, getting him off for no reward. Is that right, Diana?"

Strands of hair stuck to her cheek as she nodded. "My party was the same for you, wasn't it?"

She went to nod again when a bee stung her face. Diana blinked. It wasn't a bee. Ann's hand hovered over her face.

"Was my party the same?"

Diana shook her head no this time. A rush of pain rushed through her arms as she did. Ann leaned forward and brushed the hair off of Diana's face and behind her ear.

"And do you know who made it different this time? Who gave you what you were dying for?"

She could see each eyebrow hair powdered with filler as Ann leaned closer to her. The stale smell of tobacco wafted off her underneath a fragrance. Tropical but different. The sun would feel amazing on her skin. The beach. The wind.

Another jolt fell across her face.

"Stay with me, Di. You're nowhere near an OD yet."

Ann asked her again if she knew who made her feel different. Diana shook her head. There was nothing she knew for certain anymore. She was getting lost in the sensations of everything. *Too much*, she thought.

"At least you're being honest about it," Ann said. "Too late to learn though, remember? This is fun. Not educational."

Diana watched as Ann's long arms reached over to the nightstand. She felt as Ann parted her lips with her fingers, before wrapping her hand behind her neck and tilting her head up. She hated how good Ann's skin felt on her own. *Drugs, she had said something about drugs.*

She wondered what she had given her to make everything feel so good when she was broken, bound, and terrified. With her free arm, Ann gave her more bitter liquid from the dropper. The light pressure of Ann's manicured fingernail tracing along Diana's neck sent shivers down her spine. Ann kept dragging the edge of her nail down further, past Diana's breasts, almost to her navel.

Diana's loose shirt had bunched up in its wake, leaving most of her exposed.

Her heart was beating faster than it had in her life. She felt breathless and warm. The feeling intensified as the cloth from Ann's jumpsuit grazed against her skin. Diana could barely focus on what Ann was saying. The blood was pounding through her ears, and agony radiated through her hands.

Diana tried to speak, but the words were lost. Ann slid further back, lowering herself, following the path for her nail with a trail of kisses. Hair rose on Diana's arms. She wanted to kick or move, but her body wasn't listening. It could only feel Ann's touch, the thin cotton of her shirt, the silk-blend sheets, and Ann's breath. Diana arched her back, trying to focus on the pain Ann had caused. Trying to fight the feeling of the drugs she had been given.

"I took care of you," Ann said. She pressed her lips into Diana's hipbone, then her bikini line, finally her thigh.

Razor blades kissed her skin, tearing it to shreds. "And you couldn't even say thank you," Ann said. She spat a large chunk of something out onto the floor. "Instead, you said *his* name as if he could ever do for you what I did. As if he ever made you come. I listened. I *heard* you. All the things you want to try. The things he judged you for. You think I'm a prude, or a tease, or whatever everyone says behind my back. The difference between us, Diana, is that no one is good enough for me."

Ann stepped off the foot of the bed and walked over toward the mirror. She plucked a tissue from the dresser and blotted her face. Diana didn't remember her wearing lipstick earlier. But her lips were glossy and red. She jammed the tissue into the pocket of her jumpsuit.

"Unfortunately, the only one who can do good enough for you *is me*. And I've given up on you."

She looked back at her reflection.

"Maybe I should buy a tube of blood red," she said. "I think it works with my skin tone."

Diana watched as Ann walked back to the side of the bed. Picking up a small bottle, she pulled the stopper out and dropped one single drop "for good luck" into Diana's open mouth.

"How do you feel, Diana?"

"Unnnnuh." Words, like her body, were failing her.

"Good," Ann said. "This is going to hurt a bit. At least I think it will, I haven't really tested it out before."

Diana's mind was in and out. Her head rolled to the side.

She could barely concentrate on anything. Ann was holding something in her hand, but it wasn't clear what. The lights moved; her stomach danced with them. Her arms ached. She yearned to be touched, but she hurt. She was having a hard time seeing straight.

Something red on the floor caught her eye. It circled in her blurred vision. It looked like a spit-out strawberry or a fat worm. Pinkish and red. A hunk of inside-out salmon skin!

Skin! The word lit up in her head, but before she could follow the thought, something like a train whistle erupted in Diana's head. A million ants had to be chewing through her flesh. It seared and felt like fire erupted. Diana's eyes remained open, but the world blackened, and a ringing sound started and stopped. She blinked. Ann's face hovered above her own. Her body jittered against the bed, and her whole body felt wet and freezing.

"Damn," Ann said. "And I was going to go all Tyler Durden with lye, but I think the acetone worked too! Of course, he had that poetic kiss—this'll be a bite mark. Right where I left the other one." She looked at Diana, a crease forming between her eyes. "Ugh, you'll probably be out before I get downstairs," Ann said. She walked over toward the bed and jammed a few pillows behind Diana's head. "If you puke, don't choke."

Diana sank into the dense clouds. The room around faded into vibrating sounds. Heels clacking, the clicking and twisting of the old television, the ting of Ann's voice like a tuning fork calling out from somewhere, "More games to play later, Di!"

chapter fifty-one

<u>Ann</u>

Ann pulled on her steering wheel, cutting across the right and exiting lanes. It was hard to focus on the road as she replayed the afternoon in her mind. It hadn't been what she expected. *Of course*, when left to make her own choices, Diana always made the wrong ones.

For years, Ann had been telling Diana to leave Arnold. But no, she was comfortable. Things weren't bad. On again, off again. Trying to make it work. Nana Rosa taught her this, and Nana Rosa wanted that. What Diana hadn't understood was that Nana Rosa was dead now, and Arnold was just a deadbeat.

It should have been perfect. Diana barely noticed how often she was fainting or forgetting. Arnold was even less aware. But no, not Tim. Tim noticed. And somehow, even with all her hidden cameras and coordinated efforts, he had gotten to the punch before Ann.

And that was unforgivable.

Her car beeped as she approached the vehicle ahead of her, stopping at the yellow light. Ann swerved around them, barreling through the intersection and blaring her horn.

"LEARNHOWTODRIVEYOUPIECEOFSHIT!"

Ann's knuckles turned white as she gripped her steering wheel, thinking of the other driver's neck. Didn't anyone realize that the world would be better if they all just stayed out of her way?

She nearly clipped the gate turning into her driveway, then screeched the brakes, throwing it into PARK. Ann wasn't sure if Diana was ungrateful or unteachable. From the second Ann saw them snuggled on the couch, having a heart-to-heart, it was clear that she didn't want to be her strong-willed self anymore. No, Diana was happy to have someone save her.

Too bad for her that she picked the wrong person, again. At first, she was going to pin the murders on her, but Tim and his documentation of her health would be a problem. No. Now, Ann could play with Diana like a rat in a lab until she expired. Then Tim would take the fall. It wasn't perfect, but it worked. She'd ensure that it would.

Ann stormed inside and made her way to the kitchen. While she had things to do, she needed a clear mind to work. Filling up the tea kettle with water, Ann leaned against the island as it boiled. Picking out her tea, she went with something that would ease her tension and help her relax, something with cinnamon, kava, sarsaparilla, ginger, and cardamom. She walked over to the stove, grabbed a mug, and shut off the water as the whistle blew loudly.

"Enough water for me?"

She almost dropped the tea kettle from shock. Turning around, she saw her father standing in the kitchen.

"Sorry, Daddy. I didn't know you were home. There's enough. What kind of tea do you want?"

"Whatever you're having," her father said, nodding at her.

Ann reached up into the cabinet and grabbed another mug.

She looked at herself in the metal hardware on the cabinet. She seemed put together. Not that her parents ever appreciated how she looked. They cared more about what she did, *bleh.*

Reaching over to the tea drawer, Ann pulled out a second tea bag. Pouring the tea into both mugs, she returned the kettle to the stove. Her father was seated at the table waiting. Ann grabbed both cups and joined him.

"Something bothering you?" her father asked, smelling his tea.

"Just a little tense, I guess," Ann said.

"You picked a good tea for that," he said. He smiled, but she heard the concern in his voice. "Ann," he continued, "Tommy's parents called."

Ann lifted her cup and blew on her tea, waiting to take a sip.

"They haven't seen him since the party. I saw you two hitting it off." He kept his voice even. She could hear him measuring out each word. "You haven't seen him since then, have you?"

She returned her mug to the table, wrapping both hands around the hot sides. The sting of the heat kept her alert.

"Daddy, I haven't seen him since Sunday. He kissed me. It was nice, but..." She stopped and cleared her throat. "We had been kissing when he kept trying to take things further. I told him no and that he had to go. He hasn't spoken to me since then. Not even a text."

Picking her tea back up, Ann continued to blow on it, inhaling the scented steam as it rose, embracing the sense of calm as best as she could. She hadn't tortured him like the other two, but it wasn't like she could ask him now if it was a better experience. He really had the best X and GHB in town. It was a shame he hadn't paid attention in health class. Drugs killed, or could get you killed.

"Ah," her father said. He put his hand on her forearm and patted. "You're a good girl, Ann. Sometimes I worry about you, but what father doesn't worry?" He stood up, picking up his tea. "I'm going to enjoy this outside," he said. "Your mother is still at the ladies' event. I don't remember which one. If you need anything." Her father's voice trailed away. As he got to the door, he turned around. "How's Diana? We didn't get to see much of her on Sunday. She still with that guy?" her father asked.

He waved his hand toward the ground. Even *he* could see Arnold was dirt.

"No, Daddy. They actually broke up after the party. He had been cheating for a while and just left her for someone else," Ann said.

"Sad, but better. She needs a good man. Like that one, you know, the one she brings around sometimes." Her father paused, a big smile stuck to his face, and looked down at his tea. "Ahh, I'd better stop. Your mother tells me that I'm worse than any yenta around. When you see Diana next, tell her we say hello!"

Her father nodded once more and headed out the door.

Ann walked over to the sink and threw her cup into the silver basin. The mug cracked in half. Hot liquid sailed through the air. Turning on her heel, she stomped into her room. She closed and locked her door and put on the Pop Top 500 station on Sirius. Ann combed through her walk-in closet, collecting various shoe boxes and dropping them on the chaise lounge in her closet. There were five altogether: one red, one yellow, one blue, and two pink. The two pink ones were baby sizes.

When she had grabbed everything that she needed from the yellow and red boxes, she returned them to their homes next to the pink ones. Only the blue one remained. Opening the lid, Ann felt her heart expand and chirp. Grabbing the tissues from her pocket, Ann added them to the box. It fell next to a clipping of Diana's hair that she had bagged up.

With her new plan, she could shave Diana's head and make a wig for her collection. She should have practiced with Amber, but it was never *too* late for a good idea, just too late for Amber's hair in this case. She still had the red one she used as Diane A. Diego and the platinum one, too.

Ann looked down at the pictures in the box. So many of them together, of Diana when she was sleeping, of her naked in the pond last year, photos from this year's party. Her favorite was one of Diana lying down in the guest bed of the pool house with her back arched. The focus was on the bite mark Ann had left, just visible in the background were Diana's nipples. She had printed it in black and white, and it looked tasteful and stunning.

Ann thought about the night that she cleaned up Arnold's beer. She knew it bothered Diana, because who wouldn't be bothered by spilled anything? Arnold, of course, didn't mind. She knew Diana would be out cold. Drinking water bottles with drops of GHB, or more often, a crushed-up cocktail of high blood pressure medications that she didn't need and wasn't prescribed, kept her fainting, sleeping, and generally confused.

She had looked so perfect that night sleeping on the couch, snuggled into her blanket, the sound of her breathing synced with the sound of Ann's scrubbing. It had been its own form of music to her ears.

Goosebumps formed on her skin as the breeze from the open porch door swept in. Ann couldn't resist. She just wanted to take care of Diana better than she was taking care of herself. She had pulled the blanket over Diana, as anyone would do for someone in their care.

Diana hadn't done her part. Ann had given her multiple articles and tips for staying hydrated, how important it was, and how it helped keep skin looking young. But no, even with all of those efforts, she liked to abuse her body and neglect her water intake with no consistency!

She ranged from a sip of water a day to 100oz. That day, she hadn't finished all of her water; if she had, she would have stayed asleep as Ann closed the back porch door. She didn't. It hadn't been until she was out of her townhouse and at the top of Diana's block before she allowed herself to breathe again.

That was the problem with plans that involved other people, Ann thought. They didn't always cooperate. Especially Diana. But this time, she was going to listen, and everything would go according to plan.

Elizabeth Scozzari

Everything.

chapter fifty-two

Diana

Diana rolled the upper part of her body as far over as it could, given that she was chained to her bed. She felt pain, and like she was drifting along a river. The flashing lights from the police cars on the television floated around the room. They were angry and violent. Closing her eyes was somehow worse.

The red patch on her thigh glowed in the light of the TV. The sight of it sent chills through her body. She looked away and saw her big toe. The room still moved around her, but that was her big toe. It was attached to her body. Using it as an anchor, Diana worked to orient herself.

Everything kept swaying.

She breathed in deeply, forcing her breath out in quick succession. Instinctively, she fell into fire breathing, but now wasn't the time.

She needed to hyperventilate and push her body. She couldn't stop everything from hurting, but she could get rid of these drugs. There was a freckle on the top of her toe that she hadn't taken much note of before. She stared at it and yanked her hands into the chains. A wave of vomit flooded her mouth.

Rolling her head to the left, it spewed out onto the bed, pooling against her thigh.

Diana nodded in and out of consciousness. She opened her eyes, still in a nightmare, but at least it had docked. Getting some of that crap out of her system must have helped. *Thanks for the* lesson, *Ann.* Her hand felt warm and wet. She looked down; she had gotten her one hand free. Blood pooled into the vomit. She lifted it, and the sight made her want to puke again. Her pinky and thumb were at angles she couldn't describe.

She reached across her body and, using her three middle fingers, tucked the pinky and the thumb on her other hand. It was enough to make bile start to rise. Diana clenched her abs and yanked. The room disappeared behind a bloom of colors, and she pitched forward as she spewed throw up. She shivered and collapsed back into the pillows.

* * *

The light had shifted in the sky. Diana woke up in horrendous pain, but the almost constant ringing in her ears from earlier was less. It seemed the rest of the drugs had worn off, leaving her aware of the trouble she was in. She focused on the sound. It was an announcement. Diana looked toward the television. Captions she could see clearly now scrolled across the bottom of the page.

Shocking updates on yesterday's mysterious fire. Three bodies were found in the medical building that caught fire yesterday evening. No identifications have been made, but sources say there were two males and one female. The fire lasted six to eight hours. The former medical building was recently purchased in 'as is' condition. Leftover medical supplies could be the source of the rapid engulfment. Neither the current nor the previous owners have been available for comment.

Diana tried to focus. Ann had put the television on for a reason, and she didn't think it was to keep her company. Whatever it was was a distraction. She had freed one hand. That was half the battle. Using her abdominal muscles, Diana sat herself up. She couldn't put weight on either of her hands. The right had fared better. Her pinky was shot, but the rest of it was usable.

Sitting up, she looked down at her body, horrified to see that her legs were also chained. She groaned. Things she didn't even know she could feel hurt, but that wouldn't stop her. She wasn't going to wait for someone else to decide the fate of her life, not again. Diana kicked her legs forward. The posts rattled.

It was a start. Depending on how she was chained, maybe breaking the frame would be enough to free her. She just had to think beyond the pain. Lifting her head, she stared at her ceiling fan. She and Tim had worked on it for hours hungover. When they finished, she squealed, jumping up and down. Grabbing Tim's hands, she bounced with him on the bed, tears rolling down her face from laughter. She jumped too close to the edge. She leaned against the bedpost to catch herself when suddenly she was falling. Tim pulled her back up and into his arms.

Diana pulled her legs as close to her body as she could; exhaling, she kicked the bar again. It wobbled, the sound of a loose screw reverberating. Closing her eyes, she could see Tim laughing as he put his toolbox in her closet. "Not that your hammer isn't the best, but sometimes in life you need a screw."

"Really?" She had raised her eyebrows at him.

"Don't look too surprised; I am, after all, a man."

The images of Tim dissolved as Diana screamed and kicked the bar in front of her once more. Something snapped; she covered her head on instinct. Fireworks erupted as whatever it was hit her wrist. Her vision blurred; she leaned over, her stomach clenching like she was going to puke again. Diana wasn't sure what she could possibly have left to barf. The post, the one she had knocked over with him, had fallen off. She looked at the treads.

Sometimes you need a screw. Diana was hammer happy, always had been. But maybe!

An idea took form. Agony coursed through her with every movement, but she refused to acknowledge it. Small pittance, imagine being roasted in a building. *Focus, Diana!* The voice sounded like Tim's; of course, he would come to mind, cheering her on. He was supposed to be coming back! Help was on the way; she just had to do her part until it got there. Folding her left leg up close to her chest, she was able to slide the chain off the top.

"Yes!"

The word came out through gritted teeth. That was one; now she had to do the other. Diana scooted to the other side of the bed.

Reaching up, Diana used her two index and two middle fingers to twist the ball off the next post. Her back cramped, her muscles felt like they were ripping open, but she got the post off.

She lifted her right leg up and toward her body. She couldn't get it. She lay down flat, using her elbows like oars, and she inched closer to the post. She pushed the chain up with her left leg. With a loud clatter, it came off the post and fell free onto the bed. Outside, a car pulled up, the engine cutting off as if it were at her front door. Diana's heart pumped rapidly through her chest, inside her ears. Heels echoed against the concrete.

"Fuck!"

Diana scooped the chain connecting her legs into the crook of her elbow. Sweat rolled down her neck. The front door opened. She saw her baseball bat downstairs, serving a purpose—yes, but she had just told Arnold it belonged in her room, tucked under the covers, like a small child keeps a stuffed animal. Outside was great when she had been there, but she was up here, stranded. Noises came from downstairs: the door locking, the fridge opening and closing.

She had to move!

She looked around; she only had two rooms and a bathroom to choose from. Silence took over. The void was filled only by the blood coursing through Diana's veins. She took a step forward. Heels clicked their way into the hallway. *Shit*, she should have moved faster. Turning around, Diana shuffled to the closet, her chains still in her arm. She opened the door as the heels clacked against each step.

On the floor of the closet, she saw Tim's toolbox. Diana breathed a sigh of relief. She moved with the speed of a three-toed sloth, the comparison not lost on her as she tried not to rattle the chains. She stuck her hand into the box—empty. She could hear the swish of Ann's jewelry. She had nothing to fight with. The weight of the chain sagged in Diana's arm. The stairs creaked; she was almost at the top. Diana looked at the bundle of metal she was holding.

She stepped out of the closet and hobbled into the hallway. Ann looked up from the last two stairs, and Diana threw the chains at her before she lunged. Her body collided with Ann, the force sending them down. Something cold and wet pierced Diana's back. Limbs intertwined as they tumbled. Rolling off Ann, Diana's broken body collided with the wall.

Numbness attacked her left side. Pain seared through her right arm. She felt the warm stickiness of blood run over her lips, trickling into her mouth. On her side, half curled into a ball, she watched in terror as Ann, twisted and shaking, crawled toward her.

"You fucking bitch!" She hissed like a feral cat.

Ann's left leg jutted out behind her in the wrong direction.

Paralyzed by fear and the pain jolting through her body, Diana stared at Ann as she crawled toward her. Surrounding her were medical bottles, syringes, and pills. A fucking medical bag. A glimmer caught Diana's eye. Clenched in Ann's bloodied fist was a scalpel.

Diana straightened herself against the wall, inhaling deeply. Ann inched closer, pulling herself with one arm and raising the blade in the other. Using leverage from the wall, Diana went to stand up. Her body was frozen, stuck. The metal glinted as Ann slashed it across her leg. She didn't stop until she was standing. Before she could take a step, Ann raised the blade again, this time plunging it deep into her. Diana buckled. She caught herself on the wall in a sitting squat position.

"Deadbeat dad, deadbeat boyfriend, I SAVED YOU!" Ann's voice raged. Her words were wet and harsh.

Diana shot her leg out, connecting the flat of her foot with Ann's face. Two times, three times, four times, until Ann stopped screaming. She couldn't stand, couldn't feel the stiffness in her back like she had earlier. She kept going toward the door. Ann moaned, behind her. Diana looked over her shoulder. Ann was rocking on her back, blood oozing from her face.

Ann smiled, shaking her head. Diana reached out and clawed at the scalpel in her leg. She wrapped her middle finger across the top and supported the handle with her index and ring fingers, rocking it against her skin until it popped out. Blood spurted forward. She wielded the blade, trying like hell to keep it steady. Diana kept moving. Her body crouched and crunched like a beetle. She was halfway down the hallway. She focused on the doorknob.

Tim was getting a new one. He would be coming back for her.

She just had to be alive when he did.

She heard the rattle of pills behind her. Ann's manic breathing echoed in the hallway. Her anger was palpable. Diana's face planted into the hardwood in the hallway. Her leg began to stiffen like her back.

Not in my own home, you fucking bitch.

Diana pushed herself with her foot and pulled with her elbow. The back side of her body was numb, down through her leg. It didn't matter; she was at the door. Dropping the scalpel, she used her head and as much of her right arm as possible until her fingers touched the doorknob.

So close, Diana. So close.

She swatted at it until her upper body spilled out of the door onto the concrete platform in front. The grass in front of her blurred. She blinked. For a moment, it was in focus. Her elbow dug into the concrete, inching her forward. The rough edge of the concrete sliced her, but what was a little more blood? She heard a car nearby. Maybe someone could help her.

A cry like a she-wolf howled behind her. Diana looked over her shoulder, still inching away. She couldn't turn her neck enough to see, but a black, shadowy blur was coming toward her. Diana pushed herself backward, her foot pushing the door closed. It shook. She wouldn't be able to hold it for long. Diana looked up; the sun had faded. Bright lights exploded in her peripheral vision, and a chill ran over her body. The sound of screeching tires assaulted the deafening darkness around her.

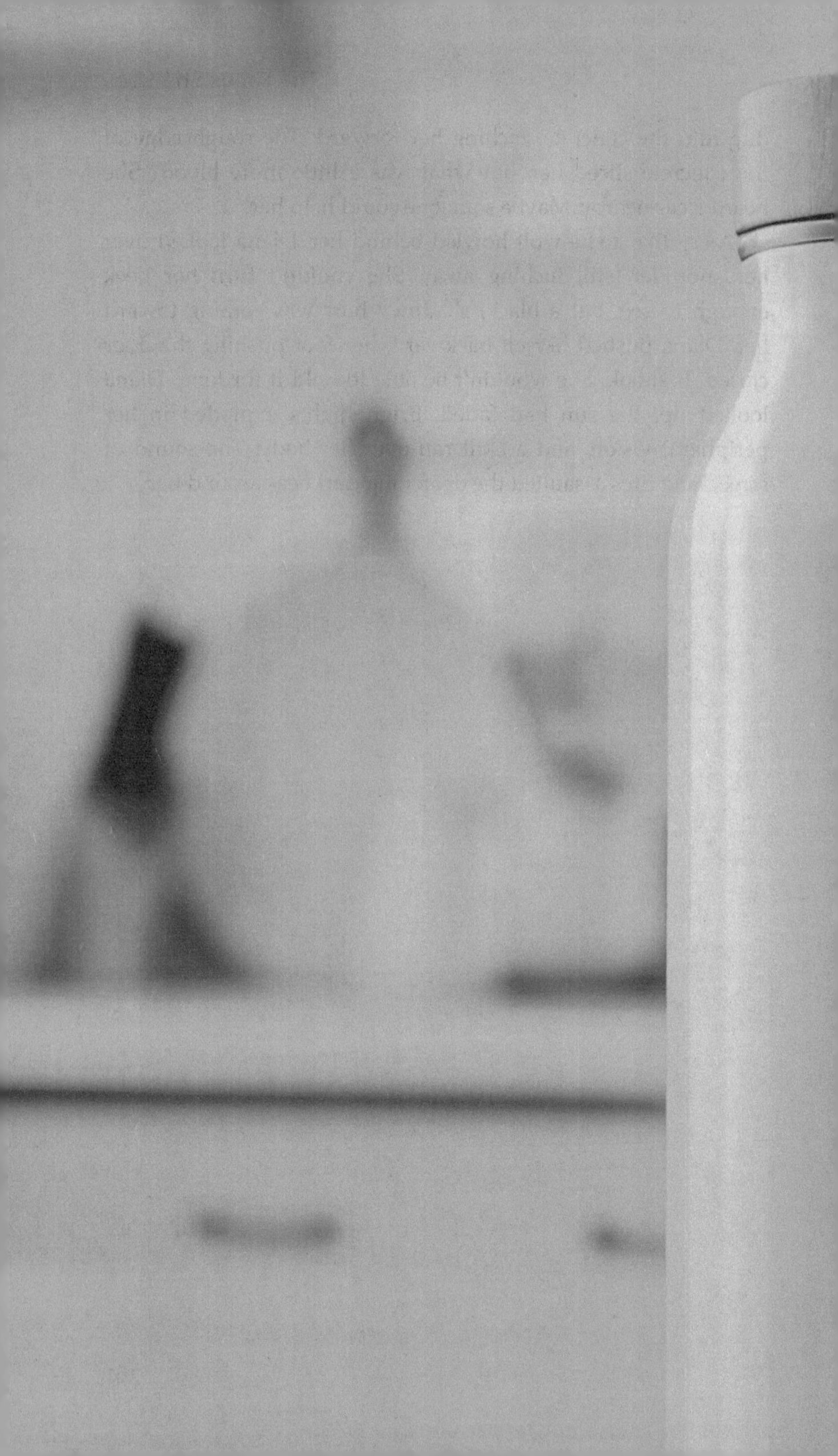

chapter fifty-three

<u>Diana</u>

Usually, Diana could sleep through the constant sounds from her next-door neighbor and the trucks that rambled up and down Route 27 all night, but something—a beeping—had jolted her awake.

Diana caught her breath as Mary, her favorite nurse, walked in to check her out.

"You're okay." She laughed. "Just me."

The irregular beeping of machines and the routine in and out of nurses was impossible for Diana to get used to. Thankfully, the doctor said she should be ready for release on Wednesday. A week and a day since she had been admitted.

"What time is it?"

"Time for a drink." Mary laughed again. "It's twelve-thirty."

"Why am I beeping?"

"You're not. But your friend in the hallway is," Mary said, lifting her eyebrows toward the door.

Diana laughed. It wasn't something she did a ton of the past week, but Mary had a way about her. Still young, mid-thirties, full of personality, a little nutty, but definitely the best nurse

Diana ever had in terms of bedside manner. Like all the other nurses, she had known exactly who the patient was before she had met Diana. Except she treated Diana like any other patient, or at least it seemed she did. Having a room to herself, she didn't see what Mary was like with anyone else.

The guard stationed outside of Diana's door poked his head in. A collective nod from Diana and Mary sent him back into the hall. Diana hadn't wanted the protection, but since it was the Hwangs' hospital and the same one their daughter had been admitted to, it had been mandated by the police. Tim had arranged for one of his fraternity brothers to watch her room. It was a compromise, and one Diana was grateful for, at least he spoke to her like a person. Though from the limited information she was told, Ann had been released with a torn ACL and other knee damage two or three days after they both had been admitted.

Mary finished up what she was doing, turned, and faced Diana. She took something out of her pocket and dropped it on top of Diana's bedside tray table.

"Since you're getting out tomorrow," Mary said.

"Thank you," Diana said. "You've been so good to me."

"I'm sure I'll see you around."

Mary winked. Diana cocked her head; she was hoping never to be back at the hospital. She waved before the nurse left. As her scrubs disappeared around the corner of the doorframe, Nate popped his head in.

"You have a visitor," he announced. A smile showed two rows of perfectly straight white teeth. "Trouble," Nate said. "Should I send him in?"

"Yes, please!"

Tim squeezed in behind Nate with a too-small backpack on his shoulders. Diana suppressed a laugh. Where Tim was tall and athletic, Nate was short and stocky. The kind of brick wall that, if it punched you, you'd fall down.

"Stealing my stuff?"

"More like a delivery service," Tim said.

Walking over to Diana's bedside, he sat on what had been considered his chair.

"Delivery?"

"Mhmmm," Tim said. Opening the biggest section of her backpack, Tim pulled out a small box.

"That one is from Paul and everyone at Mojo's." He took out another larger box, saying, "This one is from me."

Diana looked at both presents, one obviously wrapped by Tim, the other still in the delivery box.

"Very sweet, but also unnecessary," Diana said.

"Oh, but there's more," Tim said.

"More?"

"So much more," Tim said with a smile. "Your clothes for your discharge are at the bottom of the bag. There are copies of warrants, paperwork, and a few other administrative things in there. Including a list of hotels that might interest you until you can go home."

Diana's face fell.

"I know all you want is normal, but the Hwangs are using their influence to make this the most thorough investigation we've ever seen. Weird since their daughter literally tried to kill you. You would think they'd want to make everything disappear. Instead, police are still collecting samples and piecing things together. There's been speculation about their motives, but that's for another day."

"More small bites?" she asked.

"I'm going to have to get a planner just to keep track. Do you want to be excited to be sprung from this place, or do you *want* to keep staying here?" Tim said, gesturing around the room.

"You're right. You're right." Diana groaned. "I hate it. But in this case, maybe you are."

She looked around the room. While it had been good for her the past week, she was ready to move on. Looking at the oversized gift basket from Grant and everyone at SVM, Diana cringed, thinking about going back to work. She loved her job, but everyone knew. Not only what had happened to her, but by whom.

"Hiya, Dame," Tim said, throwing his voice from the corner of his mouth, "you gonna open these gifts or should I sell 'em to Nate?"

She turned back toward Tim. A smile spread across her face as Nate scoffed from the hallway.

"These two I told you about, but there's one from Judith, too," he said, reaching into the backpack.

"But she already—"

"To quote her, *the company* already. She didn't. Besides, you know better than to question Judith," Tim said.

"Didn't even give me a chance to object, huh?"

"Nope, she cut you off at the pass."

Tim began opening the gift from Judith. "Thank you," said Diana.

She had two relocated thumbs, two broken pinkies, and had sustained injuries to her wrists and carpals.

"Is she kidding me?"

She looked from the plastic case to Tim and back again. The note read:

> *Had this iPhone lying around. I had your sweet little friend set it up for you. Text me when you're home. I put you on official medical leave with pay. Talk soon—Judith PS Get well!!!*

"She is not kidding you," Tim said. "You are telephonically back once we finish the last stages of setup, which we will do when you get out of here."

Tim reached over, taking the garbage off her tray table.

"Next up are two special gifts from two special guys. We'll open up Paul's first, okay?"

"Okay." Diana smiled.

Tim wrestled with the tape, popping the box open. Tilting the box toward her, he let Diana peer inside.

"It's a menu," Diana said.

"It is. Read under *specials*!" he said, laying it in front of her.

"The Miss Mojo Platter," Diana said, looking at him. "Named for valued patron, Diana Edwards. The platter comes with Thai wings, chicken tenders, chicken and cheese quesadillas, tacos, and fries."

"And there's more."

He put a check down in front of her.

"It's a gift card for two hundred and fifty dollars," Diana said.

"Which, on your birthday, you'll never have to worry about using because you will get the Miss Mojo Platter for free," he said. "For the next five years, or something like that. There's fine print, but I didn't read it all. The last two are from me," Tim said. "This one."

He put an envelope down on the tray and slid it toward her. Looking at the envelope, Diana's face scrunched up. She struggled, but eventually tipped the weighted envelope until a silver object fell out.

"Isn't really a 'gift,'" Tim said. Diana studied the key in front of her. "None of us want you to stay at a hotel, so if you want, you can stay with me," Tim said, resting his hand on her thigh.

Diana pulled her knees up toward her chest. The stab wound on her leg was mostly superficial compared to everything else. The bite mark on her thigh had been washed, but would most likely scar. Still, her doctor had told her not to spend too much time scrunched up to help her heal better.

"But if you'd feel more comfortable, the new tenants don't move into my parents' house until September."

"No!" she shouted. Nate popped his head in the door, only leaving when Diana nodded at him. "I would love to stay with you." Tim's smile warmed her heart. "Just until I get my arms back."

"Obviously. I can't take care of you and Mark forever."

Tim and Diana laughed together for a moment. Her shoulder hurt from all the movement, but she was getting used to it. The site where Ann had plunged a syringe had developed a small infection. The infection had gone, but the irritation remained.

"Finally, the best for last. It's supposed to be a present for getting out of here, but it came today, and I'm not waiting."

He started opening the box.

"I can see that!"

He revealed another box inside a box. *How appropriate*, Diana thought. It was black and leather. Then the scent hit her nose; it smelled of old, loved paper. Glue and dust. Tim tilted it carefully, revealing a black book with an enormous red R on the cover.

"Wait, Tim. . . " Diana's voice trailed off.

"Yup."

"Yup what? I didn't even—"

"You don't have to! It is!"

"It's a first edition?" she asked.

Tim nodded emphatically.

"There's more," he added.

"More?"

"Open it."

"I can't—"

"Shit, hold on—"

With more care than she had ever seen him use before, Tim lifted the book from the smaller box. He gently opened the cover close to her, and Diana felt the warmth of the pages, the mystery, the love, all of it sweep over her.

"Holy shit!" Diana squealed. "Holy shit, holy shit, holy shit!!!"

"It's not technically signed, but it's a signed letter—"

"Thank you!" she gasped.

Closing her eyes, she chewed on her bottom lip as Tim put the book away.

"You okay?"

"Yeah," Diana said. "It's, uh, it's a lot."

"I'll bet."

"Thank you. Seriously, *Rebecca*, it's my favorite. It's your favorite. It's literally one of the building blocks of our friendship, and oh God. It must have cost a—"

"Just take a breath, Dame."

"Thank you for being here, for everything."

"Of course," Tim said, patting her knee. "Although I did forget something."

"No, no more," Diana said. "What?!"

"You're not supposed to sit like this," he said, flattening out her legs. "And this," he said.

"A card?"

"Read it," Tim said, removing it from the envelope. "Out loud, please!"

"Diana, I'm sorry for a lot of stuff. Hope you get well soon. Mark." She looked up at Tim. "That's lovely. From Mark? More than I ever expected." She chuckled a little at the thought of Mark picking out a card and signing it. She added, "Please send my thanks and condolences."

The two sat in silence for a moment. They had all lost someone. An ex, a friend, a brother. Because someone they knew murdered him before attempting to also murder Diana. And in addition to the physical injuries Ann inflicted on Diana, she had been pumping drugs into Diana's system for months. Based on the preliminary toxicology, there were at least five kinds of meds for blood pressure: Losartan, potassium, Furosemide, Carvedilol, and Klor-Con. Not to mention the additional uses of Gamma hydroxybutyrate, commonly referred to as a "roofie," and ecstasy. Diana looked over at Tim, who had been studying her profile. He stood up.

"Everything will turn out okay," he said.

He kissed the top of her head.

"Of course it will," Diana said, as he pulled away. "It's us, Mister. I've yet to see one of us not pull through, especially when we're together."

"Nate, she's being nice to me; are you allowed to protect me?"

"Miss Edwards, do you need assistance in there?"

"Traitor."

She tried not to laugh as he shook his head in disbelief.

Tim left, reminding her he would be there first thing in the morning for her discharge. Visiting hours were over. There was time before dinner; usually, Diana liked to relax and recoup. It unnerved her to be so scheduled, but Nate was outside at all hours, and she trusted him. It was also his job.

Diana figured that private security whose jobs ended in murders or break-ins didn't often get rehired. At least she hoped not. Turning on her television, Diana put on her favorite channel to be greeted by one of her favorite food competitions. She smiled, realizing it was Tuesday, which meant a Chopped marathon before a new episode premiered. A little bit of normal.

Next to the clicker, Diana saw the gift from Mary still sitting there. A milk chocolate square. In all the excitement with Tim, it had slipped Diana's mind. She was able to grab it with minimal pain. By the time she opened it, she was practically drooling and sweating. Biting into half the chocolate, she flattened out the aluminum foil to read the message inside. This time, there were two wrappers. *Weird.* Diana spat out the chocolate onto the tray. She had learned to be a little more aware and a little less trusting from the entire experience.

The note read:

*"Sorry things got out of hand. Just an apology
chocolate. Wouldn't want anything to happen to my
BFF. When you're better, you should come visit—Diana."*

She screamed. Nate burst through the door, eyes wide and
hand on his holster. Beeping erupted throughout her room. As
Diana's doctor came bounding into the room, her eyes began to
close.

"Chocolate," she gasped out. "It's from her."

Nate had called the police and Tim within minutes after the
doctor arrived. Diana thought about being angry, but she was
too shaken up. The doctor had taken her vitals before and after
unplugging all her IVs. Nate looked like he was ready to break
something or someone.

Tim came to her side as soon as they would let him.

Having both seen Mary earlier, he and Nate gave full descriptions of the woman to the police. The note and the chocolate had
been taken in for evidence. Diana repeated the story to him for
the third time.

"What a fucking loon," Tim said. "How did she even get in
here?"

"I thought she was a nurse. She told Nate she was a volunteer. The scrubs all look alike, and she had a badge. Everyone
thought it was a good idea, having someone to come cheer me
up, someone other than just you," Diana said. "It's weird,
though."

"You think," Tim blurted out. "Thanks, Poirot—"

"Anytime, Marple."

"—it's all bizarre, but I meant the note. The way it reads. It
was more like she was signing it Diana, and less of a 'come visit
me, Diana.'"

"That's creepy," Tim said, "and your impression, even more
unsettling." Diana stuck her tongue out at him. "Oh, and in case
I didn't mention, also not going to happen."

"Definitely not," Diana said. "I thought this was over. This whole nightmare was supposed to be over."

The doctor explained that everything still looked good and normal, all things considered. There were still amounts of drugs and other toxins in her system that she would eventually flush out. There was still the risk of dizziness, fainting, headaches, lethargy, and dehydration, to name a few.

"Due to the circumstances, we are going to release you tonight. However, the police need to talk to you first, okay?"

Diana nodded. As her doctor left, the police entered. Diana looked up at Tim.

"Miss Edwards?"

"Can he stay?" Diana blurted out. "Please?"

"We actually would prefer it if he did," the officer said. "As you know, this is currently an active case. You were here due to injuries you sustained. My understanding was that you were getting discharged tomorrow."

"I'm sorry," Diana said, "but can I please see your badge?"

He was in plain clothes. Diana watched as the officer put away his notepad and pen, taking out something that looked like a wallet. He opened it, and Diana leaned forward to look at his badge. She didn't know what she was looking at, but it was a start. Tim looked sideways at Diana. He raised an eyebrow, but she could see the hint of a smile.

"Of course," the officer said, pulling it out. "Lieutenant Bryant. I'm the one handling this matter. We met briefly before, but I don't expect you to remember. There was a lot going on at the time."

"Thank you, Lieutenant," Diana said.

"Miss Hwang was arrested for aggravated assault and attempted murder in your case. However, there are other open cases we feel she might be involved in."

Diana sensed a *but* coming. Maybe even a *however*.

Whatever it was, she wasn't sure she liked it. She stared as the lieutenant cleared his throat and continued. Tim squeezed the back of her neck.

"Miss Hwang's preliminary court date is scheduled for early next week. Off the record, her parents are pushing for her to be sent to a mental health facility. We just want to keep you and the rest of the members of this community safe."

A pang ran through Diana's heart while a wave of nausea crashed through her stomach. The warmth from Tim's body spread through her as he wrapped an arm around her.

"We ask that you keep Nate, or any guard of your choosing, hired until we can confirm if the note was sent by Miss Hwang, or if it was a cruel idea of a joke from the nurse. Other than that, you're free to go."

Diana sighed, her shoulders relaxed, and she leaned in to Tim.

"Ready to skedaddle then?"

"Can we please stop at Mojo's along the way?" Diana said. "I'll call it in for pick up."

Both Tim and the detective chuckled. "The usual, Dame?"

"Yes, but with extra fries, please."

Tim wrote out Diana's order, handing her the list. Diana reviewed it once and nodded, "Don't forget to see what Nate wants," she said as she stood up from the bed and walked over to the window. Looking across the tray, Bryant whispered to Tim, "That's all for her?" Tim nodded.

"If I'm lucky, she'll keep to her own fries."

"I heard that, you know."

Diana turned back around and tried stacking all her get-well cards. Eventually, she would like to reach out to Mark to acknowledge him. They had already feared the worst as things started to unfold, but hearing that Arnold and Amber were really dead? It was surreal.

Tim came up behind Diana, clearing his throat. She turned around, looking up into his eyes. It was definitely going to be a long, drawn-out hike ahead. Diana was grateful that Tim would be with her every step of the way.

"You ready?"

"Am I ready?" Diana giggled. "I'm always ready; the question is, are you?"

"Dame straight," Tim said, holding out his elbow.

Diana laughed as she carefully slid her arm through her best friend's. She was very much ready indeed.

"Let's go home, Mister."

epilogue

DIANA SAT in front of her mirror. It was smaller than the one she had at home. Everything was smaller here. Smaller and dingier. It was nicer than the hospital, but not by much. She understood that everyone kept telling her it was for her own good—she could even imagine Ann telling her the same—not that they had spoken since.

They were all wrong, though.

She knew what was best for her. For starters, being allowed out in the sun, near the pool. Spending time with the people who mattered to her—her friends, her colleagues, herself. That was the key to getting past this ugliness.

Combing out her long hair with her fingers, she wished she could get it done. It had gotten too dark and straight from being cooped up all day and all night. The trial would start and finish, and then she would be free to live her best life. How she could have ever taken it for granted before was almost unfathomable. She thought about Ann, and how it seemed that no matter what her intentions were, she always made the wrong choice.

Closing her eyes, Diana pictured little Ann, standing alone in the observation rooms, watching her father perform surgeries. The medical students *oohing* and *aahing* over him, her mother standing there so proud of him using his skills to showcase the hospital's newest technologies. It felt like most of her life had been in the hospital observation room.

Little Ann, with her long hair braided in pigtails, glasses perched on top of her nose, her small index finger always pushing them up with her knuckle, a seasoned pro already at seven or eight. She was curious and smart. One afternoon, with both of her parents out and the babysitter taking a nap with her boyfriend, Ann grabbed the cat from the living room and went into her mother's study. From the large, ornate birdcage, Ann plucked a small, beautiful finch. With great care, she transferred the finch to a smaller cage. One by one, she moved the three other finches over.

They weren't as beautiful crammed together, but Ann had a plan. Like all scientists, a hypothesis was critical; once you had that, you had a plan. Now she had the last finch in the beautiful cage. Ann nabbed the cat by the scruff of its neck and dropped it on the pellets that lined the birdcage. Seconds passed. They turned into minutes. After years of playing various string instruments, she knew how to count time; 12 minutes passed before the cat began mewing and coughing up feathers. It looked so thirsty.

Being the ever-prepared scientist, Ann was ready. Placing a small bowl of milk into the cage, Ann watched as the cat finished most of the milk. It took less than five minutes for the cat to begin convulsing. After eight minutes, it was dead. Remembering to remove the milk from the cage and add in new pellets to cover up any spilled milk, Ann released the birds back in one at a time.

Scooping up the now dead cat with gloved hands, Ann brought it to the bay window.

Her operating station had already been set up. Taking the cat apart layer by layer, Ann worked until she had found the remains of the bird. Having not yet been digested, Ann was able to peek inside that animal as well. With great care and precision,

Ann cut and probed at the carcass. Unlike her father, her patient was already dead, leaving her with more freedom to explore. After a while, she grew bored, and the cat had begun to smell. Ann returned everything to its place, including the bird, and sewed him back together. It sounded like the babysitter and her boyfriend had stopped playing their wicked games and had actually fallen asleep.

Ann took the cat outside and left it behind the front wheel of the boyfriend's pickup truck. Going back inside, she threw away her rubber gloves, the newspaper, and the rest of her operation supplies. Then she dumped the milk down the drain and washed the bowl before putting it into the dishwasher.

Little Ann, standing in the kitchen, wondered what it looked like when humans ate dinner.

The Hwangs had been furious at the babysitter for having her boyfriend over. They had been more furious when he had run their cat over with his truck. It was after that, though, that Ann was not allowed to watch her father perform operations anymore. Ann blamed the babysitter. Had she ever come back, Ann had a special game in mind for their playtime. One that would end in a different form of sleep.

She had shared her studies, her findings, and her plans with Miss Michelle, her very own "friend" whom she saw twice a week all the way through middle school graduation. A friend she found out later that her parents had paid to spend time with Ann. Once she began high school activities, they had scaled back to once a week. No longer was Little Ann a curious and smart child, but a tall, beautiful, and unique young woman.

Ann's principal had noticed just how tall and beautiful she was, but just like the cat, he had started to stink, and she had grown bored. Michelle had tried to explain how damaging it could be for Ann to entertain married men, or any man in a position of power, but Ann was oppositional. She was defiant.

Michelle tried to tell her parents their daughter had a disorder.

Ann hated being branded. She liked name-brand labels, not *being* labelled. Michelle—like the principal, the babysitter, and the cat—had passed her expiration. At least Michelle, like the babysitter, got to live, even if her career as a child psychologist was destroyed. The cat and her principal, though, their suffering only brought them to the grave.

"Too beautiful to live," was how Ann had first described Diana. Forgetting the social graces she didn't have, she had gone to touch her skin. Unlike everyone else, Diana had let her. It was the moment Ann had let Diana in. They had become so woven together. That moment was a mistake. As Ann had always warned her, Diana should have known better than to let someone so easily into her life.

Diana punched her polished aluminum mirror. Ann was not right. She did not know what was best for Diana. *She did!* And the other people here listened to her. They adored her.

Everyone wanted to be her friend or to seek her counsel. Diana was finally living the life she should have been enjoying all along. Life as a queen, as someone to be cherished. While the technicalities of the trial and whatnot weren't over yet, she could run this bitch like high school without the facade, or Michelle, or her parents trying to rein her in. It was like a high school she could reign over with unfiltered freedom.

The nurse poked her head in from the doorway and cleared her throat.

"Ann."

"That's not my name," Diana snapped back. "They made a mistake on the paperwork. Ann is a nickname. And a stupid one. It's Diana, like Princess or Ross."

"Well, *princess*, it's activity time, and you've been royally invited."

"If you wore makeup, you'd do a lot better in life. Even with the shitty attitude."

* * *

Minerva had been a nurse for 20 years, ten at this location. She had heard all about Ms. Ann Hwang and what she had allegedly done to her "best friend" and three other folks. Never in Minerva's 20 years had it taken less than a week for a patient to be transferred from the county jail to the secure psychiatric hospital. Then again, she had never met a patient like Ann before. It scared her something awful to not know if the girl was the most ill patient or the most talented actress she'd come across.

She watched as the tall, malicious thing walked down the hall, her height seeming to soften, and her walk becoming less prideful and more welcoming. There was a shift in her demeanor that changed her physicality. *No ma'am*, a brain like that scared Minerva down to her core. A lonely chill ran down her spine as the other patients erupted with joy.

"Diana's here! Diana!"

acknowledgments

This wouldn't have been possible without the love, support, and encouragement of so many people. While I did shout out my Arnolds in the dedication, they are few compared to the many bright lights I have in my life—I'm so grateful for each of you.

In no particular order, I wanted to acknowledge:

You, my dear reader.

All of my people at Santo Family Chiropractic—a piece of my heart lives in that office. Fun fact: it's where the first draft of the first chapter of this novel was written.

Taylor, who, without meaning to, literally reminded me that I'm allowed to have the book I want, that I don't have to accept anything less than. Wild right?

Steve and the Art Academy of Milton, for making the launch of this book the special and magical event I was hoping it would be!

The Wayne Public Library, which was the first library to carry my book and make my lifelong dream come true.

My "investors" who took charge of my well-being, and who always support my writing, but specifically cheered this project on.

Thank you all!

about the author

Elizabeth Scozzari writes unapologetically raw and brutal fiction. In 2013, she won the Terri Ann Armstrong Short Story Contest and has written over 200 short stories. The Faces She Sees is her first published novel. Worry not, more are on the way! Nearly incapable of sitting still (give her a good *book* or put on Clue, 1985), she is always learning, traveling, and creating. She thanks you so much for sharing this story with her and hopes to see you again in the future!

short stories, naughty novellas, & more

coming soon

COMING SOON